Alun Richards was born in Pontypridd in 1929. He was educated at Pontypridd Grammar School and then undertook teacher training in Caerleon before spending time as a Lieutenant Instructor in the Royal Navy. After a long period of serious illness as a tubercular patient, he studied at Swansea University and subsequently worked as a Probation Officer in London. Thereafter, although he had periods of employment as a secondary school teacher and, late in life, an enjoyable spell as an Adult Education Tutor in Literature at Swansea University, in essence from the 1960s he was, and successfully so, a full-time writer. He lived with his wife Helen and their four children near the Mumbles, close to the sea which, coupled with the hills of the South Wales Valleys, was the landscape of his fiction.

His output was prodigious. It included six novels between 1962 and 1979, and two collections of short stories, *Dai Country* (1973) and *The Former Miss Merthyr Tydfil* (1976). Plays for stage and radio were complemented by original screenplays and adaptations for television, including the BBC's *Onedin Line*. As editor, he produced best-selling editions of Welsh short stories and tales of the sea for Penguin. His sensitive biography of his close friend, Carwyn James, appeared in 1984 and his own entrancing memoir *Days of Absence* in 1986.

Alun Richards died in 2004.

DAI COUNTRY

ALUN RICHARDS

PARTHIAN
LIBRARY OF WALES

Parthian
The Old Surgery
Napier Street
Cardigan
SA43 1ED
www.parthianbooks.co.uk

The Library of Wales is a Welsh Assembly Government
initiative which highlights and celebrates Wales' literary
heritage in the English language.

Published with the financial support of
the Welsh Books Council.

www.libraryofwales.org

Series Editor: Dai Smith

Days of Absence first published in 1986
The Former Miss Merthyr Tydfil and Hon Sec RFC
first published in *The Former Miss Merthyr Tydfil* in 1976
The remaining five stories first published in *Dai Country* in 1973
© The estate of Alun Richards 1973, 1976, 1986
Library of Wales edition published 2009
Foreword © Des Barry 2009
Publishing Editor: Penny Thomas
All Rights Reserved

ISBN 978-1-906998-15-8

Cover design: www.theundercard.co.uk
Cover image: *Tom Jones smoking*, Wales (1974).
Photographer Terry O'Neill © Getty Images

Typeset by logodædaly

Printed and bound by Gwasg Gomer, Llandysul, Wales

British Library Cataloguing in Publication Data

A cataloguing record for this book is available from the British
Library.

LIBRARY OF WALES

FOREWORD

On 8 May, 2004, a blue Saab 9.3 pulled to a stop on the lower end of Michael's Road in Blaencwm, and from the passenger side door a tall man, a broad man, dressed in a dark suit and dark glasses, stepped out onto the road and waited for the other occupants to join him on the street. From the driver's side appeared a significantly shorter man, with close-cropped grey hair and moustache, an equally dark suit and dark glasses; and their wives emerged, elegant in tight dresses, no less charismatic, the whole vision like a valleys version of the Corleones. The women walked beside their husbands up the road toward a small crowd gathered in front of a house; the terrace of which it was a part was framed by an arc of mountain, cliff and waterfall under bright blue late spring sky: a fusion of Rhondda and Hollywood, much like the prose – fiction and autobiography – of the taller of the two men, Alun Richards, writer and raconteur. He'd come to unveil a commemorative plaque to his friend, the Rhondda prose gangster, Ron Berry.

Alun Richards' trajectory – partially revealed here in this extract from his autobiography and the short stories collected from among his prolific work – was a little more genteel in the early years, but no less troubled than Berry's as life went on, and the two writers shared adjacent turf, albeit a few miles distant from each other, and a life that connected the valleys to the sea. Richards, like Berry, saw himself as an outsider, able to comment on the constrictions and celebrate the odds-defying victories of life in South Wales from the mid-thirties to the end of the twentieth century.

Richards was an outsider from the moment of his birth, a boy without a father, a marked man, even to the extent of the mole upon his face, which gave him his schoolboy nickname. One of the many pieces of delightful prose in this collection is his description of how, at the age of five, he escaped the vigilance of his grandmother, and set off on a mission to the Pontypridd marketplace in search of a father. It's a vision of pre and post Second World War valleys life, full of lags and scam artists, mams, grans and valleys girls, the social matrix that still underpins the rich texture of post-industrial South Wales. The writing is unashamedly and unsentimentally exultant in its sense of place, while at the same time, in the first sentence of his autobiography, Alun Richards sees himself as 'a spy in another man's land'. This dual sense of belonging and estrangement, and his broad experience of life outside the valleys, equipped Alun Richards to become a writer of novels, plays, scripts and short stories; and the hilarious memoirist of *Days of Absence*. And in person, Alun was a raconteur extreme.

The maternal side of the Richards family were of farming stock, pre-mining people who had to adjust to the influx of industry and a population boom in a once rural area. They were people who belonged to Pontypridd. Richards writes about the town in a voice that's poetic and angry, painting a picture of the valleys at the confluence of the Taff and the Rhondda Rivers that sparkles out of darkness like a canvas by the visual artist who was his contemporary and co-paisano, Ernest Zobole.

The section of his autobiography published in this volume takes us from his birth to the end of his schooldays and illustrates the changes in valleys life from the poverty of the thirties – which he largely escaped, though he witnessed it through his friends and neighbours – to the tragedies of wartime deaths of relations and friends. When his father does appear, it's as a silhouette behind frosted glass, an image from a Bogart private eye movie. And if his father was absent, so too was his mother, most of the time. Alun was brought up by his Methodist grandmother, with all the warmth and generosity that Welsh grandparents always seem to have the luxury to lavish on their grandchildren. There is a deep affection for her in the prose. Then, when Alun's mother appears in the story, she has a Hollywood glow. She's slim and beautiful, not like the image the young boy thinks of as 'mother' when he compares her to the mothers of his friends. She has just stepped out of the cinema screen for a moment; she's in glorious black and white. And, just as ephemeral as a movie, she's gone when the lights come up, and the young Alun Richards goes home to his ever-secure gran. No doubt this tension between mother and grandmother, and his place in it, affected him in his relationships and his perceptions of women, which he very candidly reveals in these pages.

The chapel played a big part in Alun's psychological formation, the influence of which he readily admits, while at the same time he chronicles both his successful and unsuccessful attempts to escape from it. In his fiction, the Puritan values of the Methodist chapel seep into even the most dissipated of his male characters. It contrasts with the sexual ease embodied in the common sense of many of his female protagonists. The uptightness of Methodist mores leads to a longing in Richards' male characters for sexy, earthy valleys women, which Richards explores in 'Frilly Lips and the Son of the Manse'.

'Dream Girl' presents the vision of a more mature married man revisiting his childhood fantasies for a would-be starlet who has returned to the town of her birth after a life in pursuit of a showbiz dream. It reads like a brilliant and tawdry tale of ambition and geekdom, told from the point of view of a now well-balanced valleys plumber. Richards' characters seem to yearn for a sensible middle way, where sex and relationships are healthy; where characters aren't seduced by glamour or potential riches whether real or imagined.

Inevitably, in making a choice for a single, book-length selection of a writer's prose, this isn't the whole picture. This selection by the Library of Wales concentrates on writing about the unfolding of changes in the valleys in the years from 1934 to 1976. It gives us an historical thematic taste of a writer who wrote six novels, two collections of short stories, an autobiography and a biography of the Welsh rugby player Carwyn James.

The short stories collected here concentrate on the emotional and physical constrictions inflicted particularly on the male characters, all deeply flawed. A boy bonds with a father deprived of his son by an act of police brutality. The adolescent son of a Methodist minister falls in love with a free-spirited girl of 'bad reputation'. An impotent collier seeks mean-spirited revenge on a macho tormentor. A macho rugby player spreads innuendo about the secretary of the club who still lives with his mam, antagonism that is underpinned by a deeply repressed homosexuality. A London Welsh artist affects the stereotype of French existentialism of beret and Gauloise, and finds redemption with his no-nonsense Welsh wife. Only two of the male characters are spared the deep cuts of Richards' unflinching scalpel: a married tradesman who runs his own company and hasn't succumbed to the temptation of expanding his business beyond his means, and a cameraman who works for the Cardiff media and commutes back up the valley to his wife who refuses to move house the short distance from valley to city.

Perhaps this search and finding of balance is reflected in Alun Richards' own life story: his marriage to Helen, his raising of four children, his publications, a life engaged with the wider world, rooted in Pontypridd, and lived out next to the sea in Mumbles.

This collection is necessarily a focus on a particular part of Alun Richards' prolific production of prose. A collection, whose theme is the changes in valleys society in the second half of the twentieth century, doesn't so much tell us about the successful personal journey of Alun Richards as the Royal Navy officer, playwright, script writer for the *Onedin Line*, survivor of years of hell fighting TB but it does give us a rich taste of his prose and the desire to search out further fictional tales and the full autobiography that is packed with yet more brilliant stories of hilarious adventures; and the stomach-churning description of his hospital incarceration full of nightmare, feverish coma and physical terror.

In life, Alun was a huge character. Perhaps I was lucky. I always found him a joy to be with, a constant source of comic anecdotes told with sharp wit and deep affection in equal measure. While reading these stories, I could hear his voice, just about sense him looking over my shoulder. These words of his autobiography and his short stories bring Alun Richards to life. What a delight to hear that voice again.

Des Barry

DAI COUNTRY

Contents

AUTOBIOGRAPHY

DAYS OF ABSENCE

ONE

As a boy I was a creature of disguises, a spy in another man's land. There were facts about myself which I could not bear to face and in order to avoid doing so I began, at an early age, to spend a good deal of my day in reverie, slipping off into daydreams which provided another world where I would not be found out. My secret, the bitter truth about myself, was never told to me in a single sentence, but rather descended like a cloud which followed me over the years of my childhood, and when I finally realised what it was, it was as if bits and pieces of information at last came awkwardly together like the separate pieces of an old and worn jigsaw. It did not happen suddenly or dramatically, but slowly settled on my consciousness, imprinting itself, it seemed then, for ever. I was marked. I was not wanted. I was a nuisance. I was not like other boys. I did not have a father. It was better that I did not ask questions – they were painful to others – but there, those were the bones of it, my mark was that of the fatherless child.

If one is not careful, one speaks now in generalities. Sentences arrive as bland as fudge, all insidious. One tragedy is soon dwarfed by another. Even a one-legged man can be comforted by the sight of those without hands. But generalities have little effect on the wart at the end of your own nose. In my five-year-old mind, it was imperative that I should not ask questions. Questions would upset. Best to say nothing. Talk about something else. Lie low.

I don't think anybody actually briefed me with those precise commands but still, I knew them, and followed them dutifully until my adolescence. I learned at an early age to watch, to gauge a mood, to know when it was time for me to speak. I also learned to listen, to eavesdrop, gathering what bits and pieces of information I could. I listened from corners, behind doors, on tramcars, to hushed voices drifting out of the vestry after chapel, to the gossip of neighbours talking in the street. If two people talking on a corner greeted me, I would reply politely, then creep back to hear what they might say when I had gone.

'Whose boy is that?'

'Oh…?' This with a marked exclamation of interest, sometimes a clucking 'Pity for him!' in a very Welsh way.

There were other sentences, words:

'A waster, a thorough waster.'

'An animal in his drink.'

'Poor dab.'

This was me, I knew, the dab. The other was Him, my ever-to-be-absent father.

8

I kept these phrases to me, hugging them in the secret place. I had other problems. You see, I was marked in another way too. I had a birthmark that stretched for almost two inches down the right side of my cheek, an ugly brown thing in the shape of an inverted exclamation mark. A full sideboard was how the barber diplomatically described it, bleeding me every time he ran the clippers over it. To me, it was another punishment for something I had not done. And there was trouble coming, I knew. Soon I was to be known by my enemies as Moley.

Until I went to school, I did not have any enemies that I knew about and, but for the mark upon me, I was cradled in an affluence that was later to make me feel deeply ashamed. In 1934 we had a lavatory and a bath inside the house. I had two pairs of shoes, one for best, as well as for the day. When we sat down for meals, there was a table-cloth on the table, knives and forks, doilies on Sundays, a separate spoon for the jam. The jam pot was not allowed. We could afford crumbs for the birds and we did not soak the tea leaves over and over again. Tramps and vagrants put a mark on the gatepost to indicate that this was a good place to call. We could always afford a crust.

Outside in the backyard, there was a brick extension built under a stable which housed my grandfather's horse. This was called the wash-house and it had a door that would bolt from the inside, a fireplace, and a large galvanised tub in which I would sit, paddling my way down the rivers of my dreams while the horse fretted in its stable above. If the driver forgot to clean the stable, sometimes the drains would become blocked and the smell of warm horse piss would come pungently down from above and then I would be up against it, paddling away with a 'kerchief over my nose. There was also a rickety glass shelter leading from the kitchen door, and when it rained the rain would thunder upon it, drumming down, drips forming on the wooden underside so that when a shower was over, the drips went on long afterwards, staccato reminders of what had come before. I used to listen to them in the silence of my bedroom, or crouched in the tub, my arms resting on the long-handled appliance used to baste the washing. I liked the rain and the sound of water because they were part of my escape. In my mind, I have been an escaper all my life and I have never been happier than when near the sea, if not actually afloat.

Another of my hiding places was a space under the Welsh dresser in the kitchen where there was room to curl up and you could see the light of the fire reflected in a large brass-topped hob that was kept beside the fireplace and on whose cool smooth surface I would rest my forehead if I had a cold. There was also a forest of brass on the mantelpiece, a regimental file of candlesticks and two large brass shell cases brought home from France after the first war and in which my grandmother kept Bills Paid and Bills Unpaid, and since they were curved and highly polished, you could sometimes see people's faces in them when they talked. From my hiding place, I could peer through the fringes of the tablecloth into a world of fire and brass and when I was on my own, I sometimes inspected my own face in the shell case. Unlike a mirror, you could manoeuvre it so that your mole did not show.

It was in this hiding place that I heard my grandmother say that I was filthy when she got me, three days after I was born, brought by car in a basket because they did not have a cradle and I hardly had a stitch to put on. I was, as it happened, a clean little boy and I can remember looking at my hands and fingernails when she said it. Photographs of this period survive but they have nauseated me ever since. There is no indication on my face of what I felt at any time. I was a little podge posing for the photographer, tubby in red woollen jersey and short grey flannel trousers with properly pulled-up stockings held in position by elastic garters bought in the Bon Ton, a draper's shop whose owners came to our chapel. My round solemn face is turned to hide my birthmark and I look the kind of plump little boy who sits unobtrusively in the presence of adults, is well behaved, does not ask for second helpings or fidget, and does not get on with other boys. I do not recognise myself when I look at it, nor do I recognise my grandmother or mother in other photographs in the sense of what they meant to me. Perhaps it is that we are all creatures of disguises. At any given time, the turmoil of feelings is deeply buried and has no adequate visible expression.

Certainly, my grandmother did not realise how much I knew about myself because of my espionage work and when I think of her in those years, it is usually in the absence of my mother whose difficulties began with her separation from my father three days after I was born. While I am inclined to think now of my arrival as being catastrophic, then I had no inkling. All I knew was that my mother was young and attractive, and so 'smart', people said, 'she'd look wonderful in a dishcloth!' But she was frequently away from home and so the person to whom I was closest, who really brought me up, was my grandmother. My grandfather was still alive in my fifth year and I remember him clearly but it was to my grandmother's apron strings that I was firmly attached, and in many ways I never left them completely since it is her face I remember and her voice I hear whenever I tread the paths to home.

In my fifth year there was a good deal of quarrelling between my mother and my grandmother and very often there would be voices raised and sometimes my mother would run in tears from the table, occasionally out of the house itself; and my grandfather, if present, would say, 'Leave it, mother. Leave it.' But there were some things my grandmother could not leave alone. If the quarrelling was fierce, I would start to cry and that might bring a lull but usually this was followed by more accusations and then I would slip into one of my hiding places and listen to the slamming of doors which at last marked the end of the raised voices. Now I can look back and offer all sorts of explanations of that part of our lives, but then they eluded me and I did, I suppose, what any cub in its lair would do – draw closer to the loudest voice and the strongest figure, and since this was my grandmother's it meant, I see now, that I was drawn irrevocably from my mother's side to my grandmother's lap. My mother, I soon found out, could not cope with things. That she was not allowed to, took me thirty years to realise, but I could do nothing then and the only power I had was as a mute figure who was sometimes bundled between them, once stolen by an uncle to be paraded for an afternoon at a horseshow, then put back in the box so to speak. When my mother went away to work, or was away from home, I watched her go with a feeling of relief. With my grandmother I was comfy. In that warm embrace, all happiness was contained, and if I was separated from the true umbilical cord, it did not matter then. Retreating to the safe houses of my imagination while the quarrelling went on, I would re-emerge to be cosseted and spoiled for a time – a time for confidences when it was that I slowly began to realise, not so much who I was or where I was from, but the facts about my grandmother's life and the town into which I had arrived. In those early years, it was as if I had skipped not one generation but two, for my grandmother was nearly sixty then, had brought up a family of five children and I had come to be the sixth and last, and was, moreover, a trapped audience compelled to listen when I was not in hiding.

Although I say that I was relieved when my mother was not home and the quarrelling stopped, matters did not end there and I had, by the age of five, given at least one sign of the mark that was upon me. For once, after a stormy episode when my mother had left abruptly, I slipped secretly out of the house upon a peculiar quest. I cannot be sure exactly what the argument was about, for this time I was banished from the table and they made sure I was upstairs before they resumed it, but I had caught one phrase, 'You're not seeing him again?' And then, one of my grandmother's favourites: 'After *everything* that's happened?'

Somehow I seemed to know that 'everything that's happened' referred to me and the Him that I was soon to banish from my mind, my father. All this I kept to myself, but later I slipped out of the house alone and unseen, drawn for the first time to search for some explanation of the mystery about myself. Why did I not have a father? If he was being seen again, where was he? Perhaps he had a birthmark too, and if he had, could he confirm or deny the gypsy's advice that if I spat upon it with fresh spittle as soon as I awoke, it would go away of its own accord? I had, as my grandmother said, 'spat myself out' since the gypsy told us, but not one ugly hair had disappeared and the lump remained livid and immobile. So I had certain pointed questions to ask.

I was also in some confusion about my mother. She was slim and elegant whereas I had a deep-rooted conviction from local observation that mothers were fat. They were to be seen pinafored and aproned, arms akimbo, half-bathed in suds as they scrubbed steps, hair awry, with laddered stockings and worn slippers, when they were not haranguing tradesmen and not having any nonsense. My mother, as my grandmother had to admit, always looked as if she'd stepped out of a bandbox and there was little opportunity for her to do much at home since my grandmother was a compulsive worker – one of those tireless women who could not bear to let anyone do anything she could do herself, although often at the same time complaining that she had to do too much. She had the penny and the bun, as well as the privilege of complaint which was one of her greatest and most eloquent joys. Like the Greeks, the Welsh enjoy their woes and they nourish them in abundance, often preferring remembering to living.

My grandmother, like myself, was never quite free of guilt, even for the smallest of tasks left undone. Even in her seventieth year, when I once returned unexpectedly to find her – equally unexpectedly – sitting down with a woman's magazine, she got quickly and guiltily to her feet and said, 'I've only just sat down this minute!' and then proceeded hotfoot to the coal shed to hammer a sizeable lump of best anthracite before I could stop her. Even in my teens with my school colours for rugby football, I was not entirely to be trusted with a coal hammer.

But at five it was all a conundrum. So I felt myself impelled to search. I did not say, 'I am going to look for my father', but yet, one grey day, I knew I was going about that forbidden task and so put on an old pair of summer sandals which I had ceased to wear because it was autumn and the leaves were sticking to the roads – I had an intuition that I might have to be fleet of foot. In full consciousness of wrongdoing, I tiptoed downstairs, avoided the creaking telltale loose board on the landing and flattened myself against the wall of the little passage, avoiding the beady glass eye of the mounted fox which my grandmother's brother had caught some years before he was killed in France. (The brush was on top of a wardrobe upstairs but I was not allowed to play with it because it had some kind of mange and she was always on the point of throwing it out, but never got around to it. Like me, she was a great hoarder.)

Down the stairs I went, along the passage where there was a grandfather clock whose ticking pendulum punctu-ated my days and nights, past the closed door of the front

15

room which was not used in the week unless there were special visitors and which contained such treasures as an ostrich egg in a Swansea china bowl, two mounted Florida butterflies – gifts from an uncle in Philadelphia – all the coronation mugs since King Edward and Queen Alexandra, and a three-corner china cupboard over which war was later to be declared and litigation threatened. There were also hidden photographs of my grandmother's brothers, including an Uncle Jack who, robbed and rolled on the waterfront at Sydney, enlisted with the Anzacs, was wounded in Gallipoli and thereafter returned home to drink himself into such a state that he would be put in the wash-house – my wash-house! – to sober up before being allowed to make his way to his own home. I was already into these treasures and a great dipper into drawers and cupboards, searching for some clue to my father, but now I went to the latch of the front door. Here I paused, listening to that clock ticking. Then I looked at the door whose upper part was partially leaded with coloured glass panes and so composed that you could only see the shape of whoever was outside but could not recognise them, an affectation that was brought back to conformity by a brass strip along the sanded doorstep below which was scrubbed and polished every day. Now I put my fingers up and gripped the knob of the lock through the sleeve of my jersey, just managed to open it, the door swinging inwards. I know I did not close it since this was evidence later used against me, but while it opened easily enough, it was a heavy door and clunked noisily when closed, and I did not risk that. Then I was off, hurtling down the step past the postage stamp of a lawn, not using our gate but stepping over next door's wall and through their gateway where the gate was never shut, and then I was gone – out on to the hill and the other world that was waiting for me. Like Ali Baba, I knew where to look for strangers. You went to the market. They had everything there, and what is more, the local tradesmen, of whom my grandfather was one, did not like the itinerant marketeers. They paid no local rates and did not contribute materially to the town. They were hobbledehoys, my grandmother said, riff-raff all, and what is more, respectable people did not go there, or at least, did not like to be seen going there – only the Rodneys from the Rhondda Valley.

Although my grandmother would never admit to it, we actually lived on the extreme tip of the Rhondda Valley as our house, one of two built back to back, was sunk into the side of the hill where the valley narrowed and the River Rhondda met the River Taff to form the confluence town of Pontypridd which had grown around the site of an old fording place. That Pontypridd was an old marketplace did not seem to occur to my grandmother as she and her family had lived and farmed there for years before the coal rush and she had an antipathy to change and a feeling of belonging which gave her a sense of ownership so aristocratic that she made few tentative statements at any time. Instead she pronounced, granted audiences, expounded, as if it were part of her heritage to do so. She had that confidence in the self which very few people have, an assurance that comes from land and place, a sense of belonging which is essentially the inheritance of country people.

The marketplace lay some way off, however, and when I

left the house surreptitiously by next door's gate, I stepped first of all on to a steeply inclining hill road which bisected a much grander road a few yards away. This I came to know as the kingdom of Tyfica (Tee-vicar). It should never have been called a road at all as it was more like an avenue, rich in chestnut trees and copper beeches where grand houses, some detached and most removed from the road, lay in splendour above the uneven roofs of the smoky old town below. Here, it was said, lived the people who mattered, who *were* Pontypridd. I knew some of them and later in life marvelled at the splendour of swing chairs in the garden by the imitation wooden pagoda and the studied elegance of creamy long-legged women who smoked Craven A through long enamelled cigarette holders and spoke casually of London as 'Town'. Yet the extraordinary fact of our environment was that a mere hundred yards further up the hill where the mountain rose and the slope steepened, a green patch gave way to a crescent of back-to-back terraced houses with unpaved roads, cobbled paths near a little shop which sold lump chalk for the colliers to mark their trams underground. On sunny days, a bearded old woman half-clad in sacks often sat outside the shop on an orange box. She wore a man's cloth cap, chewed shag tobacco and spat copiously when she was not clacking and muttering to herself. All of us, as it happened, faced the opposite side of the valley where there was a leaden slug of a coal tip and the inescapable metal debris and sharp contours of a mining valley; but up above the tip and the pit wheel, the larger contour of the mountain reached up to the sky. At night, the lights of the terraces stretched out

18

endlessly like a necklace of frail cobwebs circling the town, finally going out street by street as the last footfalls of the drunks and shiftmen echoed up the hill and only the darkest shapes were visible – a wall, a tree, the slim spire of the town clock – all standing as still as grass. For me, it had then, as now, a kind of ghostly beauty and I never thought of it as a ravaged industrial terrain because it was always a place of warm associations.

But I put my back to it all and went on down the hill, past the chapel which we did not attend although it was the nearest, past the corn stores – a haunted house with fat lodger rats – then, avoiding the greasy river, ducked up behind the cells of the police station whose frosted glass and bars sealed them off in entirety and hurried on towards the Arcade which had an Inspector with his official title engraved on his peaked cap. A small, short, hangdog, bloodshot-eyed man, he had been, my grandmother said, a full-blooded Oyez town crier but had come down in the world. I was to offend him later as, following the family tradition, I tried to drive a bowley, a metal hoop, through the Arcade with a stick but was prevented and the bowley was confiscated. I had heard my grandmother describe one of my Uncle Jack's exploits: a horseman of repute, he had once ridden a horse through the Arcade in a wild moment, a feat of some daring since it opened out quite near to the police station. The event was related, not with pride but as evidence of his condition at any given time. And there had been other wild spirits in our family, as I was to discover with the story of yet another uncle – obsessed by tradition – who drove a borrowed sports car through the Arcade making a smart exit past the police station. The Arcade, like the market, was always crowded, and it was here that I began to study faces as I always did. For obvious reasons, I had a premonition that my father's face would be flushed and angry and his smell would be ripe with hops, that beery Saturday night smell which came from the shabby cloth-capped men who lined the street corners, endless files of them mufflered and despairing – their hopeless waiting reflected in their faces and in the muttering silence that would become known to me as I wandered amongst them later, still searching as I collected cigarette cards. There were areas of the town where men, always men, congregated in these groups of unemployed, and near my grandfather's shop was the Labour Exchange with more endless queues, so many of them that the solicitors' offices put vicious metal spikes on their windowsills to prevent the unemployed sitting down.

But the Arcade was always busy, dog-watched by the Inspector who always had a trowel and sandbox on hand in case nature intruded. Here there were bread and cake and sweet shops, school outfitters with Welsh woollen vests and long combinations lumped beside the cap of dreams which indicated admission to the county school and on whose crest the town's one-span bridge was etched like a small rainbow. I was heading for rougher territory, to the opening of the square where the stallholders had their pitches in the open, and no matter what was being sold – china, mousetraps, goldfish, carpet cleaners or patent medicines – they always seemed to be sold at the top of someone's voice, and at the last minute.

Articles were not so much sold as knocked down to you, cheap at the price, for this was Bargain Country.

I could not at first get near the open stalls and the stallholders I particularly wanted to inspect, so I made my way into the covered market where there was an air of respectability. Here the fruit stalls gave way to the carpet stalls where mats and rugs were piled to the roof. Nearby were religious books, home-made sweets and toffee, and the knick-knack stalls. Finally I arrived at the very centre of this universe where the ripe and homely smell of faggots and mushy peas came from the kitchen of the market café. There were seldom any young men there, I was to find, only the old tired men with wheezing coughs and ashen, blue-pitted, coal-scarred faces, the shape of their skulls sometimes standing clearly out of their skin; men who asked for cough medicines, wore strips of red flannel 'for the chest' and who sometimes sat alone, silently staring into space. I somehow always associated this part of the market with the old and hurried away from it, not realising that this was the only place where you could sit down and those who came here often did so because they had to, ordering only one cup of tea and receiving 'looks' if they stayed too long.

There were all kinds of faces in the market, but this day I studied the men. I was looking for a face like mine, for a mark like mine, but I had no idea how I would look at an advanced age so it was the birthmark I concentrated upon and, since I had seen no photographs of my father (nor have I ever done) I had in mind a kind of stereotype of evil – there is no other word – and somehow this was concentrated upon the mouth. It was half-grinning and half-snarling, the leer of a gargoyle, and the head went savagely back as did the head of a man I had seen once beating a stubborn horse. So I kept my distance from those I examined, and here began the first of a procession of melodramatic incidents in my life – real incidents which defy the art of ordered narrative and often send reason scudding out of the window like frail clouds blown by the winds of reality, my reality, the ever-present sense of things as they are, or seem to me.

I kept my distance from the figures that I passed but watched just the same. Perhaps the first inkling came when I heard his voice. I had gone through one end of the covered market and out the other, past the fish stalls with their tubs of Welsh cockles, the great marble slabs of fish and into the hall of china where the crowds did not gather until closing time because the knocking down of the knock-down prices did not begin until later – and out into the surging crowds again. I heard the voice before I saw the man. It was hoarse and gravelly but it had an overlay, one of those large and confident South Wales voices which was syruped with a faint American inflexion that gave it an added persuasiveness. It was not quite as coarse as the cockney stallholder next door who sold women's silk stockings whose seams he would show you with a flourish, holding them up for all to see.

'Madam, you can look behind you when you're walkin', and you can see for yourself... them seams, straight up the back of yer leg, all the way from toe to heel right up to the Blackwall Tunnel!'

He could be nothing to do with me. No, it was a cajoling voice, this other voice, rich and confidential. It was concerned with what might, or might not be, lingering in your stomach – in particular, your intestinal worms, and in describing them, it gushed fulsomely with an expansive aplomb.

'Let me tell you, Ladies and Gen'lemen, the intestinal worm's no more'n a cousin to his brother in the earth but can't be operated upon 'cos no surgeon's knife can find him and the only way to get at him is by persistence, by feeding him what he don't know he's takin', and buildin' him up until at last you got him and he don't know which way to go, which way to burrow – until all he wants is the light o' day. A miner's worm, he is, a little tunneller, as true as I'm standin' here. Well, see for yourselves...'

There was a movement in the crowd and through a space I first saw Broncho, a market salesman who, I later found, belonged to a separate and distinguished group, the quacks. Unlike those who only sold patent medicines, they seldom offered reduced prices and stood gloomily by their stalls, mournful beside their silver-wrapped cough sweets, or the strong, smelly, liniment rubs, applicable, they said, to both animals and humans. Broncho was unexpectedly different in that he presented an act and dressed himself up in a large white stetson hat with real sheepskin chaps and carried a six-gun in a holster with which he sometimes fired blanks to attract the crowds. His speciality was the invention of a purple mixture for the banishment of worms from the intestines and unlike the pill and liniment men, his stall was crowded with huge jars full of methylated spirits in which you could see writhing masses of yellowing worms. Beside the stall, there also stood the thinnest and most unhealthy-looking boy of about eleven, his deathly pallor and haunted features making him a picture of abject misery – all evidence of the timely arrival of Broncho with his worm mixture; for, as I later found out, Broncho would state flatly that it had taken him a month of regular dosage to extract the entire contents of one of the specimen jars from this very boy.

'All them worms... Look for yourself. Pounds of 'em! Arrived, I did, in the nick of time! You only got to look at him to see how thoroughly drained he is.'

Here he put his tattooed hand – blue lovebirds imprinted on the skin between finger and thumb – on the boy's thin shoulder and asked gravely: 'Well, was you, or was you not at death's door until I come across you? Until your mother come to me and begged me on her bendeds?'

The boy nodded gravely. At death's door was one of my grandmother's phrases and the boy, with that awful chalk pallor and the limpid embarrassed eyes, the dirt ingrained between his fingers and the sores about his ankles, was the living embodiment of ill health. But for a fleeting moment, such was Broncho's eloquence and confidence, you thought, this is what worms can do.

Broncho was not just a quack, he was a consultant quack, and when he shook the specimen bottle, some of the tentacles seemed to stretch out towards you, swirling and beckoning in the blue liquid. You could not but wonder if they were still alive. 'Pounds of stuff I got out of him,' Broncho said impressively. 'Pounds. By the cupful!' He cupped his hands to indicate the amount, using the measurement as a specialist might to indicate the gravity of the situation to a layman.

Then he went on and on. (It was his business to, like mine!)

'What I ask is this,' he said, very reasonable; 'why, when the evidence is in front of them, why, oh why will people not take the simplest elementary precaution and put a bit of liquid liner in the stomach as a preventative? You flush a copper pipe.... D'you think your own intestines is not worth a moment's thought? Pains in the morning, have you? A little flatulence? Tell you it's wind, do they? Wind! That's all they know....' It was my first acquaintance with *They*, the people who thought they knew.

Now I have to invent to order the narrative, since I cannot remember the exact words he used. But the ridiculous details survive: the fact that he carried the badge of a Deputy Sheriff of Montana, had a crumbling parchment to prove it, and later said he had learned medicine man's talk from the Seminole Indians in Florida – all of it is so unlikely as to suggest a spoof on my part. But it is not, and you have to see him as I saw him on that day and later, half-illuminated by the flickering blue light of a solitary naptha flame in a copper bowl, a relic from the previous decade, a hoarse-voiced and earnest figure in a place of shadows and mysteries. If his human worm repellent – very reasonable at sixpence the bottle – is a hoary joke now, my feelings then were not, neither were the suppurating sores on that boy's legs, and the week-old layer of dirt. Thirty years later I saw the boy's image once more in the face of a shoeshine boy in Fiji whose ulcerated legs and hangdog look caused me to empty my pocket of coins. It was a futile gesture, perhaps, but another indication of the childhood that holds me prisoner still.

Even now, I have a picture of Broncho as he took off his stetson, noting at once that the leather sweat band was removed in order to get it on his head at all. He had a high forehead and a peculiar way of staring down his nose, an expression of irritated puzzlement at times which I see now as quite like my own. I too had a very large head with a double crown and could never get a school cap to fit me. His eyes were also like mine – green, hurt and sometimes evasive, and there was another similarity. Shortly before my fifth birthday, I had extracted the gunpowder from a firework and exploded it by striking it with the blunt end of a hatchet causing an immediate flash and resulting in what was to be a permanent bloodshot corner of my right eye. These blotches Broncho had in profusion. It is true, I had no idea of his age, but he was fatherly looking, enough for me. He was also tattooed and those tattoos spelt sailor, wanderer, absentee, another item on the ledger which I had begun even then. The fact was that he had all the credentials of an absent and never-discussed father, and while I could not quite see him sitting down at the table with my mother or any of my family, everything about him spelt movement and disappearance. There is another thing. Although the idea of any physical coupling with my slender mother was quite impossible, this was something I knew nothing about. So complete was my innocence of such matters, it would not even have entered my head. Indeed, I was nine before I saw any sign of physical affection between a man and a woman, and that unexpectedly in the doorway of Woolworth's when a young man, obviously arriving late, suddenly clasped a young woman. She reached up and kissed him, tears of happiness in her eyes and they stood together embracing for a moment, her fingers clasping and unclasping at the back of his neck. Standing across the street, I noted this extraordinary action with complete surprise, almost a sense of shock, just as – about a year later, once again in the market – I was witness to Broncho's disgrace as, tired at the fag end of the day, he paid off another boy even more anaemic than the first and then, partially concealing himself (but not from me!), he poured the remainder of his elixir down the drain in order to lighten the bottles. These he then bundled into a battered old suitcase, eventually wandering off moodily into the night, six-gun, stetson and chaps having long disappeared in the hard weeks before. The worm repellent was not a line that lasted, perhaps being too seasonal, as they say in the trade.

Now, looking back, I smile but never laugh at Broncho, or his itinerant registrars who helped him, their grimy fingers shuffling the bottles forward into eager hands when the going was good.

There were for years, whole areas of my life which lay buried and which I pretended had not existed, ghosts from shadowy places who inhabited corners and danced like spectres on occasion, mocking me for that pretence of normality which I so desperately tried to assume. It was not to be found then, not even at sixpence the corked bottle.

TWO

My grandmother had the kind of face which I find almost impossible to describe. If I see her in my mind's eye, she is bent and old, her mouth slightly sardonic after she had suffered the first of several strokes; a short dumpy woman, both hands swollen with rheumatism and legs misshapen with varicose veins, but her face – strong even at the end – was ever animated by the brightness of her eyes. They were sharp, brown and intelligent, sweeping at you under a frizz of grey hair, missing nothing. Around her neck she always wore a black velvet band, sometimes with a diamond clip, sometimes not, but I never remember her without this remnant of Victorian fashion, and hardly a photograph exists without it. I suspect she must have been very vain of her neck and in photographs as a young woman you can see a firm chin, a wide humorous mouth, all the evidence of a strong face, full of character. She was small, neat, and in one profile she wears her hair close-cropped, again with the velvet neckband, and here she is full-cheeked and there is an imp of mischief which belongs to someone else. I don't think she was ever pretty, there is too much chin for that, and even as a young woman it is the kind of face which stands out in a crowd because you sense there is something capable and reliable about it. There is not just the animation of the eyes, a natural shrewdness, but a steadiness too. She had, she used to say wryly, the kind of face that caused people to leave their children with her on trains. And yet, you would not call her plain. There is something too striking there.

The face I knew, however, was marked by life. Experience had riven it until it was homely, and it was at its best seated opposite me by the fireside when we were alone, with perhaps a treat in an unexpected tin box of Allenbury's glistening blackcurrant pastilles, normally reserved to prevent coughs in chapel. These were the happiest moments in those early years and it was then that I got a sense of the past which never seems to be like anything I have read.

My grandmother's family can be traced to the previous century, hill farmers all in that most beautiful but happily unknown of terrains, the hilly mountainous country between the bottom tip of the Rhondda and Aberdare valleys, just north of Pontypridd, at whose centre is the parish of Llanwynno. Here my most famous relative, the bard Glanffrwd, is buried; a Welsh poet and cleric whose rise from the obscurity of miner to Dean of St Asaph is a period Welsh success story, the stuff of legends. He was born in 1843 in a small thatched cottage in old Ynysybwl, the eldest of seven children, and his forebears were the descendants of lay brothers who lived at Mynachdy, a sheep farm supervised for the benefit of the monks at Margam Abbey. When Henry VIII dissolved the monasteries, the brothers lost their living but settled nearby, and one descendant – Glanffrwd's grandfather – prospered and became the owner of almost all the land he could see between Mountain Ash and Abercynon. His lease on the land was drawn up in the old-fashioned Welsh way, 'to last while water flowed in the River Cynon' and for as long as he paid rent at four pounds per annum. However, he sold it for a trifle in a drunken bout with the result that Glanffrwd began life as the son of a woodcutter, only saved from illiteracy by the patience of a deformed schoolmaster. After a spell in the pit in the early years of the coal rush, he became a pupil teacher, then a Nonconformist clergyman, finally entering the Church of England for which he was prepared at Oxford, where he is said to have consorted with Matthew Arnold and other notables. His end came spectacularly. He collapsed on the platform at the National Eisteddfod at Brecon in 1890 while conducting a choir. He was then taken to his brother's home in Pontypridd where he died. My grandmother was in attendance. He was forty-seven.

His wife, a well-known singer (Llinos y De), was a beauty in more respects than one, according to my grandmother, who would dispense with all this historic preamble with a flicker of the eyelid. The poet Glanffrwd was her father's brother, but the marriage was not approved of in the family, particularly not by my grandmother who, in emergencies, had the job of lighting coal fires in the beauty's bedroom and fastening up the forty-odd buttons of the button boots she insisted on wearing despite a lifelong lack of manual dexterity – onerous tasks which were sometimes palliated by the beauty's fame, for when she was singing, courting couples were said to come from miles around to listen to her. But on the other hand, the old enemy reappeared again, for during Glanffrwd's lifetime she would very often dispense with half a bottle of eau de cologne in the bedroom before a performance. My grandmother actually helped to dress the corpse with the swigging going on next door, if you please. Her own father at this time was a Deputy of the Tŷ Mawr Colliery, given a silver plate by the men on the occasion of his marriage. One of Glanffrwd's sons emigrated to America but the other, like my grandmother's brothers, was to perish either in France or as a result of the first war. Their photographs haunted me as a child and seem now almost as real to me as my own uncles, two of whom were also to be victims of war. To this day, their medals lie in drawers, a Distinguished Service Order, a Military Cross, a Distinguished Flying Cross, all unlooked at. They perhaps explain why the only time I ever saw real fear cross my grandmother's face was when I also returned home in uniform, but that was at an easier time, and a long way ahead.

In my fifth year, it was all a mystery, but an entrancing one. On the surface of things there was a mask of respectability, composed of selected facts, but not far below there were the scars left by anguish now long-past, heartbreak which yet had not resulted in any basic change of ideas. We were never pacifists and I was never discouraged from children's games of war, unlike some of my contemporaries whose families also suffered drastically, Welsh casualties being greater per head of the population than any other country in the British Isles. So in my child's mind, I led charges over the top and got at the Hun with cold steel, amply provided with props from the commodious cupboards upstairs – a Luger pistol greased in its holster, a bloodstained bayonet, a Sam Browne, a military tunic with the colonel's crown and pips on the sleeves and, of course, the letters home from the Somme.

> Dear Mother,
> The food is as well as can be expected and we
> are seeing quite a bit of the countryside.

But there was another reality, I knew, and my grandmother saw that I knew it, not consciously perhaps, but she was sometimes overcome by the uncontrollable surge of memory that defeats all propaganda because it is full of sights and sounds and smells – sometimes, of unrelated images like the one she had of the outbreak of that first war of 'the boys marching through the main street of Pontypridd in 1914, a sea of scarlet tunics and polished brass, laughing and joking as the girls followed them to the station'. I, too, was to be a witness of such circumstances in the second war. But we remained patriots all, seeing ourselves in the larger context of the British Isles, regarding ourselves as part of the main-stream, and this never altered.

As it happened, my grandmother never told me of these things as an ordered body of facts, and now when I attempt to bring them together, I can see inconsistencies which passed undetected then – largely because so many of the things she said came as an aside. A death would be announced in the obituary columns of the local newspaper, and my grandmother would say, 'She led our Willie a dance!' She also liked stories with a moral and as she grew older, her mind would slip back to her girlhood and the early days of her marriage, one of the reasons being, I suspect, that the first war brought with it a time that was too awful to recollect. Everything changed after that. Avoiding it as an area of damage, my grandmother turned instead to her origins, indulging a predilection for the bizarre stories of country life. Her favourite concerned her expectations in a will; not all the family land had been sold, and she had an uncle and aunt who farmed quite near us – the aunt had promised my grandmother several fields. As a girl, she would go there to help out, she had nursed the aunt in one period of sickness but the time came when the old lady was dying and, suddenly and abruptly, the door was barred to my grandmother and all communication was forbidden. The little farm became a prison.

'She couldn't even get a note out,' my grandmother said emphatically.

She remembered going to the farm, taking a whinberry tart as a gift, but she was greeted by a servant girl who came out into the yard, barring the doorway behind her. The uncle was away and Auntie Leah did not want to be disturbed.

'Too far gone,' the girl said.

My grandmother couldn't understand it. Knowing her as I did, I was surprised she did not thrust her way into the house; but she did not, although she did not leave the whinberry tart either. A week later when the aunt died she discovered the reason for her uncle's absence. He had gone to see a solicitor in faraway and hostile Neath, had brought him back to the house that very night with the result that the will was altered and my grandmother dispossessed.

'A good job I didn't leave the tart,' my grandmother said. This was what she described as a dirty trick, but you never got a dirty trick story without its sequel and I got so as I used to wait for them. It was not just that I knew she would not have told the story unless it was to prove, as ever, that your sins would find you out. It was how and with what severity the fates struck which were the intriguing things.

Her uncle's name was John. He had been no more than a servant man when Leah married him, a kind of hired help who, however, lived in, according to the custom and was in most respects treated as one of the family. Soon, with the expected indecent haste, Uncle John married the girl who had barred my grandmother from the house, and within no time they were putting on the dog, he with fancy waistcoats, she with her hats and button boots. My grandmother, newly married, began to have her own children and, apart from an occasional sighting, had no conversation with her uncle. Three of her five children had been born, and were all under four years old, when a boy from a neighbouring farm called, bearing a note. Her uncle was ill, too ill to leave the farm, and begged her to visit.

In all my grandmother's stories, people begged you to do this or that. Messengers arrived out of the night and left abruptly, doors slamming behind them. Indeed, some of these doors even came off their hinges and she told me that too.

My grandmother wanted more information when she saw the note.

'Where was *she*? – "the servant girl that was"?'

There was no precise information.

'He's on his own,' the boy told her, shifted his feet, then confided he had been called into the farmyard from the bedroom window, but that Uncle John would not let himself be seen, throwing out the note together with a florin.

'He wants to see you right away,' the boy said. The wife, it seemed, had deserted him.

Something in the boy's manner convinced my grandmother of the urgency. All her life, she was consulted about illnesses, had a handwritten notebook full of herbal remedies, and was an experienced – if amateur – nurse. But she was not free to leave immediately unless she took the children with her so, in the end, that was what she did. With grandfather busy in the shop, she saddled the pony and trap herself, gathered up the babies and set off for the farm.

I have pondered that journey. It was not very far, but still difficult with young children. I have also wondered what was in my grandmother's mind and although the obvious thing is that she was expecting a vengeance of some kind to have descended upon the farmhouse, it also strikes me that there was a strong element of curiosity. She had a great interest in people's dying words, and since she had been barred from Auntie Leah's demise, she must have wondered what had been said. At any rate, it was late afternoon when she guided the pony and trap into the farmyard, and she left the children safely in the trap. The blinds were drawn, and there was evidence that the animals had not been properly fed. The place had gone down, she said. So she pressed the bell and for a long time there was no response; but presently she heard a movement upstairs and then there came footsteps descending the stairs, and finally the same shuffling footsteps came hesitantly along the stone flagstones on the other side of the door. In the last few yards she could also detect another sound, of liquid dripping on to stone.

When the bolts were withdrawn and the door opened, a sight so horrible greeted her that she moved to one side so as to obstruct the children's view from the trap. Around his mouth, her uncle held a bloodstained scarf. He was dying of some incurable and advanced cancer of the jaw. The dripping she'd heard was blood. She told me he had sent for her, to apologise, to confess his guilt.

'Jessie, it's done me no good.'

But my grandmother put a harsher construction on the matter. His lies had found him out, she told me. I saw the deadly logic of it, vengeance taking physical shape and striking like a dart at the offending organ, the mouth itself. My grandmother sent for the doctor but it was too late, and when Uncle John died, it was found the whole place was heavily mortgaged and no one benefited in the end. So the fancy waistcoats must have played their part as well.

'Just as well he died,' my grandmother said, 'otherwise it would have been the workhouse.' Temptation, Drink, Debt, Ruin, the Gutter, the Workhouse, these were the bogies of my fifth year and I considered them all gravely.

I have, as it happened, told that story twice; once to one of my own children who greeted it with shouts of disbelieving laughter, and at another time – bizarre circumstance! – in the dimly lit corner of a nightclub in Nairobi to an African writer who listened avidly. We had defined a category of grandmother stories – to the outside world, tall and far-fetched, as simple as cartoons; but to residers at the inner hearth, the stuff of life. Kikuyu whores with blonde wigs and slit skirts did the twist behind us, slapping their bare feet on the dance floor under psychedelic lights which transformed me, as one of the few white men there, into a garrulous albino private eye as I sat hunched in the corner, a bottle going, as we exchanged one story after another. His grandmother covered up her father's habit of coffin-robbing until she covered it up no more when he fell into one and choked himself to death.

In later life these stories were to cheer me up immensely the most dire moments, and strangely enough, they did not strike me as being at all odd at the time I was told them. I liked a simple view of things and when, much later, I tried my hand at the odd macabre tale and was sometimes greeted with ridicule, I hugged to myself the private knowledge of events which made the things I had written about front-parlour stuff. I was also to think of the noise on those flagstones years later as I lay helpless in a post-operative ward, temporarily abandoned because of a greater emergency, when a blood transfusion which I was receiving came adrift and I heard the same slow tap-tapping of blood on the hospital floor. I had other memories of that farm. I was once ordered off it in company with other children. We were blackberrying and trespassing.

Some ran, I did not.

'It's rightly my land,' I said exaggerating. 'Rightly' was one of my grandmother's favourite words.

Later, I boldly went to the farm to ask for a glass of water. There was a more amenable woman there then.

'The tap is round the back,' she said. 'Why did you come to the front door?'

I did not answer. To my disappointment, the flagstones had long been covered over and the stairs were not visible. So I never went there again.

The workhouse, where paupers were sent, figured large in my grandmother's stories and while it might be thought that we were quite well off (which we were by the poverty-line standards so close about us), the fear of poverty was never completely absent. It was everywhere visible – in school, on the streets, in the eyes of one of the members of our chapel whose threadbare respectability was just main-tained as he wheeled an ancient cycle around the houses of the congregation carrying an old suitcase on the rear carrier from which he sold lumps or sticks of home-made toffee. If we were unlikely prospects for the workhouse, others were not, and it was this same institution which was the indirect cause of the only occasion when I ever saw tears in my grandfather's eyes. My grandfather was not a Pontypriddian and he was not allowed to forget it by my grandmother who, when not talking about the world's ills, the evils of drink and the ever-present likelihood of degradation, swung to a completely different tack and struck an altogether more aristocratic note for which her well-rooted, if not landed, background had prepared her. Mentally, as it were, she claimed the fields of which she had been disinherited and was quite likely to strike a certain air as a consequence of being the last survivor of one of Pontypridd's oldest families, as she put it. She meant those who were indigenous, natives before the coal rush which had changed the very air she breathed. Others had prospered and moved away but she had not and never did, and she retained that proprietorial interest in her particular patch which was evidenced by the number of people she knew who inevitably stopped to talk to her.

She had met my grandfather at a Sunday School treat, an annual chapel outing to the fields at St Fagans, near Cardiff, where the National Folk Museum now stands. His journey in life had been more dramatic. A blacksmith's son from the Carmarthenshire village of Conwil Elvet, he remembered doffing his cap as a boy of twelve to Lord Dynevor and made his way to Pontypridd by way of Edinburgh where he had been made an Inspector of Shops by Sir Thomas Lipton, the grocery tycoon. ('He is widely travelled,' my grandmother said; 'he has been everywhere, including Edinburgh.') Starting as a shop boy putting down sawdust on the floor, he prospered in the Lipton's organisation until he came to Pontypridd and finally, after meeting my grandmother, opened up a small grocery business on his own in rented premises formerly occupied by the composers of the Welsh National Anthem. At first he did well, and at the time of the Depression was a deacon of his chapel and a member of the Board of Guardians appointed to supervise the running of the workhouse. One of his duties was to visit this ugly grey Victorian building on Christmas Eve when a children's party was dutifully organised. He was a generous and kindly man, and I have never met anyone who knew him who did not comment on his generosity, but I think now that there were times when life got too much for him. I can remember him coming home from that visit and sinking into a chair, the tears streaming down his face. My grandmother immediately feared the worst, trouble in the shop. There had been endless discussion about the substitution of the horse for a second-hand motor vehicle to make deliveries and then there was stealing by one of the bakery roundsmen from the daily takings ('Trouble with the baker's bag'), and I was in my hiding place when these matters were discussed. But it was some time before my grandfather could articulate his pain. He had arrived too late for the children's party but had been taken by the Workhouse Master to see the children safely abed in their dormitories. Even though it was Christmas, their shoes had to be left outside the doors and it was the sight of those regimented lines of shoes, stretching down the corridor in neat order, size by size, which had unnerved him – the meticulous order of it, the Workhouse Master's pride. My grandfather was not to live to see the premature death of two of his sons, but those shoes upset him more than anything I can remember, more perhaps than my grand-mother's constant quarrelling with my mother when she was there. There was seldom silence in the little kitchen. Now there was. Even my grandmother did not speak at first and I can remember him removing his spectacles, pinching his nose and wiping his eyes.

For all that, I doubt if I would have remembered it so clearly were I not, years later, to learn of a similar incident. This time I was in the company of another writer, Goronwy

Rees, and puzzling over the works of Theodore Dreiser whose clumsy prose style had caused an American critic to call him the world's worst great writer. Goronwy had met Dreiser on one of his pre-war jaunts and gave me the core of the man. Once, in Paris, at the height of his fame and the darling of the left, Dreiser had been asked to present prizes at an orphanage. It was a duty he could not escape from but, rising to his feet before an array of cups and certificates, he had looked at the scrubbed faces and shaven heads in front of him and suddenly burst into tears, breaking down completely so that he could not speak and did not do so. This was the heart of a man whose compassion overwhelmed him, and such a man was my grandfather, I have no doubt. At home he was not one to say much, but our doors were open to all and all my life I have never forgotten the procession of beggars who came to our door at his insistence. Eventually I was big enough to open the door myself and once when I did so, I nodded gravely and went dutifully back along the passage to the kitchen. 'I'll have to ask,' I said as I was instructed to say. But I returned to find the beggar had gone. Seeing the telephone wires, he probably feared that we might have called the police since begging was an offence, sometimes punishable by imprisonment. I was soon told to run after him with half a loaf and a handful of currants which I scooped myself. My grandmother's influence was such that I knew it was imperative for me to run to catch up with him, and run I did, not of my own volition but at her expectation and, having found him, watched while he tore the crust apart with shaking fingers, his face riven by a grey despairing hopelessness. It was an experience that was to be repeated

41

many times in my life; my first disappointment in Russia was in finding the same despairing faces, the same outstretched hands of children begging; and again in New York, similar sights in Times Square caused me to wonder whether, like my grandmother on trains, there was something about my face which encouraged them.

At home, as a little boy, the endless procession of beggars that went on until the outbreak of war was a sign of the times, like my neighbour at school being forced to attend in his sister's shoes. There were, of course, worse and better things to come, but I am glad that I felt my grandfather's pain at an early age. I was not sheltered in the way that so many are sheltered and on that day – uniquely, in our house – there was a new experience in finding someone speechless.

When my mother came home, it was a time for treats. There were visits with friends of hers, including a couple who lived opposite and had a car. We went to the coast, to Porthcawl and the Kenfig sandhills, or sometimes up to Caerphilly or the Brecon Beacons when we would climb up and out of the valley and my mother would always breathe a sigh of relief. These friends of my mother's, I soon discovered, were lah-di-dah and inevitably spoke with pronounced English accents – a sharp contrast to my grandparents whose first language was Welsh, although they always spoke to me and most of their children in English. Their speech was often peppered with metaphors which had their origin in the original Welsh phrases. Thus someone might squeal in one of my grand-mother's stories 'like a pig under the knife', but my mother's friends were out of a different drawer and were as smart as she was. It was in such company that I discovered a different set of manners. Once, at the table of a household of some affluence, I made a horrible mistake and passed a slice of bread with my fingers.

There was a hushed silence. Fortunately my mother was not present as I had gone with a friend, but the head of the household looked at me over his spectacles and said coolly in the clipped, mannered tones of the English upper class which I came to marvel at: 'I cannot accept that.'

I cringed, but managed, 'I'll eat it if you don't want it.'

When I told my grandmother, she informed me that the speaker's father had begun life as a baker's roundsman with a basket and a brown sack to cover his loaves and not two ha'pence to rub together. What is more, one of the daughters would cross town to get a penny off the price of a lettuce so I was not to worry on that score. It was not that my grandmother did not have precise standards, but they were more related to the character than the bread bin.

Away from home my mother was free (except for the encumbrance of myself) and she would light a cigarette with relief and if, in the company of friends, she went into a pub for a drink, leaving me to play with other children, I was bidden to say nothing about it when we went home. I did not do so, but I could never see that my grandmother was so old-fashioned as everybody said, and for a good deal of my childhood I accepted her standards. I could not get away from them and while I see my mother's predicament now, I did not then and was often sullen in her presence. Even when she took me to school, her youth and elegance made me uneasy and for years I have had to overcome an aversion to being seen with smartly dressed women. Once in a bizarre period of utter craziness in my life I was bidden to squire the American actress Katharine Ross to a meal at the London Hilton. I felt my throat dry with embarrassment as I greeted her, as lovely as a ripe Californian peach but 'done up to the eyeballs', as my grandmother would have said. On another occasion Siân Phillips turned up for a theatre date wearing a large floppy broad-brimmed black hat like a catamaran running free under full sail, but I could have hidden, there and then. Fortunately she took it off during the performance, but I did not then want – nor have I ever wanted – people looking at me. Exceptionally attractive and specially groomed women are an embarrassment; better they be in the old Welsh idiom 'shrewd in the marketplace, devout in chapel, and frantic in bed'. That I was certainly the envy of other men did not occur to me, I felt the same uneasiness I had felt before, holding my mother's hand as we walked to school. It is not reasonable. It is not defensible. It is laughable, but I have to recognise that it is, and always has been, me.

I see now that I inhabited two worlds as well as the world that my imagination was carving out for me. For when I entered my mother's world, I did so with my grandmother's critical sense and often a knowledge that I should not have had, for she was often indiscreet and let slip things I should not have known. Even the bank manager neighbour over the road had marriage problems, and despite the respectability of the bank, there was a tug of war going on between the young step-mother and an old and faithful domestic servant whose love for the child – a girl of my own age – was obsessive. The step-mother wanted to get rid of the domestic, the husband was in two minds, the child played one off against the other. Soon the family moved, and I watched them go with a knowledge of what was happening that was beyond my years. I learned that there were other straws blowing in the wind than those which were above ground.

My grandmother also had a nose for trouble, as she said, and so have I, and while it now appears to me that sometimes I have put myself at risk, she never did. The world and its ills and woes came uninvited to that little house but through it all for me there was always sustenance. When my grandfather died of a heart attack in his early sixties, my grandmother broke down for an hour only. They got rid of me on the day of the funeral but when I returned, my grandmother caught me up in her arms and held me to her and I felt her tears cascading on my own cheeks.

'Never mind,' she said to the world at large and me in particular. 'We still have you.'

It was the comfort of my life, my succour, a lifeline to the future, a love that never wavered and without which no rewarding emotional development is possible, the one love in life that is given unreservedly and without self-interest.

Shortly afterwards there was a ring at the front door bell but since there was now no man in the house, I was not allowed to answer the front door in the evenings. My mother's oldest brother was soon to come home to run the business but on this occasion we were alone once again. I can remember peering down the passage to see a man's trilby hat and shoulder silhouetted against the leaded glass panes and straight away I sensed trouble. We did not get many callers at this time of night. He stood motionless, with his hand on the bell, ringing persistently.

I went into the kitchen.

'There's a man there.'

My grandmother looked down the passage as the bell rang again. Then she removed her apron.

'Stay in here.'

I could sense her alarm, felt a quickening of the senses myself.

'Mind,' she said again. 'Stay in here.'

She went out, closing the kitchen door behind her. Since it had net curtains, it was impossible to see down the passageway and, obediently, I did not look but sat on the brass hob by the fireside. The visitor was shown into the front room. There was a conversation but only my grandmother's voice was clearly audible since it was frequently raised. Presently the man left, my grandmother closing the front door and putting the catch on the lock. When she came back into the kitchen she put the kettle on and composed herself. I did not say anything. I knew the stranger had upset her but I did not want to add to her upset, whatever it was.

Presently, she told me. 'That was your father.'

I said nothing. I did not know what to say. It was not that my curiosity had evaporated but now I did not want anything to disturb me, or to upset her. There had been too many other shocks, even some talk of my going away to an aunt when my grandfather died.

'I know what he wants,' she said. 'He wants to live here.

Thought there was money left, but there's precious little. I don't know how we're going to manage as it is.'

Again, I said nothing. I was like an animal in its lair that senses movement outside in the stillness, but lies inert, hoping the danger will go away.

'But don't you worry,' she said. 'He won't get the better of me.'

I was relieved but said nothing, asked no questions. I had already begun to cauterise this hurt part of myself and my earlier curiosity had gone. That trilby hat seen through the glass was all I remember of my father. He never came again and the visit was not discussed further.

I was Grandma's child for another decade.

THREE

Once as a young man, when I thought I was dying (and was indeed in a tubercular ward that was to prove terminal for most of its occupants), I often lay in a state of coma and would awake at all hours of the day and night, opening my eyes and seeing – not what was in front of me – but images which my unconscious mind had formed before I awoke. As usual, there was an element of melodrama because I was suffering from – among other things – an eye condition known then as Eale's Disease whose symptoms were vitreous haemorrhages, bloody floaters which appeared to hang inside the eye, forming a reddish tide like a minute seaweed-strewn foreshore which moved gently as I turned my head, the whole miniature landscape encapsulated within the eye. My other eye was heavily dilated with morphine drops so that for a good part of the day I could see only vague shapes which meant that when I first awoke I saw, not what was in front of me, but what my mind had put there. It was often a scene such as you might come across in those toy glass baubles whose swirling artificial snowflakes will – if allowed – slowly settle to reveal a log cabin with a fir tree, perhaps a central figure like Father Christmas leaving home for what is obviously pensionable employment.

I, however, very often saw the face of my grandmother, sometimes accusing me, for in two years of what was described as strict bed rest I had ample opportunity to go back on the life I had led. But I also saw the homely contours of the Pontypridd I had known as a child which emerged like the gaily painted fresco of spires and houses on a Swiss cuckoo clock, principally the uneven sloping roofs, the three crowns of neighbouring hills and mountain, the smoke rising lazily above the chain works and some-times the rain beating down from Cardiff. The rain always came from Cardiff, my grandmother said as a matter of geographical fact, and it was in that direction that she always looked when she got up and, indeed, during the war when Cardiff was being bombed and we could see the flashing orange lights of ack-ack fire and sometimes a loom of light faraway in the sky as the searchlights came on, we said, 'Cardiff's having it again!' in tones that were dark and treasonable. We implied in the safety of our hills that anything wicked Cardiff received, it somehow deserved.

But the outline to which I awoke was the view from my bedroom window, my back to the Rhondda, seeing the town below me, a higgledy-piggledy collection of awkward jutting buildings, some big, some small, some minute and white-washed like pieces of confectionery, some Victorian in style, some Rhondda baronial with forests of drainpipes and guttering, some straight marzipan Cardiff Rialto, the whole a representation of architectural untidiness that looked as if the entire town had been carelessly dropped from the sky and had come together by accident around the leaden river which trailed like a black slug through the centre. In the sunlight, however, it was a place of drama. For shadows cut across courts and gullies, bisected streets, blacked out whole terraces, the uneven and lumpy terrain offering up sharp contrasts, and I often thought that nowhere in the world could there be a place where the shadows formed such a variety of shapes and where voices were often disembodied, seeming to come from everywhere, even below the ground. Always, there seemed to be the clank of shunting coal trucks, coupling and uncoupling and, at intervals, pit whistles blew while at other times of the day the roads echoed with the clink of steel-tipped colliers' boots, their faces black then as they came up from the pit.

But let anyone say it was ugly and I would bristle. I never saw it except as a whole, a place of many associations. As I looked at the buildings, there were so many of them which I identified with people because my grandmother had a story about each one. This was where so-and-so had lost a tooth falling off a tramcar, that was where Tommy Ping Pong, a public schoolboy gone wrong, first began selling baby tortoises which he would instruct you to keep outside near a light at night and then steal back for re-sale; here my grandfather first felt his hernia come on, near the back of the fairground, and there, near the Penny Bazaar, was where her cousin, Freddie Welsh, the world flyweight champion, lay in bed one night and surprised a burglar, laying him out with one punch. A world in which an unwitting burglar chose the world flyweight champion's house fitted in hugely with my notions of rough justice at the time, but my grandmother's air of familiarity was not just with such notables but with everyone she spoke about. Freddie Welsh, whose real name was Frederick Hall Thomas, like Glanffrwd's son emigrated to America, was commissioned in the US Army, later opened a gymnasium in New Jersey where F. Scott Fitzgerald was proud to have boxed three rounds with him. All my life, Pontypridd's connections seem to cover the world. Lord Nelson, after all, didn't like the look of Merthyr; it was *our* chain works which anchored the SS *Great Western* and the thumping of the great steam hammers which we heard daily was like the beating of the heart of the town. Small towns, I was to find, were discoverable in an intimate way whereas the vast anonymous deserts of suburbia produce only anonymity and a grey sense of unbelonging. When a distant relative described my home town as ugly, I felt my gorge rise.

But it was the shapes that came first to me in my partial blindness: the lovely contour of the town's famous one-span bridge over the River Taff, the slim white towers which formed the impressive gateway of Dr Price's never-to-be-built mansion, the hills and mountains – even the clouds I remembered, drifting away above the ribbons of terraced houses, and the seven trees I could see from the window of the last classroom I attended and from which I was later bodily removed by the headmaster and momentarily expelled. They were a visual sustenance as I lay in bed immobile, very frequently semiconscious as I was at first resistant to streptomycin and experienced daily comas as I was being slowly desensitised. It was the shapes, always the shapes, which would help me to escape from the torpor of disease, and they could be very necessary at times since there were moments when I thought I might never see properly again and once when I awoke unexpectedly, I just made out the outline of the consultant's face peering at me, shaking his head sadly and expelling breath with a disparaging grunt as if to say, 'No chance.'

But I was a reluctant hero in my mind, there being no alternative other than to expire with the minimum of fuss – hardly a family tradition, and so the shapes returned again. One was the gaunt outline of the Calvinistic Methodist chapel which we'd attended – a grim Victorian monstrosity plonked into the centre of the town and directly opposite an equally ornate public lavatory whose main offices were below ground. The roof of the lavatory was topped with thick, bottle-green glass tiles which caused an eerie subterranean light to filter down to the urinal stalls below. Across the road in Penuel Chapel you might be personally threatened with the imminence of hell and damnation in a sculptured world of highly polished African mahogany as you sat among a sea of pews below a raised and carved bardic pulpit like a lift-off platform to the other side, but when you went to pee, you were in a green Atlantis down below. Here, to complete the illusion, there was a continual sound of running water coming from a drinking fountain for animals and humans above. ('In Ponty, we never forgets the horses!' a councillor told me once.) One could have been the world of Flash Gordon, the other was the place where God found you out – and what was more, he found you out in Welsh too, for the important services were all conducted in what Pontypridd's only historian delightfully called, 'the ancient Kymmeric tongue'.

To my grandmother, Penuel Chapel was the hub of the universe, a centre of social intercourse from which she derived much pleasure and she had been, all her life, what she liked to call 'an active member'. Her standards were chapel standards, couched in simple sayings, 'Do as you would be done by', and in so many ways she was the embodiment of the Christian ethic; but I attended only because she wanted me to, often spending a good deal of my time daydreaming in a state of blank incomprehension since most of the services were in the Welsh language which I never spoke or understood, although I remember hymns to this day.

I see myself now in my best clothes, seated in the corner of the pew with one weather eye lifting for the ever welcome box of Allenbury's blackcurrant pastilles, the other narrowing to look across at the heavily carved woodwork of the Big Seat where the deacons sat directly under the pulpit. Here the Minister often stood on high, sometimes waving his arms like a gaunt bird of prey, intoning, cajoling, haranguing, usually drawing grunted expressions of assent from the congregation. But it was not only above me, it was beyond me. Like an African savage, I waited patiently for the free gold-coloured medal inscribed with the head of the founder, Thomas Charles of Bala, the free Testament and the Sunday School treat to Barry or Porthcawl where elderly men supervised sack races and older boys got off with girls on the ghost train. I learned my verse in Welsh, duly recited it, then hastened to be anonymous once more.

I see now that I was born into the end of one era of Welsh Wales and Welsh Nonconformity. In Penuel Chapel when I was a boy, the age of the congregation was increasing; there were fewer and fewer young people and the Sunday School classes grew smaller and smaller in my lifetime until finally the building was demolished. The chapel and its religion declined because it ceased to appeal while the Welsh language was like something to be cosseted as if used 'for best' on a Sunday, then put aside for the working week in the houses of all but a few stalwarts whose children – usually sons of the manse – were unexpectedly, and often undeservedly, to prosper in later years. For them, in broadcasting and other circles, the Welsh language became a caste mark, like an old Etonian tie, and people like myself became outsiders, easily excluded for a long while.

But my grandmother had known a flourishing and youthful congregation in the aftermath of the Revival, and Penuel people were for the most part old Pontypridd people who had struggled along against the competition and the invasion of outsiders in the great population explosion after the coal rush. Then the valleys were opened up; the industrial population doubled in a very short space of time, adding nearly a million souls to what had been a rural area. They came, like my grandfather, from the Welsh countryside and from the other side of the Bristol Channel like the parents of so many of my schoolmates who brought with them the names of remote Devon and Cornwall villages whose names were to puzzle me so much when I read them in obituaries. I was impatient with the lack of youth and vigour about my chapel, the plain foolishness of so much Welsh when the streets were alive with the vernacular; impatient at the dos-and-don'ts of simple people, even at their piety in a world which grew more violent every day, and my restlessness drove me into those same streets which seemed to me to be the real world. I had enough places in which to daydream, but my grandmother saw to it that I was the instrument of her chapel duties; for I became her messenger, first accompanying her when she took home-baked cakes and delicacies to invalids and others, all members of the chapel, and later when she was unable to walk, making the visits myself, a shopping basket forever under my arm. This I did all through my childhood, changing to a more masculine briefcase which I inherited when my mother's youngest brother was killed in the second war and, once again, these visits were a happy accident of my life since it meant that I crossed doorsteps I would not otherwise have crossed. They also led to some strange memories when I lay in hospital; for I was in a ward full of colliers, most of whom had silicosis and heart conditions as well as tuberculosis, and the images which returned to me were rich and varied – all to be sifted, even treasured if they hastened the endless slow procession of days.

As a child I had no direct knowledge of the colliery, only my grandmother's stories of her father's involvement, but I used to visit one old collier who had suffered an accident underground which had paralysed his hand. With the little compensation he received, he had opened a backstreet sweet shop, one of those tiny front-room businesses which sold humbugs and cough sweets and simple household requirements and whose trade was virtually confined to the terraced street in which it stood. Here you would sometimes see men who had come directly from the colliery, their white eyeballs and teeth gleaming in their black faces as they performed errands for their wives with simple requests. ('A packet of Reckett's Blue and ten Woods on the book!') The old collier, whose name was Rhys Jones, carried on with the shop after his wife died, struggling to lift the heavy sweet bottles with his withered arm, and every week I would make my journey with a plate of Welsh cakes or teisen lap – a delicacy made with sour milk – and then I would listen while he told me stories of his struggles with stubborn horses underground. He never allowed me to see his withered arm which he kept wrapped up in a woman's black silk stocking, but he welcomed my company and even came to depend upon it as I listened gravely to his comments while the war approached.

'Myself,' he would say airily, shaking the screw of caster sugar over the Welsh cakes, 'I think that Stalin is only bouncing!'

I grew used to the sound of his voice and was pleased at his excitement at my visits, for I was one of the few visitors he received and whenever he saw my grandmother, he would extol my virtues – once stating that in his view I was a likely candidate for the Nonconformist ministry, which showed a shrewd judgement of what would please her. I was a good listener, he said, implying that it was a rare attribute in that calling.

In hospital I also thought about my schooldays and I would try to remember the names of the children who had sat next to me and the games we played in Infants' School. I suppose I was trying to recapture a sense of innocence and now, going back on it from afar, I realise that I am attempting to lay incidents of my life on paper like a card player would lay a hand upon a table – saying, as the autobiographer does with a flourish, 'Here I am. This is what made me and this is what I made of myself.' But I can detect no conscious pattern of events, and if there is any danger, it is the professional writer's curse – the dangerous habit of trying to please. I have always thought that every autobiography should contain something disgraceful, and yet the loyalties which bind you are like tentacles so that it is often painful to go back, each layer of memory having to be lifted and unstuck like an adhesion. The facts are easy but the least important. You ask yourself, how did you really feel? Perhaps the best guide is to watch your own children as they grow up, and then it is often a matter of revealing the contrast – then and now.

At first I see myself as a little cosseted pumpkin again, Grandma's boy still, standing at her side outside chapel, the sort of chummy little boy whose hair adults cannot help ruffling. I remember I had a tam at one time which I could pull down over my mole like a paratrooper's beret, and I stretched it as much as I could to hide the mole; but when I went to school, it was the mole that interested everyone. There was also the embarrassing matter of my clothes since, by the bitter poverty-line standards of the 1930s we were well off and I had new shoes, a clean red jersey and short grey trousers from the town's largest emporium, kept by a wealthy man whose ill-fitting ginger wig was a source of constant fascination since it slipped continuously, revealing a totally bald pate. I was, I see now, the sort of nice little boy whom schoolmistresses were glad to have in their class. This was to change markedly but, on that first day wending my way into the Infants' School yard, the most obvious contrast was the condition of most of my schoolmates; while there were a few as tidy as myself, my difference was immediately noticeable in the newness of everything I wore and this became one of the first of the stigmas to mark me out from my fellows. I did not have boots which most of the other boys had, but shoes, and I did not have handed-down clothes some of which, I soon saw, had the advantage of being able to stretch over your extremities and could be very useful in wiping your nose. At first, there was not a darn in anything I owned.

Many of the boys wore rubber daps or plimsolls, some did not have socks, and now I became acutely aware, not of rickets, nor malformations of the limbs due to malnutrition, but clanking leg irons which were worn by several children in every class; and it soon became apparent that there were those who suffered from epileptic fits which fact was entered upon a card and the susceptible had to be placed in desks near the aisles so that the teacher could get at them quickly if they began to choke. Leg irons on top of fits constituted a special hazard since the braces could become jammed in the metal supports of the desks. Of course I cannot remember exactly and in what order my perceptions came, but within three days I had made a bosom pal and somehow I knew now beyond any doubt that it was my mole which drew him to me, just as his awkward comic gait had struck me from the moment I saw him in the schoolyard. His name was Albert. He came from the gypsy caravans. He had been run over by one of them when a horse bolted and his legs were permanently bowed so that he could not walk in a straight line. Instead he rolled, a comic opera roll like a sailor in a musical comedy – his whole body rolling, shoulders and legs moving from side to side, his head following as if bowled along by the wind. Albert always had a smile on his face, as if by way of apologising for his oddity and his face, an old man's even at five, which was swarthy, dark, gypsyish and – astonishingly – a hint of his hair receding at the temples. I think he had unruly hair and his mother kept it firmly plastered down with grease. He was none too clean, bit his fingernails and was the owner of a multitude of boards and wheels and bits of broken skates which could be assembled rapidly into a wide variety of gutter transport which whizzed him down hills. He would never walk normally, somebody said. But he smiled, smiled, smiled, and went on smiling. He was a clown but with soft appealing eyes like a spaniel's. He would never hit anybody. He never shouted. He could do a kind of cartwheel, throwing himself sideways and landing on his little bent legs like a cartoon man. He could also whistle with two fingers in his mouth, giving out a real piercer. The first time I spoke to him, he put these two fingers to his mouth, wet them, then fingered my birthmark and we touched like dogs. I knew there was gypsy in him but it did not make any difference to my birthmark – he knew me straight away, from the very first playtime. Then we sat together, went home together, and he used to wait for me outside the house. Every day he had something different to show me, a gobstopper in a piece of rag, cigarette cards galore, a spider in a jar, and always bits and pieces of wheels which he hid in various hiding places along the road. I think some of his family collected and sold the debris at the back of the market. They were market totters, trading in scraps, and the last of the haul was Albert's. He got what nobody else wanted, the very dregs, but out of it all he created a wonderland of possessions and within a week he was calling for me.

'Is Al in? C'mon, I got the bogey.'

Once my grandfather saw us on the road.

'Who is this?'

'This is Albert.'

My grandfather gave us money for sweets. We ran up to the shop, purchased an ocean of pear drops, shared them out: riches!

At first, Albert wouldn't come into the house but shouted over the wall.

'Is Al in?' That was his cry and I loved it.

'Yes,' I said. I was always 'in' to Albert.

We stuck together. If somebody asked him to do something in the schoolyard, he'd jerk his head at me. 'I'm with him.'

There was a boy who was such an uncontrollable farter that he was sometimes sent out of class and when he performed, Albert would look at me and roll his eyes. The roll of his eyes alone was soon enough to send me into hysterics so that, out of consideration for me, he stopped doing it.

Then I went out of the house one morning and Albert wasn't there. He wasn't in school either. After a few days someone said, 'They're on the road.' I mooched about the caravan site near Mill Field but never asked any questions. I never saw him again but if I had a sense of loss, I also had a status. I was Albert's pal, someone who had been enjoined. I had somehow lost the prim niceness with which I had begun, and although it was years before I was habitually in what was frequently described as the wrong company, my friendship with Albert had taken its toll on my clothes, my shoes, socks, shins, knees. I looked as worn as he did. But I belonged. I was, I might have said, when I was not having fantasies about my never-mentioned father, 'lovely and normal!'

'Clothes do not grow on trees,' my grandmother said resignedly when she looked at me.

A long time later, our class suffered the impatience of an ageing war widow who went berserk with an ebony ruler, causing an eruption of parental complaints and the intrusion of the headmistress. We felt as if we'd been under shellfire and I who, together with others, had wet myself in fear, remember thinking gravely, 'I'm very glad Albert is out of this.' He was the first pal I ever had, one of the few people in my life who could make me laugh uncontrollably, an experience no one should be without.

In hospital, memories came like interrupted film sequences, drifting hazily into my consciousness. Now as I try to recall my primary school, I do so with gratitude. Overall and general impressions prevail over the particular now, but they did not when I lay on my back, and while I have always been fascinated by the idea that a drowning man sees images of his past life and I have heard a man of seventy calling in his death throes for his mother, one even murmuring the name of a long-dead greyhound, I am not so sure about the precise order of the recall. I suspect that any conception of form is wishful thinking. Even an attempt to impose order at this very moment somehow diminishes the heat of experience. Perhaps one only snatches at the truth. Perhaps it comes by accident, a stray card falling into place in the ever-fading hand of lost happenings.

In those days when you left the Infants' School, you went to the Big School, boys and girls separating out. In our case you went upstairs, skipping a floor which was the girls' school, to the toppermost deck of a huge three-decker building which stood, and still stands, in a prominent position overlooking the town. When you went up to Big School, you literally went up and up a steeply sloping asphalt pathway like a runway extending up the side of the hill parallel to the main building above which, higher still, there was a large playground, walled in but the wall surmountable and giving way to woods and open space behind. The school seemed monstrously high, a gargantuan building, and at seven the path and steps adjoining it were like an ascent into the sky itself and seemed never-ending. It was so steep that latecomers had no chance of catching up if they hurried. You could never hurry for if you were not bent double halfway up, you had already collapsed. When you got to the top, you entered a dark lower yard, bordered by the still-towering building and a banned area under a wall known as the shrubbery where misplaced balls could lie until they rotted amongst dank foliage which seldom received the sun. The main playground was higher up still, but this yard was the place for lining up before we went into school, for fire drills, for being 'tooled' by bigger boys anxious to inspect your private parts, and a game known as Bumberino when a file of boys gripped each other, heads bent and feet wide apart to form a caterpillar which ended with a strong boy holding the others firmly against a drainpipe. The caterpillar formed, a jumper would attempt to leap the whole, and sometimes two teams competed with each other and the cry 'strong horses, weak donkeys!' would be heard. This was the formal game, but more often than not, it went off at half-cock: there was no more than one team and the aim seemed to be to manoeuvre the biggest and fattest boys into the line of jumpers so that their descent was like a six-chamber game of Russian roulette when everybody got hurt. Sometimes you would be grabbed to form the caterpillar and automatically expected to take your medicine and be a bumberino. Strangely enough, despite injuries, it was never stopped completely and as juniors it was always our aim to escape into the bigger yards where it was never played because of the lack of supporting drainpipes. It was really a licence to cause pain given to the fat boys, but it became a boast to be able to say, 'I had Fatty Watkins on top of me today.'

It was in the lower yard where the teachers blew their whistles calling us to order, and at first we judged them by the fear they were able to inspire. When the whistle blew, you were expected to freeze on the spot and there were boys who made it their business to wait for the master on duty to appear. The moment he put the whistle to his lips, they would deliberately adopt the most lunatic postures so that they would be embalmed in them as soon as the whistle blew. These expressions and stances they held until the second whistle blew, instructing us to go to our classroom lines. Some boys would be perched like storks on one leg, their mouths yelping derision; others would stuff their fingers up their noses, or somebody else's, the toolers would be about their tooling, and even the bumberinos would be immobile, especially if some weak donkey was in danger of suffocation. You had the cane if you were detected in the slightest movement, with the result that the attitudes of even the most innocent of boys resembled those of a lunatic asylum caught at the pitch of madness. But we froze twice daily, enjoying the licence to pull the most frightening jibs as a matter of pride once we got older. Then the second whistle blew, legs would come down, fingers would be removed from whatever orifice they had found, the bumberinos unscrambled and we would lawfully proceed like sheep to our class lines before the command, 'Monitors!', came when six of the bigger boys would move to yet another set of steps and supervise our progress upwards once more.

It was on the stairs in my very first year that I basked in the glory of unexpected privilege. I had what I have so often lacked in the dark Welsh sense, influence! My cousin David, the son of farming relatives, having failed the eleven-plus examination, was a monitor and since he was easy-going and kindly, especially looked out for me so that I was sometimes privileged to receive an extra bottle of free milk, the distribution of which was one of the monitors' perks. I have seldom been more grateful for a friendly face, not that the school was unduly rough, but his cheerful wink on the stairs set me up for the day. As it happened I did not like milk but I soon subcontracted the privilege, enjoying my own influence in turn. Like the Rhondda councillor with a full glass who is offered further obeisance and says 'I'm all right for now, but I'll have a large Players' since you're offering!' I had entered the scheme of things, and throughout that year I basked in the shadow of my protector. I liked school. I was happy, and the early voices remain.

'I want a noun! Give me a noun! What is a noun?'

'A naming word, sir.'

'Very good. Give me a noun beginning with B. *Hands*!'

I can see the hands now, a forest of them, for we must have been forty in the class and a boy called Cookie blinked when singled out.

'Bum,' he said informatively without a trace of mischief.

Hysteria again. We had learned to laugh at the misfortune and ignorance of others, and there was nothing funnier than when the teacher's false teeth fell into the tadpole spawn. It wasn't long before I learned that I was expected to pass the eleven-plus examination with three or four others in the class. We were not the ablest, but the most parentally driven. Others were required to leave school at fourteen and work, but they were better off than young people now since they were almost certain of a job. For all the crying waste of that society of the thirties, it did not enfold the young with the hopeless and never-ending blight of present-day unemployment where the haves have become even more impervious to the have-nots.

By this time I had taken the eleven-plus, the second war

65

had broken out and that led to another chapter in another place. In the all-age school, or Lan Wood, as it was then called, I learned the greatest of gifts, to pass unnoticed in the crowd except perhaps for my propensity to accidents for I was cut, bruised, stitched, scoured, disinfected and bandaged more than most, especially flying down the escape ramp but I wore my scars as comforting badges of normality and suffered little. I took pride in never fainting which was quite commonplace then, perhaps because of malnutrition or, equally likely, the massively efficient central-heating system; for on some days the radiators steamed with the burden of drying clothes so that each classroom resembled a laundry. But that was all normal and I regard the school now as a humane place with none of the evils of bullying which many associate with such schools in big cities. It was in all respects a neighbourhood school and if we learned little more than to read and write, it was a sociable place and the masters kindly. We chanted our tables, fed the goldfish, watched mustard seeds germinate on blotting paper, wrote happily and at length about 'A Day in the Life of a Penny' and once we even had a visit from a writer – Jack Jones, massively handsome with his silver hair and resonant voice. He called in to present a pair of gleaming working boots to a virtuoso, a boy who had not been absent or late in the whole of the seven years he spent there. I can remember thinking, he probably had never even coughed aloud either. He was an unknown boy, unseen, never heard to speak, one who had kept well and truly in the background. He might have been a lesson to us all. The prizes came to those who were most easily managed.

So the memory deals the cards – seven years gone and a chapter closed. But my time in hospital preserved the memories and there was one day which came back to me almost in its entirety since it seemed to be more truthfully part of my life than the cosier reminiscences with which I sometimes indulge myself. In the intervals between bouts of pain, men will recall the joys of their lives, the most recountable incidents and, like all storytellers, will attempt to show themselves in some kind of acceptable light. But as the days go by the tall and the long stories give way to exchanges of a more common kind, incidents at first simple but often more revealing. Almost all Welsh children have a memory of a school trip, usually a visit to some desirable venue which can accommodate large numbers of unruly children. There was a minimum age limit, usually fixed at nine, and for weeks we looked forward to the expected day – particularly those who had never been beyond the boundaries of the town, or at least as far as cold, wicked Cardiff. Sooner or later we would be told the venue and in this case it was Bristol Zoo, which was a manageable distance in the space of a day.

Once announced, the excitement generated was quite incredible. As the day approached some boys confessed they could not sleep. The whole school was going, the upstairs boys and the downstairs girls, and for a week there were exhortations as to our appearance, the necessity for socks, handkerchiefs if they could be managed, above all cleanliness. The headmaster, a peppery little man who sometimes played soccer in the schoolyard and was a dustbin cricketer of repute, gave us to understand that People Would Be

Watching The Lan Wood Boys and, what is more, as a special privilege we had been granted what seemed to be the freedom of the ancient City of Bristol because we would be welcomed and marshalled from the railway station and the police had been told of our impending arrival. I did not know until I got to our own railway station that the privilege had actually been granted to most of the schools of the lower Rhondda as well as Pontypridd, but this was the first of many such speeches I was to hear in my life and, indeed, to compose myself a few years later. But at the time I listened gravely. The headmaster had decided it would not rain so that raincoats would not be carried and since refreshments would be provided, there was also no need for sandwiches. Sandwiches made a mess and the Great Western Railway had inspectors especially briefed to diagnose a Lan Wood mess. There was also the matter of being sick on the train. 'Now I'm warning you well in advance, no one is going to be sick, especially those who fill themselves up with sweets, whose parents have more money than sense. There's no reason why we shouldn't all enjoy ourselves, BUT...'

Dutifully, I bore it all in mind. I have since tried to define a day in my life when I began to see through such exhortations, a time when I no longer bluntly accepted everything that was told to me, but it was a long time ahead, and I would not then have disobeyed a single instruction. It was to be a fun day. Bristol, we said, and paused – awed – as we might have said Mecca. And the Zoo! We spent days discussing what animals we might concentrate our attention upon. Intelligence reports from a previous year revealed that there was a hippopotamus which urinated continuously and had won a kind of celebrity for being the most disgusting exhibit, next to the chimpanzees whose red arses and wandering fingers invited hysteria, especially if you stood next to a teacher when they were performing. Perhaps we were joyously anticipating the sight of unrestrained versions of ourselves by courtesy of the City of Bristol. At any rate, we discussed it endlessly, even arranging our seats on the train well in advance.

My grandmother instructed me to wear especially clean underclothes in case of an accident. She was obsessed with the need for cleanliness next to the skin when visiting major English cities. It was a reversal of her normal positive character and showed a curious inferiority which was characteristic of many Welsh people at the time. 'Suppose you were run over?' she would argue; 'you don't want people to know where you're from!'

I had then, and later, a vision of myself as a crumpled figure in some metropolitan gutter with a police officer fingering my immaculate Bon Ton vest and pants.

'He's not from Ponty, you can tell!'

These exhortations were to become more complex when, as a young man, I attended interviews in London – one in Queen Anne Mansions in the Admiralty, inwardly the most unlikely candidate for His Majesty's Commission.

'Speak clearly and stand up straight!' my grandmother instructed me.

What the English thought of us in Bristol or elsewhere, I had no idea and did not care. But on another occasion I experienced a neat reversal of role. Descending in civilian clothes from a bus carrying a naval rugby team to Colchester Garrison, I was accosted by a sentry.

'Who are you, then?'

I told him.

'Tough shit, mate,' he gave a cruel grin; 'the Taffies are here.'

He was right. The Welch Regiment had returned from duty in Berlin and a strengthened Colchester Garrison side beat us by a cricket score.

But Bristol... ah, Bristol.

'Remember where you're from!' my grandmother said once more before reminding me of the presents her own children had brought her back from such outings. I clutched two silver half-crowns in my trouser pocket as I raced to school. The weather, as ordered by the head-master, was obediently fine.

In the yard, there was a hubbub of excitement. The poorest boys had been found an array of presentable clothes from the headmaster's charity bag, a collection of odds and ends of boots, shoes, jerseys and trousers which he solicited from wealthy friends and kept in the storeroom for rainy days when children were soaked coming to school and such occasions as this. Some children had brought games to play on the train, even tattered comic annuals to read; others, disregarding the instructions about sweets, were well stocked up and there was an air of buzzing expectancy that accompanied all such bonanza days. It was such a treat to be going anywhere.

There was first, however, a slight confusion. On such days, as in fire drills, the teachers marked the registers in the schoolyard and we did not enter the school at all, but a last minute act of generosity by a local fruiterer, known as Tommy Potatoes, in collusion with the headmaster, had resulted in the late arrival of several crates of Fyffes bananas on the previous evening. Even more welcome was a parcel of slim white drawing pencils, each one stamped with the Fyffes insignia, a golden banana on a blue oval. They must have arrived just as the school was closing and now, so that they could properly and fairly be distributed, it was decided that we had to enter our classrooms where registration would take place as usual. I suspect that the headmaster realised that there was not enough bananas to go around and so he wanted the distribution to be done in an orderly manner inside the classrooms. It might have been his intention that we ate the bananas before we left, but in any event, we were doubly elated. It was not just that we were to have something for nothing, but the pencils in particular were prized and perhaps something else that might occupy us on the train. It was such a glorious day anyway that anything that was to happen could only be an added bounty.

So we were sent to our classrooms as usual but we were not usual children and the monitors could not control us. We scampered up the steps, bounding, leaping, racing across the assembly hall, jumping into our classroom where our teacher, usually a kindly man, found himself doubly harrassed by our exuberance and by the ominously small bundle of bananas in the wicker basket beside his desk. There were also not more than twenty pencils glistening in a partially opened box.

He told us to keep quiet and to sit still but we could not on such a day and now came the problem of dividing up the gift, a complicated matter which necessitated a pencilled tick opposite your name at the side of the register. There were other such distributions throughout the year and our teacher would keep a record so that he could refer to the haves and have-nots in the past. But now he was all of a hurry as we clambered about him.

'Sit down!' he shouted.

We hardly moved.

'Silence!' he said.

We were too excited.

His problem continued. There were forty of us. There were enough bananas to go round, but not enough pencils and the pencils were the real prize, as he well knew. He made a decision. Finally, he got us to sit down and we folded our arms as instructed.

'Right,' he said. 'Stand up those without fathers!'

I think I could have died then. I certainly wanted to. In all my nine years, I had never experienced such a humiliation. I was exposed, laid bare. This was no piece of information surreptitiously received from muttered voices by me alone. It was a public announcement of what separated me from others. More importantly, the matter had never been mention-ed before. It was new information. There was dead silence. Alone, I got to my feet. I felt every eye upon me, my throat dry, my eyes already filling, my heart beating and beating away. And it was to have been such a bonanza of a day.

He realised my embarrassment immediately. He was a good kindly man. His own embarrassment was almost as great as mine for he must have been told of my circumstances. He covered up at once, avoiding my filling eyes.

'Right! Stand up all those whose fathers are unemployed.'

There were twenty on their feet straight away, all eyeing the pencils.

'We'll go backwards down the alphabet, Y, W, V, U, S, T, R...'

I got my pencil. He made sure of that for I was an R. Then we were out into the yard, made to eat the bananas until the monitors collected the skins, and finally moved in a long crocodile towards the railway station in pairs. My pal did not say anything. He had new shoes borrowed from his brother which was a change from wearing his sister's. They pinched his feet. He was suffering too. I broke the pencil into bits in the lavatory of the train, put the bits down the pan but they floated so I took them out and threw them from the window. I did not think I would ever get over my humiliation. Now everybody knew.

When we returned that night, I sat silent and tired in my seat. We enjoyed the day. We did not let anybody down. In the train, the teachers played solo whist on an upturned suitcase and you could tell they'd had a few since they did not want to be disturbed and the beery smell of hops came from them when they patrolled occasionally down the new corridors. When we went through the Severn Tunnel, I made a long journey down the whole corridor. There were shrieks of laughter coming from the lavatory at the far end of the coach. A half-dozen of the bigger boys had hold of a girl who was not quite all there, as we said. They were holding her forcibly, her knickers were on the floor, and one had his hand over her mouth. I can see her reddened face now, the pain in her eyes, her unruly mop of wild ginger hair. I didn't know what they were doing to her. 'They're tooling her,' somebody said. She was still flushed when she got out at the station but they'd given her knickers back. Another girl, big and freckled with flaming scarlet lips and mouth, had her arm around her and threatened the boys.

'I'll fucking get you tomorrow,' she said.

I brought a china tiger home for my grandmother, and a penguin for my mother. I said nothing to anyone, but I had discovered more about the world.

'He doesn't seem to think a lot of Bristol,' my grand-mother said, not without a certain pride.

These were two incidents in my life, my earliest memory of the reality of pain. Now I doubt if I would have remembered the one without the other. A writer's path is made with such connections. Without them, he is only a trader in information, or other people's ideas.

FOUR

A fatherless child is more sensitive to the men he meets in his childhood than other children. In a sense, he is window-shopping for the father he might have had. There is also the matter of authority. Away from the female apron strings, there are strange males to be investigated and sniffed at and, invariably, some who appear large and dominant, often figures of fear who seem to breathe a different air from normal men. In the child's mind, they can be difficult to envisage in domestic situations for they are mostly encountered in institutions, backed and cloaked by public trappings. They exist as triumphant role-players, frequently seem larger than life and, at times, their very presence seems designed to make those with whom they come in contact seem smaller and weaker. These are the rulers of their little kingdoms who do not seem little at the time because there is seldom any immediate escape from them.

Such a man was my headmaster in the County School to which I went once the all-pervading battle of the eleven-plus examination was overcome. Like Pharaoh he ruled all he surveyed, I soon came to feel, but bullrushes were in short supply. Whenever he was around, there were no hiding places. Like other rulers, I heard about him before I saw him. In the hazy summers after the war broke out, I often played with children who had made the all-important transfer to the County School. Since colliers and collier boys invariably came home blackened from the pit, the contrast between the two kinds of education, ours and theirs, was often dramatically illustrated within days of leaving school. A boy who left at fourteen could literally appear the next day with working boots and tin jack, his eyeballs and teeth gleaming brilliant white against his blackened face and helmet. One day, he might be a neatly jerseyed monitor on the school stairs, the next he had joined the working world of men who spat and swore, the steel tips of their pit boots clanking and striking sparks as they walked by their former classmates who passed them self-consciously in blazer and short trousers and the peaked school cap it was then obligatory to wear. Fourteen was the age when normal-sized children passed into long trousers, but many continued to wear short trousers to school long after and so the gulf remained immediately apparent.

Now the boys with whom I played were all destined for higher things, if not the County School, then private school – more exclusive still as they entered the world of 'hols' and tuck boxes and 'fags' which all figured importantly in the 'public' school stories we all read avidly in the comics of the day. It was never expected that I should fail the eleven-plus and I came thirty-first out of about ninety entrants, among the top seed as it were, and those a year older who had gone before soon informed me that I would be in the first stream, paradoxically called the 'B' Stream, and that meant I would have so-and-so for 'Geoga' or 'Chem' and, most important, Pig would keep an eye on me.

Pig was my headmaster's nickname, the most loathsome imaginable, and boys were known to wet themselves in his presence. These and other facts were known to me long before I ever encountered him. He was remarkable in that he memorised every boy's name within seconds of meeting him and his very entry into an assembly hall was enough to stiffen a multitude of five hundred boys into an abashed silence. The silences his presence invoked were legendary. He beat you, harangued you, and found you out. Like Stalin, or Mao Tse-tung, or Field Marshal Kitchener on the famous wartime recruiting poster, his eyes were always on you. He did not leave you alone – ever. And there was The Stick, a substantial bamboo cane which he kept in his room or about his person – down his trouser-leg, sometimes tucked up the sleeve of his gown – and then there were the fearful questions he was likely to shoot at you, muscling you into a crevice as he gave you the third degree on sight. 'Twice the half of two-and-a-half, boy!' He had caned a prefect for being caught by a farmer with his trousers down in the act of sexual intercourse on a mountain path, school cap in his back pocket, each buttock rising and falling, bringing the school further and further into disrepute with each continuing stroke. He had also struck out at a member of the staff for not wearing a gown, later protesting a justifiable mistake. When he walked down the main street of the town in the day, the streets were likely to clear of boys who had the slightest connection with the school. No Western lawman ever walked down a street with more effect. He was not known to have any hobbies or leisure pastimes and nothing human about him had been reported to me, although I knew vaguely that he had a wife and a daughter but these were seldom seen. In addition to his degrees, he had won a boxing blue at Oxford, and the fingernails of his right hand were upturned as a consequence of continually poking and jabbing at offenders with his stiffened palm. He also smoked Gold Flake which was to prove immensely important to me.

Then there was his face.

'You wait until you see him!' my informants told me. 'You won't laugh.'

I never did, as it happened, or at least, not for years. All the information I received then, I believed in its entirety. For every exaggerated claim, there was a basis of truth, and he remained a feared man, much talked about, a man who created waves.

It was like me, I see now, to get off on the wrong foot with him, and the County School. My elevation to the blazer and cap-wearing peerage was much celebrated and very soon after the results were announced, I was taken to the little school outfitters in the Arcade where the dark maroon blazer and cap with the bridge motif emblazoned upon it were duly tried on, and my grandmother regarded me with pride. I have never since felt with such intensity that I stood at the threshold of a new world, and the fond looks I was given exaggerated my sense of self-importance. I had done something at last. It was natural that having won my spurs I should want to demonstrate myself and wear the blazer at once and, indeed, did so on several occasions. So I was wearing it one evening when I played on the street with several other boys who had already entered the school. It was high summer, the chestnut trees were in bloom, one of those still evenings when you could smell the horse manure wafting up from the Co-operative stables below the railway bridge, and although the light was fading, we took advantage of the shadows as we hid from each other.

I was hot and sticky but kept my blazer on. Earlier we had bought some chips, the remnants of which I now ate from a crumpled newspaper. I think I had opted out of the game, or been caught out, when suddenly the cry came from one of the boys who had strayed furthest away.

'Pig's coming!'

'Where?'

'Down here... he's coming this way! He is! Honest!'

There were five or six of us, all boys, playing release mob – a game of seeking and finding, the person 'on it' having a tennis ball which he threw at you if he could find you before you returned to base. But now the street cleared, my playmates were nowhere to be seen, save one, a slightly older boy who cowered behind a wall near me. I looked in terror at my blazer, realising that the wearing of it was premature.

A phrase of my grandmother's came to my mind, one that has often returned.

I was not legally entitled.

Then there were the remnants of the chips in the vinegar-soiled newspaper. They compounded the felony and the charge began to frame itself in my mind, 'Bringing disgrace on the uniform you were not entitled to wear!'

I hastily stuffed the chips down a nearby drain, ramming them well down and beyond sight.

He was not, as it happened, coming down our particular end of the street, but passing it, and I soon saw him in the gloom as he moved away from me, crossing the street to head for his own home, a thickset, olive-skinned and moon-faced, trilby-hatted figure with the stub end of a cigarette glowing sinisterly between his lips. He wore thick, horn-rimmed spectacles and they glinted as he cast a sidelong glance at the deserted street and passed on, an unusual breadth of shoulder visible under his shabby raincoat, his footsteps stealthy on rubber soles. Soon, he was no more than a retreating shadow.

'He'd have had you!' my hidden companion said when it was safe to do so.

I was sure he would have.

' "Chips as well!" he'd have said!'

I'd got rid of those.

He did not live more than six hundred yards away in a semi-detached house set high above the road with a long rising pathway leading to a shrubbery which hid the bottom of the house. Later, I would look up at it half-expecting smoke to rise, or to see the glint of some powerful telescopic lens as it beamed towards me, such was the power of the myth he generated, and myths ruled me until I could think for myself. This was my problem and I soon found I could not concentrate in the classroom and had little interest in what was being taught me.

Very soon, the awful reality of war descended on us. After the initial excitement of marching soldiers and the appearance of my mother's youngest brother in air gunner's uniform, I began to realise that once again we were at the periphery of events which were happening far away from us. I remember the paper boys crying the slogan 'War declared!' and Chamberlain's quavery voice on the radio; then my mother said, 'It's not Hitler. It's the men behind him', taking a very South Walian view and pretending to be in the know. This view was shared by the local newspaper which proclaimed, 'The promises he [Hitler] has broken were enumerated in the pamphlets recently dropped over Germany. We have no quarrel with the German people and wish them well.' My grandmother said nothing, however, and now she would sit silently in the chair for long periods while propaganda took over the radio bulletins and the newspapers, and stories of German depravities became known. There were also the immediate household trappings of war: blackout curtains, sticky tape to cover the windows in case of bomb blast, and, of course, ration books.

My own war, save for some half-hearted attempts to collect salvage with the Scouts, was a very private one and at first I laid low. Teachers who should have retired, plodded on in the absence of younger men and soon there was fire-watching, the Air Training Corps for youthful cadets and the appearance in chapel of older boys, their fingers blotched and swollen with frostbite, survivors of early torpedoings. You could go to war at an early age in the Merchant Navy, the South Wales ports were at hand, parental consent forms were often forged. It wasn't long before the casualties came, one after the other. To give a factual account of these times diminishes them. As they linger in the mind, sentences return, remnants of conversations that stand in the memory like old scars that will not go away, some of them searing conversations in the classroom.

'Why are you crying, Leonard?'

No answer. But there were always informants.

'Please, Sir, his brother went down on the *Prince of Wales*.' Then there was the brother of the boy over the road, the brother of the boy up the road, brothers along this street and that, and the most dreaded sight became the telegram boy with his push-bike and leather pouch. When my own uncle was killed, shot down in a Wellington bomber over Le Havre, family connections with the Post Office meant that the telegram was intercepted, but the news came just the same: *Missing, Presumed Killed*. Again, I saw my grandmother howl, again a parcel arrived marked, *Effects to Next of Kin*. It was only bearable because it was happening to us all as it had happened before, and somehow we survived while others who had lost an only child began visibly to shrink as the weeks went by. My grandmother began to regale me with old exhortations, addressed I suspect as much to herself as to me, saying 'Best foot forward!' and 'Stick at it, John Willy', both sayings from her own childhood which she repeated automatically, no stranger to the numbing chaos of loss and war. But she never lost the will to go on, literally to put one foot after the other. Surrender of any kind would have been unthinkable, even to morbidity and she gave herself more and more to tasks, caring for this one in chapel, visiting another, several times being the first caller in a house where another casualty had been reported. She was more and more welcome as one who had experienced most things. You could tell her nothing about grief and yet she managed a smile, invariably a little gift, or a comforting word. Somehow it is hard to convince young people now of the feeling of impotence which everybody seemed to feel in the first years of the war. Generally there was a total scorn for pacifists, little understanding of any intellectual or religious objection to war. South Wales was ever a rich recruiting ground for poor men's sons anxious for foreign adventure. The feeling persisted, 'Everybody is in it together', and was shrewdly manipulated by newspapers. The exhortation 'to do your bit' was general. There were, of course, attractions – escape from the confines of a small town, the excitement and glamour of uniform, the almost universal distortions of reality in the stories servicemen told to civilians when on leave and, to those who stayed at home, a feeling of missing something vital. And yet, as each casualty was announced by telegram, the sense of loss was total and near at hand: the baker's son, lured to sea by an older friend after a quarrel with his father over a trifle – whether or not he should help out with deliveries after school; the butcher's son, recently proudly qualified as a doctor, dying of wounds in Java; the air gunners, the radio operators, the seamen, the grammar school boys who formed the bulk of air crews who were being decimated with heavy casualties – this was somehow so normal that it became a daily fact of life. If I wept at night for my own kin, part of my grief was my sense of personal loss, but the consequence of all those other deaths seemed to make my elders even more determined to redouble their contribution to the war effort. No matter what happened, you conformed and I had no experience of any kind of rebellion – except perhaps in my grandmother's howl of anguish, repeated across the road by a neighbour when yet another *Regret To Inform You* telegram came. It was as if she had no vocabulary to deal with these events, and no real comprehension of them, only of their effects. It was a gap in her armour, I sensed, and when the time came for her to go to Buckingham Palace to receive a posthumously awarded medal, she became so concerned about what she should wear that I sided with my mother who felt an indifference to the occasion. Uncle Ithel was dead. Nothing would bring him back and I wished my grandmother had been her usual forceful attacking self, but she conformed, and later reported knowledgeably on the King's chalk-white pallor. His hand shook, she said. She hoped it wasn't drink!

In my own case I moved into a world of fantasy in which the figure of my headmaster began to occupy more and more of my thoughts, and beside whom Adolf Hitler became increasingly provincial and remote. I have described my first sight of him as rationally as I can, but reason became a frail friend as it slowly dawned on me that I could not cope with school. Now the consequences of my fantasising came home to me. There was so much which I did not understand. I could not concentrate and I could not take things in. I grew thinner, more haunted, and at first, very wisely tried to hide, finding my level in the back seats of classrooms with others equally anxious to be anonymous. From an early age I found my level with the masturbators and droolers, with those who came late and were often unkempt, dilatory with their homework, yearning like myself to be away. A hero's death with a sad little photograph in the local newspaper was easily achievable, it seemed, and the caption, 'Sadly missed by all his former workmates', which I read so often, was not entirely out of the question. 'Richards, A., Form 2B. Missed by his classmates in the back seats, but not by the staff!'

Now I began to develop frenetic scenarios in my mind, all of which had a sombre aspect. I had to pass my head-master's house every day and began to judge the precise times when he appeared and learned to avoid him with an expertise that was immediately rewarded, because for a year he was not aware of my existence. Nor, indeed, were the other masters for I cheated and copied most of my homework and remained undetected with hardly a blemish upon me. 'Crime *does* pay,' I said to myself with relish in the first blissful months of keeping out of sight.

I had begun to fly imaginary bombing raids daily in my mind, screaming into the intercom as I held an imaginary joystick in my hand. At other times, I might be a parched lifeboat survivor gasping for water and at any time of the day my facial expressions might resemble those of victims in the furthest reaches of pain. I considered death by burning, drowning, even cannibalism, and in the midst of some incomprehensible lesson I would sometimes look thoughtfully at the exposed thigh of the boy who sat next to me, a strange expression coming on my face and occasionally I would say quite incomprehensibly, 'I'm sorry Bevan, but you've got to go!', then retreat – masticating solemnly – into my mysterious self without explanation. Occasionally, prompted by the example of an older boy next door who had shrewdly decided on a divinity course at an opportune time, I preached to congregations. Once in the physics laboratory when a student teacher lost half the dwindling supply of the school's mercury down the sink, I made up a little sermon and addressed myself frequently in the manner of the old Welsh preachers. 'And the Devil looked out of the watch tower with a lusty leer upon his dirty chops... "Mercury," he cried. "Whereby is my Mercury?" ' At first, I kept my fantasy life strictly to myself and I became known as the silent one, an anonymous face at the back of the classroom, but the war first intervened when my Uncle Ithel was awarded the DFC shortly before he was killed and, suddenly, the two most distinguished old boys on the Roll of Honour – a copper plaque at the back of the assembly hall – were both relatives. This occurrence, together with the results of the end-of-term examinations, became known to my headmaster and my life changed. I was now bottom of the class.

'I was thirty-first when I went into the school and I've kept it up,' I told my grandmother, already putting a face on things. There were actually thirty-two boys in the class as we'd had a late arrival who only sat half the examination papers, but there was no mistaking my lowly position and poor progress. When the new term started, I stayed with my form as there were no demotions that year, but within a few days Pig arrived like a holocaust. His appearances in the barrack-like

86

extension of the old buildings called the new school, were less sinister than in the original building – a place of corridors, stairways and tiny classrooms with coal fireplaces. In the new school he could be seen in advance and he would peer into classrooms as he marched along the corridor, sometimes trailing his stick, sometimes causing it to tap sinisterly along the corridor tiles. When he entered the new classrooms, he would do so abruptly and we stood up as if electrified. In the older buildings, you could hear his footsteps on the stairs as he bounded up them. The effect of his entrance was that of some identifiable controller in a horror film, the grotesque mastermind in a world of weaklings which he could galvanise into action and bend to his will. It was invariably melo-dramatic, noisy and imperious, often with scant respect paid to the teacher who had charge of the class. You could feel the muscles of your calves stiffening, and sense the same stiffen-ing in the boys next to you. Fear communicated itself myst-eriously as it does with rabbits. He had a habit of bounding in, immediately marching up the aisle and bending his face to within inches of your own, so close that you could see up his meaty nostrils, noting your own cowering reflection in his dusty spectacles as you got the full cheesy waft of him while he asked you some probing question. Woe betide a boy sitting alone in a double seat. This meant someone had to be accounted for. The balding pate would bend towards you, the thin lips parted, then sometimes there was a vicious dig with the prodding finger before the third degree.

'Where's Millwyn Jenkins?'

Somehow you had to find an answer, to say something – anything, just to speak.

'He... he... he...'

'Speak up, boy! Out with it! Sharpen up now!'

'He... he... He've got a job!'

This was years later, but the horror on his face at this grammatical mistake became as much described as the expression on the Mona Lisa. Now he exploded, gasped, spat, shivered with wrath:

'*He've got a job?* Central Welsh Board School Certificate English Examination within a week. You can do better than that, boy! *Again!*'

This time the victim thought hard, came out with a pearler in the poshest voice he could manage.

'Sorry, Mr Thomas. He have obtained a position.'

But these repeatable jokes were in the years when we got to know him. On this day in 1942 he came bursting in, clutching one of his bulging files, briefly acknowledged the master and swivelled his eyes around us as we stood like thin, undernourished storks trapped in a pond before him. He had one query and a demand.

'Form 3B?'

'Yessir!' we said shrilly in unison, the obnoxious anxiety to please overwhelming.

'Richards, A.?' he then said, the malevolent eyes searching for me amongst the staring faces which all immediately turned to my hiding place amongst the dreamers tucked away at the rear.

I was already on my feet like the others, but now my legs went and I began to tremble uncontrollably. I had so much to hide. I was so puny by this time, gawky and peaky faced, all elbows and knees, my adolescent spots beginning. I was unable to speak. Fish-like, my mouth opened and closed. In an instant, saliva became a thing of the past. This was what he could do to you – reduce you to a thing! The boy beside me elbowed me out into the aisle, even a movement on his part an act of courage, coupled with the assurance that somebody else was going to get it – a relief I often felt myself. Somehow or other, I went sideways down the aisle like a gawky half-sized beanstalk tottering in the wind.

He glared down at me. His normal expression was ferocious. He seemed continually to be in an appalled state but was even more so in these confrontations which he continually sought. It was as if all of you appalled him, your face, your pimples, your grimy spectacles, your crumpled socks, your scuffed shoes. His very stare seemed to create a visible reduction in everything you were, or owned, as he looked. It was not just a matter of cutting you down to size, but he was X-raying you as well. I was aware that I was still in short trousers and last week's underpants showed. Neither did I know where to put my hands or feet as I drifted before him like a damp cloud. If skeletons had feelings, this was how they must have felt, I thought. I could feel fear rattling in me. It went down to my groin like an electric charge.

'Come here, young man!' he said in his oratorical voice extending the phrase like a singer.

He beckoned me forward.

I stood close to him for a second, close enough to see the homely egg stain on his smudged waistcoat. But then he moved his plump repellent face and followed it with his body, opening the door wider, but cunningly leaving a space between his crooked arm and body for me to pass.

'Come with me!' he crooned. 'Come-come-come!'

Hesitating, I eventually went through the tunnel like a lurching goldfish down the plug hole and without another word to anyone, he followed, closing the door behind him, but not before I heard the class gasp with relief at their own collective escape. Later, I was to feel that such a sacrifice now and again was worth anything to be rid of him. In war there had to be casualties. Be thankful it wasn't you!

Outside the classroom, he was on the move at once in a flurry of feet, files, waistcoat and billowing gown, his feet skidding away.

'Follow me!'

His feet seemed to dance down the corridor, the gown flew out behind him, neck hunched, beak raised, like an overfed bird of prey who has already hypnotised his victim so that I followed powerless as if drawn on a poisoned thread. Further and further down the corridor he strode, hurtling forward, up the steps of the covered way and I suddenly realised that he was heading for the assembly hall. He did not look around once. Reaching the door, he threw it open, once again standing to one side so that I would have to go through the tunnel, brushing against his waistcoat, those eyes flickering down at me. Like all predatory creatures, he seemed to caress you appreciatively with his eyes before moving forward for the actual act of destruction.

A class was taking music at the far end of the hall but he paid no attention to them, or to the master in charge, and soon I saw the reason for the summons. I have said that the names of the war dead were inscribed on a bronze scroll at the rear of the assembly hall. For 1914–18 they were ranged in order of rank, so that my grandmother's brother led the list – Lieut. Colonel W. E. Thomas DSO, MC. But now the scroll had been extended. New names were being added piecemeal, week by week, and these names were burnished in new bronze so that they shone brilliantly in glistening golden letters and among them was my uncle's name – Flying Officer Ithel Jeremy DFC – and somehow the lettering was altogether more bold and pronounced, more real for me because, of course, I could put faces to these new names. In Ithel's case, I had walked so proudly with him down the main street, tried on his leather bombing jacket with its trailing electric flex and felt his hand holding mine as he took me on the dodgem cars at the Easter Fair. He was the father I would have liked to have had, youthful and humorous with a ready wink, but incinerated now and committed only to memory save for those dreadful golden letters.

'Here, boy!' Pig said, beckoning me closer.

I did not move. I began for the first time in my life to feel a dull and sullen resentment, a stubbornness that might have been born at that very moment, welling up slowly like fuel gathering imperceptibly at the bottom of a tank inside me. It was not fair that I should be so singled out, not fair according to any accepted case law, in that my spurious homework had not been detected or the evidence laid before me, crime proved. Neither had I said a word out of place, or ever sought to be anything but inconspicuous, lost in the crowd. I had just been sitting there in my desk minding my own business. It was all I ever wanted in my life – to be left alone to dream.

Something of my resentment must have showed on my

face. Surprisingly, I was not in tears and the exertion of the long march had left me calmer. At any rate, the stare which I now fixed upon him was as slow and probing as his own. And equally as insolent. It went up from his shoes, the grubby grey woollen cardigan which he sometimes wore under his waistcoat, over these, past the egg-stain and up to his sallow porker's face, finally to the narrowing impatient eyes as he evidently waited for me to perform some act of obeisance. Exactly what he expected me to do, I cannot think, but I did not do it, did not move at all and he gave a gasp of impatience, seized me by the neck and thrust my face forward towards the scroll so that I could feel the raised bronze letters under my nose. I was pressed so close to them that they must have left a physical impression on my face itself. And the bronze was so cold, cold, cold.

'A family of heroes,' he said in his most scornful and biting voice; 'and what are you?'

My tears had begun by then. I tasted them under the pressure of his hand. But when he released me, I kept my head bent, taking my time before I looked up at him. I was choking with resentment now. In that moment, perhaps, the worm turned for ever after.

'Alive!' I said, choking at the back of my throat. I spat it out. I bored at him with my eyes, thrusting my own eyes at his. I was aware at the same time that we were being watched. The form taking music had the enchanting diversion of the monster and the mouse at the rear end of the hall. I distinctly remember a loose and nervous note from an oboe as there were some of the school orchestra under tuition there as well, but all eyes were turned to look at the two of us as we stared each other out.

I was not then aware that I had him, in a sense, as the saying goes. I did not realise that I had more or less summed up the position so neatly. I *was* alive – just. I had survived Pontypridd's one night of bombing, seen a stick of screaming bombs come down a searchlight, picked shrapnel off the schoolyard, and had also gravely considered the intelligence that the entire enemy raid was directed at Pig's greenhouse which lay at the exact centre of the bomb craters. I had also heard that the traitor, William Joyce, known as Lord Haw Haw, had once kept a stall in Pontypridd market and had old scores to settle. All these pieces of dubious information remained with me, but were hardly pertinent at that precise time for Pig gasped, stared at me, seemed about to explode but – incredibly – took no further action, and the famous prodding right hand lay sheathed in the folds of his gown.

We must have stood there looking at each other for a full minute. I kept my eyes on his because, somehow or other, I knew that it was the only thing to do. When I said no more, he was confronted with a problem and was dumbfounded, it seemed.

'Ha...' he said. 'Hm...'

I did not think it then, but now I realise that he must have been aware of some of my feelings and the consequence of his classroom abduction. I am sure he understood that by any standards he had gone a little too far. There was also the unexpected nature of my reply. I have not forgotten how I looked, perhaps more insolent than wretched when under pressure. And I had snapped the word out at him, 'Alive!' More important, I see now, was that I had yet to learn one cardinal fact about him. He had a weakness for a villain, being one himself. So not only had the worm turned at that precise moment, but a career had opened up for me.

He folded his arms, rocked back and forth on his heels, considered me. I realise now that he was putting on his act. This was the formidable presence that quelled the five hundred every day in morning assembly. But I did not alter my gaze.

Presently he spoke. Above his folded arms, the lips moved; now came a grimly insinuating note of threat:

'From now on, I shall be keeping my eyes on you, young man.'

I said nothing.

'Richards, A., Form 3B. Disgraceful end of term report?' he said.

I continued to say nothing. He had rubber-stamped my report with his signature and the comment, *Must try harder.* If I had said one word, I knew he would have struck out, or invoked some punishment. And, besides averting retribution, my silence and glare were having a positive effect of their own: he did not know what to say.

'Cut along,' he said finally. 'To your room!'

So I left, slinking away, just hearing him turn on the audience at the far end of the hall. His voice was full of confident shots once more, as he raised it, imperious and in full command again.

'And what does *this* form think *it is* doing?'

From that moment on, I acquired a certain notoriety as One Who Was Watched From Above.

'What did he say?' they asked in the back row when I got back to the classroom, eager for news of my demolition.

'Nothing much,' I said shrilly, putting a hard face on it and concealing my alarm. I felt that in some way I'd won a victory, although I knew there was a price on victory. But I had already joined the ranks of the army of Them, the put-upon, the hard-done-by, and those pronounced guilty without trial. I had also, I was to find, entered into a much more select group, one marked off from the common run by the headmaster's penchant for a rebel – a pronounced preference of his which overrode all other characteristics and was to last throughout the tumultuous years of our acquaintanceship. Unlike any academic I was ever to meet, or any person in such authority, he regarded the wayward as being exclusive members of his special parish and ministered to them according to their demands. I was now one of them, marked, the villain from a family of heroes and from that moment on I might have had a special patch sewn upon my uniform rather like a jailbird who is considered a top risk escapee. I had ceased to be anonymous. Before long, 3B found it had a liability in my presence for his visits became more and more frequent and now I experienced a second feeling of rejection – this time from those who liked a quiet life and felt my presence to be dangerous. This I came to enjoy and, indeed, suffered a loss of status later on when the sins of others transgressed my own. But by this time, in one subject, at least, I had become what I had earlier despised – a swot.

FIVE

For a year, Pig declared war on me and never left me alone for long. He would sweep along corridors, come bursting out of the shadows and back me into some tight corner whereupon he would pepper me with his sharpen-you-up questions, sometimes laying the tip of his cane upon my exercise books whose neatness, if nothing else, markedly improved. I felt his eyes upon me everywhere as he seemed to hurtle around the school, sometimes in the company of uniformed old boys whom he would dragoon into giving us pep talks. You might be sitting in the classroom listening to some boring account of the Wars of the Roses – we read history in turns from a textbook – and then he would burst in with a hangdog, grinning flight sergeant whom we remembered as an oafish prefect on the stairs.

'Flight Sergeant Jones, David! Just returned from a bombing raid over Bremen! Give him a big hand!'

And we would applaud, relieved of our boredom.

My own war was more private. Now that I had ceased to be anonymous, I decided to take him on. Still obsessed with the idea of being demoted, it was some years before my experience of failure gave me an intense desire to prove I was good at something, no matter how long it might take. At first I hid, then, being detected and singled out for the headmaster's attention, I developed – as it were – in fits and starts, as if like a ball being bounced on a hard surface, my shape altered imperceptibly, responding to the pressures of contact. For years no one took much interest in me except my headmaster, and although I felt at the time that but for him, I would have escaped undetected, now I see things differently.

At thirteen, I looked a miserable specimen. The chubby, jerseyed little boy became an elongated, bespectacled freak who suffered from boils. 'Eggs,' my headmaster said. 'Eggs it is, you can be sure!' He had an answer for everything. There was, early on, another confrontation which added to my reputation as a card which I carried with me into the fourth form. One night I accidentally burned my hand while putting coal on to the fire at home. A small and painful blister developed on the palm of my right hand within seconds. This was on a Saturday night and the remaining two examinations in mathematics were on the following Monday. As I looked at the burn, it occurred to me that a heavily bandaged right hand would prevent me from sitting the examination. I knew that my grandmother would never give me any encouragement to stay away from school, but an injured hand, together with my regretful presence and pathetic attempts to use a protractor, might easily result in my being excused. I saw the scene immediately: the sympathetic teacher, my intense concentration, the reluctant failure, my own dialogue regretful.

'It's no good, sir. I've tried and tried.'

At first I contemplated moving my hand closer to the red-hot coals to increase the size of the burn, but I could not face the pain. Then I remembered a box of wound dressings which my mother, who was then nursing at an Army convalescent hospital, had brought home several days before. When I opened it, I saw that it also contained a tube of Acraflavin and very soon I realised that I would have to construct two dressings: one for immediate use – a mere plaster – and the second, much larger, which I could hide in my schoolbag and slip over the first when I left home on the Monday morning. I would need a dressing so obvious that it would not require a note or any explanation. The dressing would have to look authentic and, for some reason, I decided it would also have to smell like a burn which attention to detail occupied me for several hours. We had at the time a cat called Ginger whose hairs when singed gave out a particularly revolting smell and, mixed with copious amounts of Acraflavin, now formed the base of a kind of glove which I constructed. It enveloped my palm, a creation so large and untidy that it began to look like some bedraggled battlefield dressing, the kind you saw in pictures of the Crimean War. The yellow ointment soaked through the bandages, the cat's hairs stank, and I used so much bandage and plaster that the size of my hand doubled. By Sunday I was already beginning to refer to it as the Sebastopol Glove and on the Monday morning I slipped it on outside the house, noting the weekend's accumulation of grime with satisfaction. It was now moulded into a totally credible shape and as I made my way to school, realising that I would have to pass the headmaster's house, I also adopted a slight limp, hunching my shoulder under my schoolbag, muttering to myself as I went forward.

It was a walk I made every day and about each household that I passed, my grandmother had given me certain information, usually coloured with her own perceptions. There lived a Mr Jones who drank so much that a single scratch from a thorn killed him in an instant, leaving his whiskered widow to sit regretfully in a permanent aroma of polishes, while across the road in a much larger house the stipendiary magistrate, constantly visited by saluting policemen, came and went on foot in a shabby overcoat, often nodding sociably to me – his importance quite lost upon me until, years later, I was to trek up to his book-lined study in search of the character reference so necessary to bolster up my poor academic record. Then I passed a house once owned by a dimly remembered Aunt Polly who also had a parrot of the same name and, finally, came under the lee of my headmaster's house itself. Since it was set high above the road with a long set of winding steps, you could pass close to the gate without being seen above. I always approached it with a sense of apprehension, taking the deliberate risk of slowing down as I passed, my ears straining for any sound of him above, enjoying the tension created, and then hurtling past like a prisoner on the run. On this morning, limping, the bandaged claw outstretched, my face contorted with imagined pain, I played the same game, lingering dangerously by the closed gate, one step – two – and then I was clear! But I was hardly past when I heard a door slam high up in his house above me, and soon I was aware that he was behind me, his soft sinister footfalls audible. I did not dare to run but quickened my pace, stretching my legs so that I was almost goose-stepping, the Sebastopol Glove held far in front of me, my body hiding it. Fortunately, a woman came out of a house behind me and stopped to talk to him and I was clear once more.

Amazingly, none of my classmates suspected me in school.

'What have you done?'

'Oh, had an accident. Coal fell off the fire.'

'Trust you! Lucky sod. Alg' and geom' today.'

I sat manfully with the others in the geometry examination and made an attempt to complete the paper as I had planned, but now the Acraflavin began to seep through the bandage, staining the examination paper and the smell was so overwhelming that it irritated the master in charge, so much so that I feared he would send me out of the classroom to the library where I was certain to be detected since it was situated within a few yards of the headmaster's study and he made it his daily business to check who was in there.

But I insisted on trying to complete the examination paper. When it was seen to be clearly hopeless, the master told me to take out a reading book and duly wrote an explanatory note on the stained paper and I was left alone while the others continued, pens scratching away at the paper for this was the age of the relief nib and the cloth pen-wiper.

Then – of course – the expected happened, and we heard the telltale sound of boys in the next classroom scraping their chairs along the floor as they hurriedly stood up to attention, examination or no examination. The monster was on his rounds, varying his routine between the upper and lower school like a clever turnkey, his presence calculated not just to deter likely offenders, but also to remind supervising teachers that boys could be vile. In the practice of such deterrents, nothing was beneath him and in my travels in later life, I would sometimes come across old boys who had been on his list like myself and their greetings were invariably couched in imitations of his voice and special chastisements. Some of them were policemen and they would recall his peculiar habit of announcing returned ex-servicemen by rank, substituting their own with the inevitable debunking.

'Chief Superintendent Evans, J. 'B' Division. Smoking now, I see, Chief Superintendent? It'll be the young ladies next!'

Into the classroom he came, bald pate gleaming and flowing gown in a flurry. We jumped to our feet.

'Sit! Sit! Sit!' he snapped. I was sure the dressing flashed, illuminating me like a lurid beacon as I moved.

'They know they're not to borrow equipment? Nothing to pass from hand to hand?' he enquired of the master in charge. '*Hend to hend*?' he pronounced in the familiar South Wales posh.

'Yes, Mr Thomas.'

'Everything in order?'

'Yes, Mr Thomas.'

He nodded, almost amiable for a second, then against all expectations, proceeded briskly up the aisle – my aisle – and stopped beside me, peering at the blotched bandages, a look appearing on his face which was a caricature of incredulity.

His eyebrows lifted as he snorted unbelievingly. He hooked his thumbs into his waistcoat.

'*What?–What?–What?–What?*'

'Accident, sir.'

'*Accident?*'

My voice now assumed a nervous confidentiality:

'Yes, Mr Thomas. Putting a coal on the fire, Mr Thomas. The er... bucket came down on top of it. I mean, the tongs, sir. It came down. Right down. *On it,* sir.'

He stared at me and soon a delighted smile broke across his sallow face. It was like a welcome issued by the porter at Hell's gate to the inner circle of the damned. I knew I was discovered and his smile has lingered in my mind. I once saw a Royal Marine colour sergeant, six and a half feet in height and with the foulest breath in the Corps put his moustachioed face through the doorway of a detention cell – straight into the face of a violent psychopathic prisoner who had broken the jaw of an officer. The colour sergeant had the same kind of smile and when he spoke, his voice had all his world in it, the vocal chords strained by the issuing of a thousand commands to men beyond all repair.

'Hard man, are you, Sunshine?' he said throatily. 'Little bit of a tiger, are you?' The prisoner did not speak and the colour sergeant smiled again. Like my headmaster, he relished the prospect of difficulty and in confrontation he was in his element.

'Putting a coal, *one coal*, on the fire?' said my tormentor; '*cole?*' he pronounced.

'Yessir.'

He chuckled evilly and bent forward.

102

'Remove it!'

'Pardon, sir?'

'The bandage!'

The examination had, of course, gone by the board. Every eye was upon me, or rather, upon it – the Sebastopol Glove. Once again, I was the centre of events and the atmosphere was charged by the genuine interest of my fellows, one of whom dared to stand up so as to get a better view. He was followed amazingly by others, and they did so unchecked.

I began to dismantle the Sebastopol Glove piece by piece, removing the holding strip of plaster from the wrist, then unwinding the long length of grubby bandage. It came off slowly, damply, the smell increasing and the cat's hairs showing clearly until finally the original small plaster dressing over the blister lay revealed. It seemed to have shrunk in size. I turned my palm over for inspection. There might now, I thought, be an act of clemency since the removal of the final strip of plaster was an act which might be considered too painful but his narrowed eyes gave me my answer. I lifted the edge of the small plaster and there lay my blister genuinely revealed, about an inch in diameter.

I felt I had to say something.

'I didn't know whether or not to burst it, sir?' I said hopefully, as if I could promote some casual conversation.

But my classmates let me down. Those who could see began to laugh, tentatively at first, then with his obvious encouragement much more loudly. The master in charge came up the aisle to inspect it and the laughter continued.

Then a snarl silenced everyone.

'*This thing*!' he said, referring to me. He looked at me for a moment, then turned abruptly and walked out. It was the beginning of my life as a comedian. I waited for days for him to send for me, the usual follow-up, but he did not. Perhaps he forgot about it, perhaps his silence was the real poultice upon the wound of my inadequacy. I never cheated again.

There were other confrontations. I made that walk, hugging the wall of his house every day for six years, once carrying the school bell which I had purloined to take to the rugby ground at the Cardiff Arms Park when our school half-backs were capped for the Welsh senior team and again, he followed me, the bell chinking under my raincoat but this time I was undetected. On another occasion, he expelled me for refusing to go to a 'voluntary' lecture by a distinguished old boy and when, ignoring the expulsion, I returned to school the following day, he punished me for failing to bring a note to explain my absence! He was at this time, like almost everybody else, a recruiting officer and on Speech Days, although still gowned, he now appeared in the uniform of an RAF flying officer since he was Commanding Officer of the School Air Training Corps. Once, proudly displaying his First World War General Service ribbons, he proclaimed: 'Our old boys are serving in the four corner of the world! In Africah, in In-jah...' this was followed by a pause which indicated to me that he had run out of countries, but not to be undone – he was never undone! – he promptly repeated himself with aplomb: 'In er... In-jah, Africah!' On another occasion, standing magnificently in the centre of the platform, he got carried away. 'At the present time in two world conflagrations, ninety-seven of our old boys have paid the supreme sacrifice...' he began, then, pausing for effect with his customary glare around the hall, he lost his trend, probably thinking of examination results and continued volubly: 'and we have every hope and expectation that the number will reach treble figures by the end of the school year!'

But simply to quote him is to do him an injustice. He was a concerned, engaged, forthright man, never diffident or aloof, often wrong, but always moving forward, making a two-fisted attack on life, unafraid of its abrasions to the end. In some ways, for me at least, he remains enigmatic as a human being and I have recalled him as he appeared to me in those crucial years. There were at this time no effective form masters or house heads, or indeed anyone else who took the slightest interest in your progress through the lower school and we were like coins haphazardly pushed into a machine. Some set the machinery in motion, some did not, and reject coins like myself would otherwise have been left unspent. Old men pressed back into service while their juniors went to war lacked the energy to motivate us, and were further handicapped by the general restlessness in the air. But for my headmaster, I suspect I would have become an even more dire casualty. Later he was to praise me when he could and gradually I came to be chastised with a new preamble, 'A person of your intelligence...'; but in those first years, it was as if his physical presence was all that I had to think about. I was a fatherless child. I clutched at whatever root extruded from the undergrowth in which I sought to hide. Of all the men I knew up to that time, he was the most dominant and forceful and the only one interested enough in me and my fellows to pursue us, praise be, with such vigour.

This he once did carrying his cane underneath his raincoat, walking a mile to a billiard saloon where the aroma of damp chalk and the shuffling sound of greasy playing cards falling on grimy tables provided us with yet another haven from the reality of school. He drew his cane and struck out from the hip as soon as he entered. And we – a half-dozen of us – dived for cover, scuttling under the snooker tables as his cane flashed, decimating a row of cues which fell as if struck by bullets with a staccato rattling of expensive timber that merged with the roar of his voice, 'Richards! Watkins!' – and a host of other names; 'To my room!'

Thus he intruded, offended, risked making a laughing stock of himself, and often chased us hotfoot, using fear as a weapon in a world which still grew more unpredictable and violent every day. His was a physical presence, but our physical well-being was not his concern. I was to remember his concern when I last saw him, a haunted and shrunken man, his greying face weakened by the onset of a throat cancer, he of all people frail and mufflered as our paths crossed once more under the chestnut trees. I had travelled several hundred miles to attend his retirement presentation, but this was some time later. Now he could scarcely speak but he gripped my hand warmly and I think he said, 'Keep them at it!', for I was teaching then myself. I could not reply to him, nor articulate my debt and, watching him thread his way homeward, his unsteady invalid's tread punctuated by the tap-tapping of his walking stick, my eyes filled with tears for the second time in our acquaintanceship. I was afraid no longer, but he left his mark indelibly upon me for later I was to stand on another school platform in morning assembly, one hand holding a vicious metal knuckleduster, the other the ear of a miscreant, while I too fulminated.

'Make no mistake... I am not going to teach in a school where thuggery rules in the playground!'

Later a young supply teacher, a few years my junior as a pupil at my own school, buttonholed me in the staffroom.

'You know who you sound like? Pig! The image!'

It is true. Unless I am careful, on public platforms another monster lurks, loud-voiced and overbearing, looking likely to bustle up the aisle to the smokers' corner at any minute. The eyes are the same, so is the stance, but my voice belongs lower down the social scale, sounding, as a charming Old Etonian once informed me, 'like that of the shop steward British Leyland most want to sack!' I care not. Is there not another voice whispering in my ear? 'By their deeds shall we know them!'

The turning point in my school life came when I began to look ahead beyond my immediate peers to those a little older, some of whom were no more successful than I. Sooner or later an adolescent boy will recognise certain traits or attitudes in others which present themselves as likely future aspects of himself. What others have done, he might do. There will be those he likes and dislikes and also, if he is a realist, he will begin to realise that there is a ceiling to his ambitions. In my case for several years I was spoken to as if I were dull and stupid, and if praise came my way, as it eventually did from my English teachers, I had always to move into the next classroom where I had to revert to this other self for much of the school day. For four years I was a no-hoper, backward, unable to cope, some-times the butt of sarcastic remarks and I often resorted to playing the fool to entertain my friends, becoming a mimic to this end. Every group creates its own black fool because it needs him to reassure the successful and to comfort the mediocre, and for the outsider, becoming the entertainer is one way of belonging.

Strangely enough, I now feel this is an experience that no one should be entirely without at some time of life. It is a healthy reminder of other people's difficulties when roles are reversed. I have often noted that nothing is more detest-able than the way in which so many people, particularly English public schoolboys, develop the autocratic habit of brusque speech known in the services as 'good power of command' but which usually implies that they are not speaking to recognisable human beings of the same species. This was once brought home to me by a story of the African nationalist, Tom M'Boya who, backward at school, could only proceed to a technical college course where he qualified eventually as a sanitary inspector. On the first night of his appointment, proudly wearing his uniform in the splendour of the Nairobi Public Works Department, he was suddenly confronted at his desk by a planter's wife who strode in accompanied by her dogs. He stood up expectantly. It was his first moment of authority. He was in charge. But she looked through him haughtily, his black skin preventing her from seeing him as a person.

'Is there anybody here?' she said.

Like him I was a mentally absent and invisible person for much of my school life and, naturally, when I looked ahead,

I looked keenly at those boys who were castigated and treated in much the same way as myself and soon I began to see a haven. Just as in rugby football which I had begun to play, I knew at once that I should be a forward and not a back, so did a place appear where I might be contained in the shape of a form called 5U, or occasionally 5 *Remove*. This group inhabited an old and dingy classroom in the old school block and beckoned me like an exclusive gentleman's club.

Here, tucked away in an ancient room under the stairs, were the savages and rowdies who comprised the most notorious form in the school, some of whose stalwarts dominated the rugby team. They had failed their school certificate and had reassembled to resit it. They were thus bigger than their contemporaries, being a year older, and for the same reason were much interrupted in class to carry out their roles as the school's hewers of wood and drawers of water. Although seldom called by the name *Remove*, it was the name best applied to them, for they were called upon to remove all the furniture in the school when such domestic changes were required. Among them was the Dirty Jobs Squad which might be required in emergencies if the caretaker went sick, or was not to be found when some unfortunate vomited in the corridor. Here too were the valiants who could be called upon to chase wild and uncontrollable dogs, who were the bulwark of the fire-watchers when there was a threat of air raids, burly sand-and-bucket men who quarrelled over the Air Raid Precaution helmets, purloined the leaflets explaining how to deal with incendiary bombs, and often had a lawless authority of their own, sometimes intimidating the prefects who left them well alone. When they removed anything, they did it noisily with scant attention to authority, and since their resit year was the most pleasant they had experienced in the school and they were not intending to spend another year in it, they seemed collectively to adopt attitudes which were quite different from those destined – in the headmaster's words – for 'Higher Things in Education'. There were other important caste marks. Free of the pressures put upon sixth formers of their own age, they had more time to turn their eyes to the world at large – and also looked different, and this became important.

Although the war had its effect upon us in many ways, nothing was more levelling than the short supply of clothing and, as it went on, the general appearance of people became more alike. In school we were at first obliged to wear ties and blazers, but as the stock of uniforms diminished, there was a less rigorous insistence so that we began to wear clothes which would not have been allowed at other times. Many of the boys wore their blue Air Training Corps uniforms, some attended on certain days in matlo's bellbottoms and jumpers if they were sea cadets and, here and there, items of service dress like khaki or blue pullovers were seen. But for some reason 5U seemed to stand apart and, when I looked at them, it was as if I too had my first intimation of the world at large because there were a number of them who dressed at the height of pre-war fashion, often the handed-down clothes of relatives who had been killed which included fancy fawn waistcoats, lemon pullovers, and in one case – incredibly – a pair of plus fours put in an appearance for a day or two. About them all, it seemed to me, was a raffish air fittingly described by the headmaster who would descend occasionally, prodding his fingers into the elegant waistcoats as he exclaimed, 'Young man about town, eh?'

That was it exactly, and while he sometimes euphemistically called 5U the 'Army Form', as if Sandhurst were beckoning, the fact was that the demand for manpower was such that anything was feasible. It is hard to convince people now of the imperceptible changes which the war caused in schools, particularly in our youthful expectations and the idea of a career which could be mapped out, those pleasant avenues of success divided up into stages by the passing of this examination or that – all was severely shaken by the defeat of the British Army in France. Some, naturally, pretended nothing had changed, but others sensed that a more chaotic wind was blowing. A peculiar kind of local history was being made before our very eyes and it was nothing like the past. Oafs whose bulging thighs protruded from ancient desks that were much too small for them and who were generally regarded at best as 'characters', at worst as 'thicks', suddenly reappeared after a year's absence with subaltern's pips in immaculate khaki uniforms, carrying leather-bound swagger sticks and perhaps the explanatory insignia of the Pioneer Corps, or more exotic still, the familiar Prince of Wales' feathers now representing some Gurkha regiment in the Indian Army. There were others too, the well-known rebels who scorned all uniforms – these appeared in shabby mufti with a silver badge and the letters MN for Merchant Navy. The classic Welsh exhortations from those who regarded scholarship as the principal avenue out of the pit had lost their immediate force and everywhere about us we had evidence of a more quixotic fate which was laden with ironies.

There was one classic story of two friends, neither of them exactly gifted, both rugby players whose school career had paralleled mine in poor performance and general waywardness but who were old enough to leave when the war was at its height. They did not see each other for several years, but chanced to meet on the night of the Old Boys' Dance which was held in the school assembly hall. On this occasion one of the friends came down the covered way immaculate in dress khaki, his one pip, shoulder straps and Sam Browne gleaming as he tapped his swagger cane imperiously against his leg. Beside the entrance a former classmate lurched drunkenly in a shabby suit and jersey, all survivors' clothes from a recent torpedoing, his third. The seaman was coarse-faced and strong with immense arms and fists which had earned him a nickname like Bashie, whereas the second lieutenant was genial and lazy. But another world had intruded and begun to mould him. As he gazed incredulously at his former classmate, he blinked unbelievingly. Feeling a sudden physical need as of old, he then enquired in the peremptory tones of the accent we had come to ridicule, 'I say, Bashie, old man, whereby is the pisshouse now?'

There was this story and that, and the world intruded constantly into the life of the school as we witnessed the return of those a little older than ourselves. One boy of burly physical appearance, old for his age with a fond parent who had connections in the clothing industry so that he was immaculate at all times, decided that he'd had enough even of 5U. Soon he appeared in the handsome uniform of a Merchant Navy cadet with kid gloves and white silk scarf, all embellishments which we admired. Then, as did so many others, he disappeared for a year and we went about our school work or improved our snooker, most of us sexually backward in both theory and practice. Suddenly, our friend reappeared, tanned and seeming broader, smoking Turkish cigarettes, already an habitué of the fastest bars in town, some of which had been placed out of bounds to US forces. He had little to say about the Merchant Navy, although his hands bore the peculiar marks of long and persistent immersion in hot water.

'Where have you been?' we said, eager for details.

'All over,' he replied expansively. It was the golden phrase of the time. It meant, the World. But he had been to Sydney, more cabin boy than cadet. You had to learn to stand with your back to the wall, he said impressively. We nodded wide-eyed, not understanding. In Sydney, he told us, he'd got off her as soon as he could.

'Who?'

'The ship!'

As soon as he docked, he gave the mate the slip and got in tow with a woman they called the Duchess, an ex-beauty queen of remarkable prowess. Staying ashore in her flat overlooking the harbour for a long weekend, she had finally driven him by car to the gangway. There he was spotted by the captain who seized a megaphone to order him to pick up a crate of lettuce and carry it aboard. He had done so at once but upon reaching the deck, such was his physical state, that he promptly collapsed in a dead faint.

'Couldn't even pick up a crate of lettuce!' he told us, shovelling around his duty-free cigarettes.

'How many times a night?'

'Five. And three times without taking it out...'

'Bloody hell! All in bed was it?'

'Twice on the stairs, once in the bath.'

'In the bath?'

'*French*...'

'Did you have to ask her, Billy?'

'You don't in Australia. They don't give you a chance.'

We sat riveted, open-mouthed. It was the Duchess, of course, a woman who haunted my imagination for years until I began to see her as one of those sinewy, twisting, sexual athletes revealed in lurid poses on cheap editions of the *Kama Sutra,* with three or four pairs of arms and legs, the whole attached to the blonde tresses and deadpan face of Veronica Lake, the current screen pin-up who, incredibly, I later accidentally tripped up on the dance floor of a London nightclub. Unfortunately – I have worked it out – she was fifty-four at the time, an age I then thought unforgivable. Another shock was that she was as small as a large garden gnome, only the peek-a-boo hairstyle and the immobile, deadpan features remained the same as the face I had planted upon the Duchess. The vision stuck in my mind for years, as did the sentence which galvanised the school.

'Did you hear about our Billy down in Sydney?' we said. 'Couldn't even pick up a lettuce!' And it wasn't long before we added knowledgeably in our piping voices: 'You'll do all right in Sydney!'

Thus are our minds formed and the central focus of my

education began to switch to that core of experience which emanated from the snappy dressers and the studied elegance of the lemon-yellow pullovers and white riding macs of 5U, the whole ambience more 'county' than you would have expected. There was, also, rugby football which came to dominate our school life and provided another world which sometimes seemed to exist independent of the school, although the social approval which the school cast upon it was one more way in which South Walian forces moulded our lives in traditional ways. I did not know then that prowess at rugby football would eventually carry with it a kudos which would provide a magic key that opened doors to entire careers for those especially gifted. To me it was at first an extension of the kind of sub-world which existed in that gentleman's club under the stairs and on the periphery of the billiard saloons increasingly populated by county schoolboys and the local YMCA which, at the time, was little more than a services canteen with thriving snooker and card tables, and a complete absence of any kind of authoritarian supervision. Here worthies gathered for a game of solo whist or brag, eventually contract bridge, and there was a strange mixture of town and gown as the hallowed letters YMCA provided a safe haven for modest gambling and only the headmaster ever penetrated it as vigilante. Here we went after school for a quick frame of snooker and mixed at an early age with servicemen on leave and heard the stories which revealed a different world to that described by visiting dignitaries.

'Brigadier Stubbings', said the school magazine, 'talked so entertainingly on the Indian Army that the boys privileged to hear him evinced little desire to return to their studies.'

Studies also went by the board for rugby football. That we knew, since for the whole of my time in the County School we had an unbeaten school first fifteen and the aura which attached itself to the players outshone that of all other groups. When our school halfbacks, Glyn and Wynford Davies, were capped – first for the Welsh Secondary Schools team, then for the senior team itself, while still schoolboys – we had a half holiday, and the headmaster frequently read aloud glowing match reports praising the play of our heroes in the school assembly hall. But this was excellence, a stylish excellence at that. Underneath there were tiers of performance, second fifteens, form teams, club and cadet teams, an infrastructure of groups whose buzzing enthusiasms formed cadres from which the progress to stardom and its concomitant glories began.

In my own case I lacked the physical coordination for excellence, but early on I sensed that there might be a place for me. At first it was simply a matter of group loyalties, us against them – the school form to which I belonged, 4B, having taken it upon itself to respond to a challenge from our inferiors, paradoxically known as 4A. They wanted a match. They could have one.

The game was on a Saturday morning at the edge of the cricket field in the centre of the town's memorial park. We changed in the open, few of us with proper kit. I had been lent rugby boots two sizes too large for me by a boy whose brother had recently been killed in Java. I had PT shorts but no jersey and so wore an old pullover and short socks which stopped at the ankles. Those who had precious jerseys were allowed to play at three-quarter, one of the reasons being

116

that their jerseys stood in less danger of being torn or damaged than if they played at forward. There was not a single spectator. The referee was a senior boy who could be trusted with a school ball. As we gathered behind the sight screens, our shrill voices echoed in the damp air.

'Jonesie's got two pairs of socks!'

'Give us one!'

'Can't. I'm wearing them both.'

'Come on!'

'Can't. I'm playing in the front row.'

There were two boys in this team whom I was to meet later on, in the strangest of circumstances. One was even then over six feet in height, a drifting skeleton with staring myopic eyes and a habit of talking soundlessly to himself. He did not seem to have a will of his own in class and invariably followed others, joining groups automatically where he stood out like a vulnerable lathe. We called him Knocker because he was an obsequious knocker of doors, appearing like a lamplighter in the corridor windows. Now he had brought with him a large pair of foundryman's working boots with steel toecaps which were laced with strong hessian cord, and, like myself, he was without stockings or jersey and determined to play in his woollen vest which was much too large for him and hung in folds. He looked a sight with pinhead protruding from its drapes and it was as if the huge weighted foundry boots at the end of his stalk-like legs acted as an emplacement for a slender secret weapon – in fact, the great tottering length of him above. But he slipped his spectacles knowledgeably into his shoes for safety and I followed suit.

117

The other star was a boy who had three Christian names which was regarded by the master filling in the register on our first day at school as both a conceit and a wanton extravagance, since he had difficulty in writing them all down in the appropriate column.

'Name?'

'Evan John Keith!'

The master protested so we immediately called the boy Bugsy, the choice of nickname dictated by an outbreak of nits on the school bus. He was also unusual in that he wore his vaselined hair exceptionally long with the result that it flapped oddly at the back of his neck. But on this morning he was immaculate and properly kitted out with starched flybag shorts with pockets, polished rugby boots, scout stockings and a white tropical shirt of substantial cloth so that there was a touch of class about him and he outshone us all. He also made it plain when we sorted out the positions that if he wasn't allowed to play at wing-forward, he wasn't going to play at all.

We were short of a hooker.

'Rich, will you go?'

'All right,' I said.

'Good boy, Rich.'

I felt superior to Bugsy already.

Knocker had to be in the second row and when I found his pinhead sandwiched against my thighs as we tried out our positions, I could just see him out of the corner of my eye but the thinness of his bones meant that every time we packed down, he cut into me like a butcher's steel. This was to be his strength and when play began, he became a leaping, elbowing apparition, a creature of sharp edges, elbows and knees, all working like flailing scissors. But as well as cutting into our opponents, he also collapsed our own scrums and took against Bugsy who soon began to talk continuously, giving such gratuitous and meaningless advice as 'Short and take!' and 'Feet! Feet!', which Knocker thought were personal remarks expressly directed at himself. ('Whose feet, please?') So he did the opposite, stretched and writhed, the foundry boots carelessly moving this way and that, the elbows jabbing and prodding, working against all who came near him, friend and foe.

Soon it began to rain continuously and there were further complications as the weather got worse. These all seemed to centre around Knocker. First, having got the ball he never released it, not once, not even when Bugsy told him to. Then, having caught it he hid it, the rest of us binding and milling around him like infantry looking for cover behind an absurdly slim tank. But the flailing limbs created spaces in front and we invariably drove forward like a wedge in which he was as much germ as weapon, salivating, biting and grunting as he writhed on. 4A panicked, the cowards got out of the way, and only the odd stalwarts stopped him, usually by the inferior tactic of kneeling down in front of him as if in prayer. But this counterplay took time and we had made several dashes of ten or twenty yards before they grew wise.

'Good boy, Knocker!' the cry came from our captain who stood as an interested spectator in the centre of the field. It was a cry much repeated as we drove on and on, even approaching their goal line. Once, having been prayer-matted then bowled over with others, Knocker hid the ball under his copious woollen vest. At another time he tucked it under both arms and found himself attempting a somersault, the wildly raking legs in the foundry boots slashing at the air like some futuristic piece of agricultural machinery, but still creating valuable space. In this period, he seemed to be playing 4A on his own. His face was flushed, he salivated continuously, his myopic eyes peered about him and all the time his lips moved soundlessly as he continued to trail part of his private world about him. At times he was the school-boy vision of the mad professor, but his effect was that of a street fighter. The men were very rapidly being sorted out from the boys in our opponents' team, for their pack had disintegrated and become a team of wing-forwards who all sought glory hanging about on the edge of the mêlée. They had also begun to quarrel amongst themselves.

'You go opposite him?'

'No, I'm not. You go.'

'I've been.'

'Come on, boys. He's getting through all the time.'

'It's all very well for you to talk out there on the wing. Why are you always throwing the ball to him?'

'I can't get it over his head!'

'Well, shut your mouth then, or come in by here!'

There were also injuries now – injuries, stoppages, evil looks. One boy got Knocker's elbow in his eye. It swelled up at once, blackened as if poisoned by some deadly venom. Then Knocker trod on the foot of some unfortunate who only wore plimsolls and he went off the field sobbing and did not come back for half an hour. And through it all, Knocker blossomed, peering after the casualty modestly. He seemed to be unstoppable by virtue of an eerie form of hypnotism, for we seemed to be living in the line-outs and no matter which team threw the ball in, it inevitably ended up in his hands. It got so that his look was enough, the ball simply would not pass him; and once he had got hold of it, the rest of him moved at once. The ball became like a coin which you put into a slot machine. The moment it touched, the monster moved. Now 4A tried various tactics. They raced to the line-out to get there first in order to avoid him. This failing, they began to trail in the hope that being last was safest, but then Knocker began to move his position so that the line-out went backward and forwards, extending like a snake, then compressing; and all the time, he rose above it, his thin limbs extended and waving like signal flags until he pounced. Now there were hoarse shouts from 4A's captain who played at fullback.

'Come on, boys! Mark him!'

There were mutters in reply, low furtive voices already mutinous. 'Mark him? He's marking me. Come and have a look at my leg.'

Inevitably, we soon got within a few feet of their line when Knocker got felled himself. He was kicked, a half-dozen people fell on top of him, but he scorned attention and once more we lined up. Now we could smell victory. There must be a try coming. Bugsy had now ingratiatingly placed himself near Knocker and kept close to him, sensing glory. Knocker took the ball once more but then there was an accidental tactic, for 4A, led by their captain, immediately piled in like angry wasps, shamed at last into action, but to our amazement Knocker began to run the wrong way with three or four wasps hanging on to his vest. Knocker had become disorientated and so had we all, with the result that both teams hustled him into touch, combined efforts being needed in a unique emergency.

'You've got to turn him,' Bugsy said to the rest of us. 'Keep the wind at the back of you, Knock.'

Knocker looked sheepish, but Bugsy was right. Again and again, we lined up and now we shouted, 'This way, Knocker! Wind behind you!'

It would have been fitting if Knocker had scored, but he did not. It was Bugsy sneaking in on the massive heels of the foundry boots who saw his chance, picked up and went over like a rabbit, now a dirty mirage in off-white. Up went the referee's finger, a firm blast on the whistle, a try!

We had an impromptu party on the spot, shrieking and gyrating, clapping Bugsy on the back.

'Good boy, Bugs!'

'It was Knocker really,' Bugsy said modestly. Ambitious, he was playing his cards right. He wanted more. The captain told Bugsy to attempt the conversion, but before he went over to take the kick, Bugsy called me to one side. He was very excited but his manner was confidential.

'Rich?'

'What d'you want?'

He came close to me, sidling up, turning his back to the referee and our captain who stood waiting to hold the ball while 4A huddled disconsolately behind their posts.

'Favour?' Bugsy said out of the side of his mouth. 'Hold on to this for me.'

With the most furtive of expressions, he put his hand

deep into the pocket of his flybags and removed a large army clasp knife, complete with marlinspike, and slipped it surreptitiously into my own hand to hold for him while he took the kick. Then he trotted off, his vaselined hair bumping lumpily, all attention upon him.

The kick failed, he returned to me and merely held out his hand. I handed over the knife, no explanation being asked for or given, and the game finished soon afterwards. We drifted about the park, at first together, then in twos and threes – highly elated, so together that we did not want to go home or leave one another.

'How did you get on?'

'We ate 'em!' we said, again and again.

To this day I have never discovered or been able to make up my mind whether Bugsy regarded the clasp knife as part of his essential rugby equipment, to go with his white flybags and shirt, or whether – more likely – he had found the knife on the field since the Territorial Army used it for exercises. He was never an especial friend but years later, after a long period abroad, I was delighted to see him in the enclosure at Twickenham – the first homely face I was to see that day.

'Bugsy?' I shouted at the top of my voice. I was overjoyed to meet someone from home.

He was elegant in white riding mac, yellow gloves, Old Boy's scarf, the hair more discreetly Brylcreemed and in the company of two high-heeled girls, both elegantly dressed and one on each arm.

He nodded briefly, did not stop and passed on, both he and the girls displeased.

I could almost read his lips.

'At school with me. Never cared much for the fellow.'

So do our paths cross and uncross. After I left school, I saw Knocker only once, this time as a booking-hall clerk in a railway station as he argued with an irate customer, his neck extending through the glass partition like a giraffe's from its stall. He was evidently giving one of his long speeches. I never saw either of them again. But once we walked proudly together as victors.

'Good boy, Rich.'

'Good boy, Knocker!'

'Good boy, Bugsy!'

That old ambition of mine to join the select ranks of the resit form was to be thwarted. As expected I failed my Central Welsh Board School Certificate, since a combination of five subjects was required, but because I had opted for Spanish and the timetable could not be rearranged to suit me alone, I merely marked time for another year in a form of younger boys. This proved successful, since a number of events now took place which altered my life in subtle ways. Chief among them was my appointment as the headmaster's Gold Flake Boy. A heavy smoker, he was constantly in need of this special brand of cigarette and since my form-room was the nearest to his, he made it a practice to appoint a smoking factotum from this form – an appointment which he frequently coupled with the position of Bell Boy, an equally important task since the ending of lessons in the old school was marked by the ringing of a handbell which he checked at forty-minute intervals, sometimes by the second hand of his own watch. It was, he gave me to understand, a position of immense responsibility and in my case, if appointed, it would be a signal honour.

'You have a watch?'

I had a watch.

'Is it accurate?'

It was accurate.

'I am considering you,' he said, but shook his head gravely, clenching his gown and sucking at his breath as we stood in the gloomy corridor where he had summoned me. 'For, you see, there will be other duties.'

When he was talking to you in the corridor, those who passed did so with bated breath and other boys made as wide an encircling movement as possible. You could feel them wanting to be invisible, at the same time curious, like spectators at a nasty traffic accident. You were sure to be cross-examined later, for each public interrogation was a minor event. ('What did he have you for, then?')

'Other duties...' he repeated. He did not reveal their exact nature then, but he finally came to a decision.

'You will be on approbation,' he said.

So I became his Gold Flake Boy and several times a week would be sent on his tobacco errands when I had the power to swear in a deputy to look after the school bell. It was an appointment not without its nepotistical flavour since cigarettes were in short supply and another uncle of mine had returned home to keep my grandfather's shop, but this connection was seldom necessary as he had his own supplier. I was sent on these errands in the middle of the school day and somehow or other I knew I had to return discreetly with my purchases, bringing them quietly into his study. If there were visiting dignitaries present, I would unobtrusively place the cigarettes together with the change in a paper bag near the door, having first secured the nod from him but taking care not to display them. I became a model of discretion like the butler on the Kensitas cigarette packets, adopting a suitably solemn and confidential air. As Gold Flake Boy, I could often choose the lessons I wanted to miss and these occasions did not pass without comment.

'Four Eyes has gone out for the headmaster,' my former cronies said bitterly.

I had a new status. I enjoyed it immensely.

SIX

People often think that education comes to one by virtue of attendance at some place where it may be 'got'. In my own case, I 'got' very little as a consequence of formal lessons and my struggle was simply to survive. At first I went for cover, needing to pass unnoticed and undetected amongst my fellows; later I tried to find some place for myself within the life of the school. The dread of school felt by so many is rooted in fear of exposure and ridicule. Every individual craves some chance of success, a status; if not in academic subjects, then it must be found else-where – in sport or in the other activities which go on, often reflecting the enthusiasms of individual teachers whose contributions in this way are immeasurable. If the home circumstances also cause anxiety, the pressures on the child multiply and the need to escape from both sets of circumstances may provide an impetus which leads to all kinds of delinquency.

For me, reading became the only total escape until the war ended and the younger teachers returned, bringing with them enthusiasms which had been lacking for the most part – doubtless the battle to keep the school going at all left little over for extras, but I was not to be aware of that. By the time the war ended, my school life had changed completely. It was not that I grew any more or less intelligent, but that my search for knowledge of lives outside my own led me into the pages of fiction which I devoured omnivorously and uncritically, book after book. Often reading under the bedclothes at night by torchlight, to keep myself supplied I had frequently to make a daily visit to the local library whose shelves I haunted, withdrawing the maximum number of books, sometimes returning them in the same day. I read anything and everything, from Richmal Crompton and the structured world of her 'William' books, and all of Percy F. Westerman's adventures of Cadet Alan Carr, to Maugham and particularly J. B. Priestley whose voice on the radio distinguished him as a man of place, immediately identifiable amongst the bland and mannered tones of others who seemed to have a monopoly of the microphone. I often carried a book-strap and became conspicuous.

'You can't have read all those?'

'Test me!'

I obtained extra tickets to last me over the weekend and came – fortunately – to be spoilt by the local librarian who smiled benevolently upon me. That was one stroke of luck; another was the return from the army of the senior English master, Ken Railton. It was to him, a diffident and sensitive man whose disapproval of the headmaster's hectoring ways became obvious, I owed my change of heart towards school for under his tutelage I began to succeed – to win, for the first time, modest praise which acted upon me like an elixir. What is more, on one of the headmaster's rounds, I was praised publicly and it was as if the enemy had been sent packing; as if I had passed into other hands and there, in that gloomy and ancient schoolroom which had the Victorian sign 'WORK FOR THE NIGHT IS COMING' slotted upon its walls, I had magically found a way ahead. I began to abuse my position of power as Bell Boy, daily extending the English lesson by delaying the ringing of the bell and now I laboured over homework like a monk scratching at a parchment, becoming in the process another person. Then there was the school play – produced by another returned soldier – in which I was given a part, a school magazine which welcomed my contributions, and the poetry I had begun to write. This, although mawkish and sentimental, also gave me a sense of difference. It was as if a skivvy had come out from under the stairs and joined the family.

It was not an abrupt transition, but the effect of praise was dramatic. There were the usual intrusions and we continued to jump to our feet when the Gauleiter checked up.

'Sit!–Sit!–Sit! Form 5B about its labours, I take it? Hm... How d'you find Richards, Mr Railton?'

'Exceptional in every way.'

'Hm... Hm...' Words actually failed him.

On his face there was only disbelief, but there was now born in the ogre's mind that further phrase with which to chastise me: 'A person of your intelligence...' He continued to have good reason because my general examination results remained poor. But I just passed the dreaded School Certificate and the time came to think about a career, a decision which I put off for as long as possible. There was an odd form called 6B (Commercial) which existed for boys who were not taking the Higher Certificate and filled in an extra year by taking commercial subjects like book-keeping and shorthand.

'There may be a place for you in commerce?' the headmaster said expansively as if the City of London awaited me.

But there were typewriters in that classroom and the amiable master in charge had, I was to discover, a private library from which he introduced me to Evelyn Waugh's *Scoop*, an event in my reading life. So to 6B (Comm) I went, free of the pressures of an examination, and there I spent a happy year untainted by the social disapproval which still attached itself to the gentleman's club under the stairs. Miracle of miracles, I was a sixth former.

Eventually, I responded to school by doing the best I could and I was lucky, both in my headmaster and in my English teacher whose very different selves acted upon me like sharply contrasted instructors, always at loggerheads but who, in their joint efforts, contrived to keep the swimmer afloat. In the sixth form the headmaster relaxed, especially after I began to play rugby for the first fifteen and when I won an essay competition in the local newspaper and scored the only try of my career in a key match, I might have been a genuine hero for my virtues were now extolled from the assembly hall platform. There were real heroes, among them Tasker Watkins, later a Lord Justice of Appeal, who won the VC and was the cause of a half holiday. Now it seemed the headmaster never lost an opportunity to praise, and if the praise was too fulsome, the notes stentorian, often the trumpet blasts of a propagandist – it was still praise. As we got older we began to realise his limitations, to see through his bluff; but by then he had become a character, always a caricature of himself, a shared hazard and a decisive and abrasive part of our growing up.

There was another world, however, outside of school and it is from this world that images most often return. There was after all a kind of order in school – common enemies, common delights and routines which faced us all; a togetherness created by age, or simple geography. We were all in that together, like the war itself; but outside, at home, along the street, in the billiard halls we frequented, we each made our own way separately and carved our different niches. At home, my problems remained. My mother's tours of duty at the army convalescent home allowed her to return home several times a month when she often took me to the cinema which had begun to absorb me. I knew nothing of her life away from home and although I once visited her at Miskin Manor, which had been converted and was used to rehabilitate the wounded, and rowed her around the lake in a small boat, I never went again. She was too busy. I found her visits home an embarrassment, although she gave me pocket money and such treasures as brass soldier's-cap badges from many regiments and a button stick for cleaning brass which I kept all my life. Her brother Tudor now lived at home and ran my grandfather's grocery shop and I was aware of an antipathy between them, with the result that I clung closer to my grandmother who remained the constant and stable influence. The feeling that I was a nuisance as a small child ended; but as I grew older and began to have friends and a life of my own outside the house, I began to live two lives and I see now that I was already taking steps to escape. I already felt that there was so much which my grandmother did not understand about the world in which I lived, and there was a good deal which I left unreported about my own life and that of my contemporaries. Between a woman in her sixties and an adolescent boy there is a necessary reserve and I had already realised that there must be secrets, and that her feelings must be spared. I could not bear to see pain upon her face, she who had suffered so much. So I, by censorship, by slight embellishments, invented my own doings in a sense – creating a reportage of them that was acceptable to her ears, just as, I found, her own children did. It was as if I was already taking steps to become a popular author while all the time I was noting another kind of reality, keeping it to myself, filing it away, reserving it until I could deal with it. Thus, I came to have another persona. But when I addressed a simple letter of enquiry to the sports pages of the *South Wales Echo* and they printed the answer, together with my name, and my grandmother proudly flourished the newspaper as if I were a distinguished contributor and promptly announced to our neighbour, 'They do not understand him in that school!', I was quite capable of modestly bowing my head, and did.

Like all fatherless children, I had a secret wish for normality. It was never to end. All through adolescence in the houses of my friends, I would study the behaviour of fathers rather as a butterfly hunter examines a species, collating odd items of information for future reference. There were fathers who farted and fathers who shouted and fathers who sulked. There were fathers who swore, gardened, went to the pub or the club and others who never went anywhere. (What's he doing? He's moping!) They seemed, did fathers, to grow on garden allotments where on any given summer evening you might find them sprouting collarless and unshaven in clumps, and I studied them all gravely. I once saw a collier-father bathing in a tin bath, on his naked back the bright raw redness of new blood glistened through a layer of coal dust from a nasty wound. But he laughed at my alarm and when he produced a sixpence to send his son on an errand 'Over the shop for Dada!', I felt another stab of self-pity. At the other end of the social scale was the stipendiary magistrate and his rage when the maid misplaced his normal pint-sized breakfast mug for a mere teacup. And then there was our chapel minister who lived nearby – a gaunt, haunted man with sepulchral features who locked the door of his front room on days when he prepared his sermons with the air of one communicating personally with the Almighty; but he was disturbed like any father when his erring son, a pianist of note, absconded on the Irish mailboat to join Waldini's Accordion Band and had to be brought home shame-faced.

'He has gone! He has gone!' his mother announced dramatically.

We thought she was referring to the old man whose winter bronchitis was as usual severe. He always looked, as my grandmother put it, like Death itself.

'The Lord sends these things to try us...'

'No, he has gone to Ireland to join Waldini.'

I was most envious of those boys whose fathers accompanied them to rugby matches, for the most part amazingly young men. Just as I thought all mothers should be fat, so for a time I imagined fathers all to be old and grizzled. Another friend's father had been gassed in the First World War, then prematurely retired so that he was continually at home, able to take part in games with his son. Then fathers came home from the war in large numbers and I felt even more deprived, but mainly I was curious – of all of them. Again conscious of a missing element in my life, I fantasised and invented stories of a father killed in action; but I told no one, and if anyone asked me any questions, I said he was dead and dismissed it from my mind. I soon came to avoid company where I was likely to be asked such questions and my friends never referred to the matter. I must have communicated my hurt in some way and was spared the pain of answering questions by those closest among my friends, most of whom I kept for the rest of my life.

One of the great happinesses of my childhood was that I was welcome everywhere I went outside the house. At first I moved up and down the social scale without being aware of it, and since my uncle took over my grandfather's shop when the old man died, we continued to live in a condition of modest affluence – although not quite as comfortably as others nearby whose children were sent away to public schools and who returned home, gulping like lost fish. They were accented with polite manners, the boys often shooting from a sitting position on to their feet when confronted by the opposite sex – a habit which profoundly startled me when I first witnessed it. I did not envy them, but noted with satisfaction that they welcomed my company in the holidays as they became increasingly estranged from the streets where I seemed to know everyone. There was this group, and there were others – my schoolmates, including the companions of the difficult years who remained intransigents and continued on what the headmaster called 'the downward slope'. I see now that I had a foot in many camps, moved among them with ease, my bookishness hidden as I joined the card players or squinted under the lights of the snooker tables.

My conception of social class was indeed slow in growing and my grandmother put the definitive seal upon it. We were first and foremost chapel people, and that was that. Free of the petit bourgeois constraints which surrounded her, the only concession to ostentation she ever made was in her sixties when she accepted a fur coat from her surviving son in honour of her visit to Buckingham Palace to receive Ithel's Distinguished Flying Cross. Upon it she often pinned a simple sprig of artificial violets and she never felt quite at home wearing it, although her two daughters always looked at it with envy. After she was dead, it had a life of its own since my mother wore it for years in one shape or another, finally having it considerably shortened until it was little more than a cape.

As far as my own clothes went, clothes rationing prohibited any marked difference in my appearance until my late teens when I began to favour the county-set clothes affected by 5 *Remove* – tweeds and riding macs, the stiff white kind now associated with sex offenders and indecent exposure. Then they seemed to give the highly desirable impression that the horseless had recently stepped off a horse. My grandmother approved of this style for she was from a long line of farmers, although a blue suit for Sundays was for a good while the order of the day. There were, however, special constraints at home. My Uncle Tudor, a bachelor until middle age, like his father had to disguise his breath whenever he took alcohol outside the house since it was never allowed inside it. So I grew up with the firm smell of peppermint until it was replaced by chlorophyl tablets, including large-size animal chlorophyl tablets intended and advertised as very satisfactory for farting bulldogs, which I eventually came to take myself in copious numbers – one tablet for every three pints of ale, I eventually calculated. Even when my uncle became a magistrate, the deception continued and the surface appearance of all our lives was dominated by the fierce Nonconformist spirit of a little woman who would not compromise. Her great fear for me, she often told me, was that I should follow my always absent and seldom discussed father or her brother Jack, the horseman who had 'drunk himself into his grave' – a phrase that made me think of him actually toppling into it. Drink – all of it, anywhere in any company – was a demon and she never let me forget it. The attitude was not uncommon amongst older people who had witnessed the rapid industrialisation of the valleys in our chapel, and the consequent debasing of the rural life it replaced.

My mother was away all through my teens, my uncle was busy – at first resentful at having to give up the freedom of his life as a commercial traveller to settle at home, he had little time for me although it was his efforts which supported us – so that I was left pretty much to myself. My books, my reading, the forays into sport, rugby, table tennis, snooker were tendrils of normality – and I carefully nurtured them, discovering a life for myself, forming habits that would last for ever. Some of these skills, particularly table tennis, were to help me forty years later in Japan since I remembered a highly idiosyncratic service – illegal, perhaps, but it won me games and was the subject of much discussion, all a step towards breaking down barriers. In my childhood there were few barriers.

But if I had other things to occupy me, I was still a misplaced person. Under the tendrils, a disturbed self peered out at the world and my condition was not improved by the sexual stirrings of adolescence. In adult life it is easy to forget the teenager's single-minded obsession with sex, but my own perceptions were stark and stand out in my mind still. When my grandfather was dying, a nurse stayed in the house for several days. We'd had a bathroom built on to the end of the house, access to which was through my bedroom. One night she forgot to lock the bathroom door and I walked in upon her stark naked as she sat smoking on the edge of the bath, powdering herself. The amount of hair upon her body disgusted me and my revulsion must have been obvious for she sought me out later and gave me a number of cigarette cards by way of recompense. I did not see a naked woman again until, intoxicated and inflamed, I burst drunkenly through the bead curtain of a brothel in La Linea in my twenties and for years my sexual knowledge proceeded in lunatic fits and starts, comic in retrospect, painful at the time.

I lived a chauvinist life separated from girls for the whole of my formal education and most of my childhood. They might have been a different species but, of course, we talked about them constantly and later investigated. First, however, I fell in love, hopelessly and idiotically and – curious imitation of the pattern of my relationships with Knocker and Bugsy – the subject of my adoration re-entered my life in an oddly unexpected way. Between the jerseyed cherub and the bookish young man in the white riding mac, there was another figure – itchy in a blue serge suit, bespectacled and staring, the omnipresent mole remaining like a dago sideburn. I had, I am told, an unnerving stare. Like Richard Burton I practised it, as if I could will people to crumble in front of me. (But when I tried it out once on him, I lost. I could not keep it up.)

The subject of my adoration has a special significance in my life since, despite my wayward progress through school, there was always a respectable side to me, a part which wanted to behave in ways of which my grandmother would approve and so it was natural that the first girl should be a regular attender at our chapel. She was dark, neat and fresh-complexioned and pretty with high cheekbones and that gypsyish air which Welsh girls sometimes have. Her hair was quite long and naturally curly with jet-black ringlets so that when she shook her head you half expected them to chime. She also spoke Welsh and came from a family who suddenly arrived in our midst like ghosts from our own past. Her father, an inspector for the National Society for the Prevention of Cruelty to Children, known ironically as Powell the Cruelty, brought with him from the unknown territory of North Wales a wife and seven children. All of them spoke Welsh fluently and naturally as their first language and about them there was a healthy robustness that brought an infusion of life into the sparsely attended and decaying chapel. They filled a complete pew, descending in size like miniature toby jugs, and all were handsome, fresh-faced and vigorous. The eldest brother, much torpedoed, swaggered home with frost-bitten fingers; the eldest sister was in the Wrens. All had about them an air of the world that contrasted with the cowed air of many of their chapel neighbours. Perhaps because they were poor, they were not quite so ostensibly respectable; the younger brothers wore handed-down clothes and there was a liveliness to them that somehow did not belong in that gleaming mahogany temple of righteousness.

The middle daughter's name was Buddug – the Welsh for Boadicea – and although I even then regarded it as slightly ridiculous, and her friends called her Biddy, I kept that treachery to myself. I had already pressed my attentions upon her. Misusing my position as Gold Flake Boy, I had contrived to wait all morning for her outside the dentist's, just to get a glimpse of her, and perhaps a few hurried words; but she emerged swollen and red-faced and obviously annoyed to dismiss me with hardly a sentence. Both of us were in the chapel Christmas play but I never seemed to be able to get her on her own. Once a group of us decided to explore a loft in another church building and I, ever the perfect gentleman, stood aside to allow her to climb a ladder but she refused pointedly and I suffered again, for I saw that she believed that I wanted to look up her skirts when no such intention was in my mind. Another put-down occurred when an elderly woman died almost in front of us one night in the chapel vestibule. It was a violent death, the woman expiring in a fit, her cheeks blue, eyes staring, vomit cascading on the marble floor. One of the deacons ran for a doctor but the doctor was too late. It was a frightening experience and although later I attempted to put on a George Raft face and some sophistication as if to imply, 'Suckers get it all the time!', the experience disturbed me profoundly, as did the impotence of those who tried to help. It was the first death we had both seen and when I confessed my horror at those choking sobs, she said: 'Oh, you get that with asphyxia.'

I sought her company constantly and did everything I could to impress myself upon her and thought about her continually, but I still could never get her on her own. Finally the chance came when I contrived an expedition to Caerphilly Castle – a place of approved interest since we were both studying history – and she finally agreed, her bright green eyes laughing with amusement. All week I worried about what I should wear, how I should behave, and fatally decided to vaseline my hair which stuck up in sprouting clumps because of my awkward double crown. It was still the mole-time in my life, however, and much as she occupied my thoughts, I doubt if I occupied hers. I was conscious of my innocence and longed for the poker face, the marks of age and experience, all evidenced by the American film stars who had begun to influence my fantasies. But now, I thought, I would at last get her on her own and have my chance to shine.

But when I called at her house to collect her, she was in Girl Guides' uniform holding the hand of her snivelling eight-year-old brother. She had to take him. It was a condition of us going together.

'You'll have a *lovely* time!' her mother said in the effusive Welsh way.

As it happened, we had an awful time. It rained. We spent an hour looking for a public lavatory and the brat kept crying all the time. It was the end of my romance with Buddug and shortly afterwards I ceased to attend chapel on any regular basis, doing so only at the behest of my grand-mother on special occasions. There was no one reason, just my general dissatisfaction at the elderly ambience, and the echoes of the ancient language. It all belonged irretrievably to the past.

Its values would haunt me, however, and half a lifetime later Buddug's snot-nosed brother Gareth turned up in the disguise of a millionaire paperback publisher sporting a Rolls Royce at the precise time when I was busy complain-ing that most of the people you met in positions of power in London had been at school with each other.

I reminded him of that day, of Caerphilly Castle in the rain.

'D'you remember when I gave you sixpence to clear off?'

'You're wrong,' he said. 'It was threepence.'

He did not publish my books and loftily informed me

that he did not read most of what he published and promptly disappeared once more, one of the few millionaires to apply for an assisted passage to Australia. His sister became an actress, appeared in the first stage version of *Under Milk Wood*, and also disappeared. I never saw either of them again.

Such memories of childhood, I have found, are popular amongst Welsh people who tend in retrospect to idealise the past, often imbuing it with a quality of golden innocence. But in reality, it was never like that. Innocence soon changes as a conception of sin is formed and the simple black and white values of the primitive Nonconformist religions can sometimes bring on the seeds of madness. My infatuation with Buddug was both an end and a beginning and an example of normality. Later, however, knowledgeably avoiding chapel girls, I found another girl – a discovery with dramatic and lunatic consequences. Slipping my hand under her blouse in a youth club party, I found my explorations welcome; but when I returned home two hours later than I had promised, I entered the little kitchen to find it empty. Upon the table was a Glamorgan Constabulary helmet with shining steel spike and gleaming chain mail, a pair of white cotton policeman's gloves beside it. The sound of voices came from the front room at the end of the passage, from the room that was seldom used, except on Sundays or when there were important visitors. There was an unmistakeable smell of burning in the air. For a second as I looked at that huge blue helmet, my heart trembled for I immediately associated its presence with my first sexual adventure, although there was no rational way of connecting the arrival of the police with my wandering hands – my attentions had not exactly been repulsed, and the girl could scarcely have had time to get home. Later, before I was sent to bed in disgrace, I found that I had inadvertently left a candle burning in the loft over the wash-house where my uncle was illegally storing large quantities of greaseproof wrapping paper, then strictly rationed. As a consequence of my negligence, half the stock was destroyed, the fire brigade and the police had been called so that, in a sense, fire and brimstone had attended my first mutually acceptable erection and my guilty mind connected the two events as sin and punishment for a good while. My grandmother often said, 'God will find you out!'

'Two hundred pounds worth of damage!' my uncle said, striking me across the face.

I slunk away to contemplate my navel.

There were other girls but never the release I sought and I slowly began to move in different circles, avoiding the chapel girls and seeking out the more sophisticated company of those who returned from public schools for the holidays; but now and again I returned to the chapel – to keep an eye on it, as it were. It continued to be a microcosm of the old ways. One of the boys older than myself surprised me one day by the fierce dislike he expressed for a local hero whom he thought of as a glory hunter with his decorations. The boy had been a young soldier in the same military action, had been overrun by German infantry and only survived by feigning death amongst a pile of bodies for two days during which he did not dare to move, an experience that affected his whole life;

for he became a chronic asthmatic and died prematurely, a shy, retiring person. His view was the kind of contradiction of public acclaim that somehow reaffirmed my own existing suspicions that there was another side to everything.

Never forgetting the moment of terror when I saw that policeman's helmet, I became completely sceptical; but that moment also returned to me, the memory held like a flawed pearl on a string – trapped between its fellows. There were others to come. As a trainee probation officer, I was required to interview a woman whose son had attempted to castrate himself with a cut-throat razor, and had nearly succeeded when interrupted by the milkman. Upon discharge from a surgical ward, he was transferred to a mental hospital where I had to visit him and complete a standard form after consultation with his mother. One of the column entries asked for a statement describing the mother's attitude to the matter in question. I think it said, 'Attitude to the Offence'.

In the dingy almoner's office, a little woman sat opposite me, demure in a purple hat, a fox fur; on her lapel a clutch of artificial flowers of the kind which I always remembered my grandmother wearing. She had come down the valley to the hospital dressed in her Sunday best. For me it was a poignant moment but I adopted a breezy confidentiality as I questioned her.

'Tell me, Mrs Williams, what d'you think *yourself* about what Emlyn's done?'

She smiled, a tight little smile from those purse-like lips, clasping her hands primly about her handbag.

'What our Emlyn have done is wrong,' she said carefully; 'but it was on the right lines.'

I had then, as I had many times, a sense of relief at my own escape from entrapment in the dark rivers of lunacy which lie beneath the surface of many ostensibly respectable lives. This was a bizarre and extreme example of warped puritan belief but there were skeins there, part of a cobweb which connected to my own experience and also the experience of my chapel contemporaries – two of whom later developed sexual peculiarities, encouraged by an overwhelming Methodist conviction of sin that proved ineradicable.

In my own life I was to respond to many situations in life with an absolute conviction of right and wrong which allowed of no compromise and often led me into headlong confrontations, later creating a sense of guilt that at times proved intolerable. We may attack the past, but we can never destroy it, or deny it, and a conviction that simplistic beliefs are no preparation for the complexities of life does not alter what we have experienced either. Perhaps my luck was that I was never wholly contained in any one world and when I began to discover in the pages of Sinclair Lewis and John O'Hara the complexities of the small-town life which I also had led, I found myself nodding in agreement, becoming in the process an outsider myself and subtly withdrawing from the most extreme pressures of the life around me. There was thus always a part of me that did not believe, would not be swallowed wholly, and although in my other everyday pleasures I was ordinary enough, there was another self in the making during all these years of adolescence.

It was at this time in my life that I began to understand how society divides itself up, how the great inequalities of life begin and, in some cases, are structured from the start. At the beginning of the war, however, the narrowness of the wage differential in a small depressed town obscured the most obvious class divisions. While the war was on, most of the people I knew were in some way involved in 'doing their bit', as they said and, as we all knew, the casualties came irrespective of social class so that there was a sense of being 'all in it together' which made it a unique time to be alive. The collier was perhaps the one who suffered the most since the pits had no glamour and conscripts drafted into them often felt unfairly singled out. Most public officials were jingoistic and pontificated frequently in the name of the war effort about men who were caught sleeping underground, or who were detected with cigarettes or matches – age-old colliery offences which now became unpatriotic. Generally everybody believed that there was, as the song said, 'something about a soldier' and the prize of a uniform held sway for a long time.

But gradually, once the fighting moved further away across the continent of Europe and extended to the Far East, old social superiorities reasserted themselves. Rationing was not so strict, produce began to come in illegally from the country, and money reasserted its power. It was as if the common purpose and a public togetherness had been held in suspense while the pressures were on – the very presence of so many soldiers before the invasion of France, negroes from Alabama, or 'Free' Poles marching daily about the streets, encamped in public halls and

146

chapel vestries, acting as a constant reminder of 'something going on over there', words on everybody's lips. It was the great age of the cliché. But once the soldiers had marched away and the pressures eased, normality began to return and a skin that had been drawn tight began to slacken revealing wrinkles and folds where the mixture stayed the same as before.

So when at fifteen I played the drums with a friend on guitar at a concert to mark the retirement of an old drayman who had spent his life in the service of a whole-sale baker, it was not thought unusual that the managing director's Roedean-educated sister did a scarf dance by way of entertainment in a working-men's club hired for the occasion. This was somehow also to do with the war effort and that general feeling of togetherness. But within a year or two, the gaps widened. Petrol had become more freely available and once again the Armstrong Sidleys and the Morgan three-wheeler sports cars began to appear. Alongside the widening rifts, though, there flourished the stories of local celebrities and illegal goings-on told with a nod and a wink which we savoured for the tribal feelings they fostered. They were further proof of our difference.

One concerned a prominent butcher who, forceful and domineering, used to visit the local golf club every Thursday afternoon, the time of early shop-closing. Here in the company of his fellows he would play solo whist, at the same time obligingly providing a frying pan of chops and steaks which would be fried on a coke stove. It was a long-standing custom and since the golf club was situated in a remote place, illicit drinking or such rationing offences were unlikely to be detected. But the war had brought with it another problem, the difficulty of finding a suitable steward. A number were tried and found unsatisfactory, so the butcher announced that he would deal with the matter. He would make a search himself. A week or so had gone by when he announced triumphantly:

'Got the very man. From Tonypandy. Ex-Indian Army. Knows his place.'

The candidate appeared, was engaged, and Thursday became Thursday again as the friends gathered as usual, took up their positions at the card table with the comforting knowledge that the lean, white-jacketed figure at the bar was at their service. When a coal fell from the open door of the coke stove, the steward came from behind the bar to retrieve it, but at that precise moment the butcher picked up his cards and examined them – the steward pausing and glancing interestedly over his shoulder.

'Misère,' said the butcher impassively, indicating that he was prepared to lose every trick.

The steward gasped. Perhaps there was a collision of experience, between the ex-Indian Army man who knew his place and the truculent Tonypandy youth. Perhaps it was that the cards spoke more plainly to him than anything else. At any rate, he could not contain himself.

'You silly bugger!' he said. 'You're not going a misère on that hand?'

Such stories delighted us. From an early age we hoarded them. Pontypridd, like Damascus, we were given to understand, was a universe within itself, but it was always dangerous to get ideas above your station. The exception was sport, particularly rugby football where the pursuit of excellence was quite normal. This was where the real status lay so that when a young Geraint Evans came home on leave in the uniform of an RAF corporal – known as we said, 'To have a bit of a voice' – it was his brother-in-law, our international fly half, who really stole the thunder.

I'd had a taste of thunder myself by then. My grandmother, realising that my birthmark remained an embarrassment, prevailed upon the local doctor to have it removed and when I was sixteen, I went to the cottage hospital where a surgeon operated upon me and I came away with an impressive facial scar. I was moley no longer. It was an event and it was shortly followed by my inclusion in the school rugby team in which I just managed to keep my place. This gave my last years in school that sense of belonging which was so completely missing in the beginning. Suddenly, I was physically different and caught up in the most powerful of local forces. It was not just kudos that the first fifteen conferred, but the key to one of the few Welsh activities in which excellence was everywhere in evidence – and not just excellence but style, that elusive grace and flair of the truly great players which I learned to recognise because there were such a number of them on my own doorstep.

It is a matter easily exaggerated. (But not by me then. I thought of nothing else for two whole winters!) When I was not playing I was watching, hard up against the railings on this ground and that, usually in the company of my team mates with whom I had already played in the mornings. We were not so much supporters as clinicians, for we often left Pontypridd to make our diagnostic forays to Cardiff where

149

the post-war sides contained players whose individual skills, and skills in combination, were never really to be equalled in quite the same way. We went, sporting our colours and often our scars, with the conceits and confidence of Italian *bravos,* swaggering at times for we were the best, we felt, with the results to prove it. We were also players looking at players, therefore it followed that we knew what we were talking about and we conducted inquests in which our elders joined when we returned home, often to the public houses from which, quite soon, we were ourselves recruited to play for senior sides.

Never before or since have I felt such a part of things. Soon my enthusiasms reached a pitch so that, as for many of my contemporaries, the game took the place of theatre, a theatre in which there were heroes and villains, and there were moments when the touchlines were not so much touchlines as footlights. I would study individual players as if they were actors, noting their facial expressions, their stances, their every movement. When there were controversies I took sides, until I saw not players but personas and when the cool insouciant and insolent grace of our own side-stepping fly half, Glyn Davies, was threatened by the mechanical kicking skills of Cardiff's Billy Cleaver, it was as if a poet was being assassinated by an accountant and I willed bad games upon him, staring venomously through the railings. It was not reasonable, but it was me.

Such passions also produced pictures with the result that certain players of this era remain vividly in my mind, cloaked by images which reflected their style of play. There was a fullback playing for Cardiff named Frank Trott, the image of dependability, the kind of blacksmith fullback who is encouraged to stay behind the anvil until the bull runs amok. I saw him – and I see him now – as the kind of doughty and reliable figure who puts you in mind of a curly haired, barrel-chested British Tommy going on up the line in the driving rain with tin hat, full pack and cape and a shrug of the shoulders as if to say, 'What comes, comes.' There were many players I saw in this way, villains as well as heroes, and for a time nothing would have pleased me more than to have become some kind of sporting journalist, but I would have been very unsatisfactory since I was often so carried away with my enthusiasms for certain players that I almost ignored games just to watch them. It was a harmless passion but it took me into the heart of things local.

When the time came for me to think of some kind of career, I followed the line of least resistance and pleased my grand-mother by deciding to apply for a place at a teacher training college. If I had any ambitions as a teacher, it was only to emulate my own English master and I approached the forthcoming selection interview with a confidence that amazes me. Shortly before I had sat in the bar of the public house where the town rugby team gathered strays to play for its second fifteen. Noticing my interest, the landlord pointed out an ancient browning photograph of three world champion boxers, all born and brought up within a five-mile radius.

'Champions of the world, boy!' he told me pointedly; 'not bloody Machynlleth!', attributing all the aspects of parochialism to that remote North Welsh town. This was, of course, the hub of the universe talking and the landlord, like my grandmother, never let you forget it.

I was suitably impressed and when, later in the year, I sat before the Principal of the training college at Caerleon in Monmouthshire to which I had confidently applied, he had two pertinent observations.

'Pontypridd?' he said ruminatively. 'You must have played with the famous halfbacks?'

I had, and told him so.

Sport was very much uppermost in his mind, for he then told me that he had boxed with Freddie Welsh as a young soldier in the first war.

'A relative actually,' I said.

These were useful conversational lubricants, but more important was the reference from my headmaster.

'You have a very ordinary School Certificate,' the Principal said, 'but in all my years, I have never seen a reference quite like this.'

Pig, Boss, the Ogre, the Old Man, the nicknames had softened as we grew older, and in my case, on my behalf, he had done his stuff to the end. Now I had fallen into that special group for whom all his superlatives were reserved. If only half of them were true, the Principal observed, accepting me with a smile, I would be an acquisition indeed. As it happened, I was never to fail another examination in my life, and sitting there, I saw that enraged appalled face, the gleaming bald pate, the imperious manner, the prodding forefinger, the hasty flurry of his gown, and I heard that loud domineering attacking voice which scoured corners and had once struck terror into me until I learned to challenge it, and I swallowed hard. Somehow the gratitude we feel for imperfect people is more poignant than that which we reserve for saints. Soon I realised that at last I had a foothold on some kind of career. I was immediately to become a student teacher and while my horizons remained small, my life as a schoolboy had come to an end.

SHORT STORIES

GOING TO THE FLAMES

The old Stipendiary Magistrate, Ignatius Morgan fixed it;
fixed it with soft soap and the passing of time, first a day
and a night, then a week, then a second postponement of
the inquest, and all done with a word in the coroner's ear,
letting things simmer down, as if evil spirits would go
away, soft-shoeing over the tramway like vanishing gypsies
who'd done their stint of filching and were now eager to
creep off. In all the Welsh valleys, no one dared to say that
only Ignatius Morgan could fix a murder, but it was true,
and Punch Leggatt knew it; knew it at first hand and
nursed a sense of grievance which remained in his bones
until it warped him, the fixing, and the memory of his dead
son stretched across the kitchen table, a trickle of blood
coming from one ear, his face the colour of putty with the
life going out of him and those filmy eyes staring up at the

157

ceiling and not seeing the ceiling, seeing God knows what, and not saying anything that made sense, except the two words: 'Sarnt Hickey... Sarnt Hickey...'

Well, old Sergeant Hickey had paid, ended his days in a wheelchair, dribbling and drooling away, a burden to his family, cut down speechless by a stroke.

'Doctors could do nothing for him,' people said, and Punch Leggatt knew there was a God that day, a God of vengeance to be sure, but it only went to show. You got away with nothing in this life. Nothing at all. Unless you were Ignatius Morgan. But he was just a fixer, not to be blamed for what went first, him being only the cover-up man, the preserver of the King's peace, a minor Lord Muck in the area, and God forgive him for all that he'd done, but his was not the leading role.

Before it even got to the ears of Ignatius, the boy was dead anyway, and it was Hickey who'd struck him down, and Galton had aided and abetted, if you liked the legal way of putting it and wanted to hang them by their own rope. The pity was, Sergeants Galton and Hickey were both dead now, and may they rot in their graves and the boots of good, heavy men tread upon them, dead they were, like almost everybody else concerned.

But Punch Leggatt was not dead and lived with his memory, nursing it, worrying it, going over it in his mind, and gnawing away at this interpretation and that, his own constant ceaseless court of enquiry into the events of a January afternoon in the year of our Lord, Nineteen Hundred and Twenty-Seven. He referred to a killing at the gully end of Dan y Graig Street, and some day, he hoped that the truth would come out. It was Punch Leggatt's obsession.

There are some stories you wish you had never heard, and having heard them, being prompted to tell them, wish you had never started. How to get at the truth of it? How to see it as it was? How not to take sides? How to hear the cries and see the faces, and know exactly why?

I was twelve when I met Punch Leggatt. It was through the chapel. I did not know his nickname then, and respectfully called him Mr Leggatt. He had taken to religion late in life, and it was only when I got to know him better that I began to gain some inkling of a different man. At my grandmother's insistence, it was my task to take him Welsh cakes, sometimes a teisen lap, or flat cake, usually little delicacies of pastries or cakes that he could not have provided for himself. He was a widower, suffering from arthritis, rheumatism, and silicosis, all the ills of the coalface. His attendance at chapel had dropped off and he was put on the list for visits by the Minister and the good ladies of the chapel, deacons' wives and the like. He came under my grandmother's parish as it were, but like most of the wives, she had some reluctance in calling, and the task fell to me.

I did not mind much, provided I did not have to carry a shopping basket which labelled me as cissy to most of my friends. I like to think I was a quiet, thoughtful little boy. I took care to be polite. I spent a good deal of time in the company of old people and I learned to listen. If you cannot experience things yourself, the next best thing is to sit at the feet of those who have. It is not that I am indifferent to recorded experience, but rather that I love the groans and grunts of experience itself, the *aarghs* from the old men, their mouths hardening as they recall this event or that. To this day, I cannot make up my mind whether I have ever really learnt anything from people who do not take sides. I am not sure. For every statement you make, there is a contrary. But of Punch Leggatt, I am certain.

He was a hard man.

He must have been nearly seventy when I first met him, and he was immediately different from other men, standing unshaven and truculent, thumbs in his thick leather belt, booted feet apart, a striped flannel shirt open at the collar band, his stance, despite his ailments, always the stance of the aggressor. His face gave away his life, the strong cheek-bones shiny, the cheeks pinched and sucked-in, mouth bitterly downturned unless it was gasping at the air, his whole face bearing the burden of those dust-impregnated lungs. His eyes remained clear, a menacing pale green which sometimes stared slyly at you from under creased eyelids, often seeming to look at you from an angle as he moved his head to one side, viewing you on the slant and looking into you, as if to say, 'Now come-on, never mind the fan-dangle! What are you up to?' His constantly suspicious glance was made more villainous by another injury, a squashed dent carving up his large, fleshy nose, where an incisive blue coal scar gave the illusion of a break, but as he soon told me, break there was none. His most distinguishing feature, his thick, coarse, silver hair, he brought to order himself, giving it a monthly lop with a cut-throat razor, leaving himself a short fringe which fell without a parting over his forehead, then continued, basin-shape around his crown. It was a

Roundhead crop, wildly old fashioned then, strangely in fashion now. It shook when he moved like a girl's hair, his eyes screwing up with effort of movement whenever his aches and pains got across him.

Today I would be silent and reflective in his presence. Children have no such reservations.

'Trouble with the old bones today, Mr Leggatt?'

'It's the weather, boy.'

'A touch of north.'

'North? It's easterly, coming over from Graig top.'

'Your arthritis bothering you, Mr Leggatt?'

'Arthritis for a start.'

Sometimes he wheezed when he sat down, or lifted his boots over the shining brass strip of the doorstep. It was as if the effort of moving his long shanks – he was two inches above six feet – squeezed the coal dust further up his lungs. He was a hundred-percenter. No need to bother with check-ups for him. The colliery had remained with him and in him, was slowly stealing the air he breathed.

Not that there weren't times when he seemed to enjoy his illnesses, showing me his great gnarled hands with the enlarged knuckles of the chronic sufferer from rheumatism, a gold ring on one finger sometimes surrounded and pinched by red flesh, especially in the cold weather. There were days when he could not straighten the fingers and he'd hold up one hand, fighting to demonstrate a grip, wincing as he did so.

'Look at that. Look at it, boy!'

The hand in question had lost the tip of a finger, an accident with a jigger, and one knuckle was malformed from injury and whenever there was frost about, he clothed it in a woman's black silk stocking and then his face grew cunning.

'That'll show Jack Frost.'

He cultivated enemies, saw them everywhere. Nature had to be watched.

More delightful to me, was his accomplishment of being, in his own words, a spitter-and-a-half.

I should say that no one in our house had worked underground for two generations. 'They've got on, your lot have.' Only my grandmother remembered men coming pit-black into the house, and it was natural that I should think it rude to spit in public, but my visits to Punch cured me of that genteel notion. With Punch, it was a business, a matter of girding the loins, taking the strain, setting up the target and then his whole body would cavort into action as he aimed, the final expectoration proceeding in a direct straight line between the bars of the little, black-leaded firegrate where the blazing lumps of small coal would immediately hiss as he leaned back with immense satisfaction.

'Back to where it comes from!' he'd grunt and wipe his mouth with the back of his hand, much relieved.

'I got so much dust, that if I spit in the fire, it banks him up for the night!' he sometimes added, a joke that I would share. He often gave me a sideways grin afterwards and if he was particularly chesty, would hold up his good hand in warning before his performance. On a specially bad day, November fog or undue humidity, the orchestration of sounds when he was straining for breath, was accompanied by a violent change of colour in his face. He gasped then,

162

gasped and grunted, clenching his fists, knowing that his fight was against an enemy long planted in his own body.

In company, he soon recovered, would fix me with a pale eye, sniffle, settle back, reach for his ounce of chewing, and bite off a chaw.

'What has she got in the tin for me today, boy?' (I was always, boy.)

'Some Welsh cakes and teisen lap, Mr Leggatt.'

'Nothing like your grandmother's teisen lap.'

'No indeed, Mr Leggatt.'

'Fill the kettle by there. We'll have a wet now just.'

I would fill the kettle while he opened the biscuit tin, picking through the dainty serviette which had been wrapped around the cakes, then fingering the screw of castor sugar which she included so that he could give the bakestone cakes their complementary dressing. He had a sweet tooth, and his own teeth still, the possession of which gave him special pleasure.

While I filled the kettle, he would set out white rose-bud plates on the kitchen table, sometimes giving them a wipe with a grey jerseyed sleeve, and rub his hands in anticipation. I shall remember that kitchen all my life, chiefly because of the brass ornaments which adorned it. In the gloom of a winter's afternoon, the brass would glint as the flames of the fire were reflected in a dozen shapes. There was a tea caddy with an ornate brass cover decorated with a clipper ship on the dresser, several long toasting forks beside the fireplace, a brass hob in the grate, and along the mantelpiece, twenty candlesticks, the tallest about eighteen inches in height, their size diminishing until the tiny centre pair, which were no more than three inches in height. All were highly polished, like the cylindrical tobacco box behind them, and a large brass tray which was kept behind the hob. To clean all this brass, he used two new bristle toothbrushes every six months, and dried HP sauce when he ran out of metal polish. I never saw those ornaments without seeing my face as clearly as in a mirror. What intrigued me most, was that he cleaned his teeth with kitchen salt and a tobacco-stained forefinger.

For the first year of our relationship, we did little more than exchange pleasantries. Without quite knowing why, I soon came to realise that he was a man with a reputation. They did not tell me at home, but I knew soon enough. I called one day when he was out. At a loss, I knocked at the house next door.

A collier answered. He was interrupted in the middle of his bath. He had a threadbare towel around his waist. He had washed his lower half but his torso and face remained streaked with black. I could see the whites of his red-flecked eyes and glistening white teeth.

'What is it, kid?'

'Mr Leggatt?'

'Oh, Punch...'

'Punch?'

'Punch Leggatt, aye. He goes down for his pension 'bout now.'

He gave a wry grin as if to indicate we were dealing with a character, a man all on his own. I was dying to ask about his nickname. I immediately knew it referred to fisticuffs, but he seemed too old to bear a name like that, and too stern a man to encourage levity. It was months later when I was chatting to the postman that I learned that Punch had been a terror with his fists. The name had come from a classic event. He had been a haulier at one time and there was a particularly stubborn horse which had backed on him in a stall, raising its hind legs dangerously. Punch had clambered over into the front of the stall, seized the horse by the throat and showed him his fist. The fist would conquer all. He did not actually hit the horse, but he had been in trouble for striking a colliery manager. In his drinking days, they said it took three policemen to remove him from the bar of *The Bunch of Grapes* when he got violent. He was a man with whom you had to be careful, one not to be crossed.

At the time, this filled me with awe. There were scrappers up and down our street, but I was not one of them. I did not have the temperament, nor the desire to be cock of the walk.

I was content to run with gangs but not to lead them, yet at the same time, I was conscious of a feeling of inadequacy. Men fought every Saturday night in certain areas of the town. I was often hurried past, and I had several times seen policemen taking their time as they made their way in pairs to the centre of a melee. For the most part, I daresay drunkenness was at the root of it. But all I knew was that it frightened me. At the time, I was conscious that this was a weakness on my part. Perhaps I had caught that belief of so many inarticulate people that the fists were one way out of present difficulties. At any rate, I learned to avoid ugly situations, but always with a sense of cowardice which it took me years to dismiss. When I was told of Punch's reputation, I felt I was in the presence of my betters in more senses than one. Three policemen, I thought; that was some going.

Of course, I realise now that I was probably looking for heroes. A small boy is a creator of worlds as well as an occupant of a present world. Like all those who grow up close to a physical world and are not part of it, there is always a mystery, even a romance about the other man's poison. If two men are fishing alone on a storm beach a mile apart, it is an even bet that one will tend to fancy the other man's chance more than his own. It is only looking back that one sees how complicated are issues which seemed too simple. That Punch was a workhouse brat and a bastard, bandied about by the world, sent underground at the age of twelve, and had taken his fair share of kicks before he was twenty, was unknown to me then. And if I had known, I would not have understood it. He said one day that he had been sent to a Reform School. We had been talking about cricket. He had been, as he said, 'a bit of a bowler'. One August Bank Holiday Monday there was a match between the staff and the boys. The headmaster, an ex-military man, would put a half-crown piece on each stump and bat until each wicket had been knocked down.

'And the half-crowns?'

'Bowler's. To keep.'

'And how much did you get, Mr Leggatt?'

'Five bob. Yorked him.'

I could see the remaining half-crown stubbornly clinging to the stump which remained standing, and could quite imagine Punch glaring at it. He had the height and arms, as well as the aggression of a good fast bowler. It was the one anecdote he ever told me about his childhood, a shining day in so much misery, those stumps flying, sending the coins to the turf, and then his fingers bending around them, the envy of the other boys.

'Money in pocket,' he said. 'The only place for it.'

If he did not speak of his childhood, he spoke all the time about his wife. She was the making of him. 'A little bit of a thing, but strong. Off a farm, see, could wind me round her little finger. And a dab hand with the bakestone too. Turn her hand to anything, wash and scrub too, and needle – she'd make a sock last years.'

He showed me prints of his wife, but they did not tell me much, except that she was dark and small with close-set eyes, and a long aquiline nose. She looked a severe woman, I thought, but I had a sense of her, a tiny thing beside him, tidying up after him, a duster forever in her hand. He said she'd pulled him out of the gutter and was the making of him, but I did not know what to make of the phrase then. I took it that Mr Leggatt had been under-ground, had been married, his wife had died, had attended our chapel until his ailments prevented him, had once been handy with his fists, but all this was in the past. For months, I knew no more than this, but one day his cakes were not ready for me to take as my grandmother had been delayed, and I had to visit him at night.

The war was on, there was the blackout and some doubt as to whether I should be allowed to go. It was at the time when dimmed torches were carried, windows were criss-crossed with sticky tape to minimise the effects of the bomb blast, searchlights were placed at the top of the mountain, and various busybodies had been given uniforms and unknown responsibilities in the event of an air raid. When the warning sirens went first, I remember we lowered our voices and spoke in whispers, and if so much as a cigarette end were seen glowing in the dark it was felt to be a direct communication with the enemy who might be lurking silently overhead.

Eventually, I was allowed to go on my weekly journey to Dan y Graig Street, and while he was seated unpacking his tin, there came a hammering at the front door. It was sudden and violent, echoing down the passageway and startling us in the little kitchen.

He looked up, his eyebrows glowering and eyes staring wildly around him as if he were searching the room. The banging was repeated. Now he looked at me.

'What have you done?'

'Done?' I did not understand.

'You haven't done anything?'

'No,' I said. I could not think what he meant. If someone knocked at the door, my innocent instinct was to answer it. Then I heard the word, 'Police!' shouted through the letter box. He must have suspected before, but now he had no doubt. He stood up suddenly, forgetting his woes, held out his good hand, flexing and unflexing it, then nodded at the firegrate.

'Poker,' he said.

I stared at him. He breathed heavily, his wheezing returned, but on his face was an expression of such hatred as I had never seen on a man's face. His lips parted over his teeth as he clenched them and his eyes seemed to grow smaller, the pupils dilating as his breathing grew ferocious. His grey fringe positively shook all the way around his skull as he hissed at me with a massive impatience.

'Give us the bloody poker!'

I did not. I was petrified.

'Ha,' he grunted. 'You'd be no good in a bundle.'

With one sweep, he was across the room, had seized the poker, opened the kitchen door and had taken himself down the little passageway before I could move. I had a sudden glance of the tail end of his trouser leg over his boot as one leg snaked out with the speed of his move, and he hurled himself down the passage, muttering, 'Right then... right then...' as he did so. I got to my feet and stared down the passage. He drew open the door and raised the poker but took care not to step out into the street at the same time.

'This time you can come in here and get it!'

I could not see properly. I was still frightened. The tone of his voice suggested a man trying to frighten an animal. It was deep and guttural, a snarling from the back of the throat. He repeated himself.

'Come in here and get it, and you'll have it too. Mark you!'

There was a complete silence from the street. I edged my way down the passage, stopped a safe distance and peered under his elbow. A Special Constable stood there. He was a rent collector whom I knew by sight, a short, round-shouldered, pigeon-toed man of middle age, with a pouting oval face and the first pair of rimless spectacles in Dan y Graig Street.

169

We called him Makee-Learnie Williams. He had sold home-made toffee from the back of an ancient cycle during the Depression and had yearned all his life for a uniform. Now the war had given him his chance. But the sight of Punch drawn up inside the doorway, one hand raised, the other beckoning, took him by surprise. He stepped back on to the pavement.

'Blackout, Mr Leggatt,' he said in a thin, peeved voice.

When Punch had come to the door to let me in, he must have knocked against the front room light switch, switching on the light so that it blazed out into the street, an offence against the wartime regulations.

Punch paid no attention. Having got his hand and the poker into the upright position, he did not seem to want to bring it down into the empty air.

He continued to growl, 'Come on... I can take you....'

Makee-Learnie Williams was a makee-learnie policeman and did not know how to cope with the situation. He had said, 'Blackout,' with pronounced authority. Now he became ingratiatingly more social.

'It's all over the street, mun. I mean, the light by here.'

I could see his blinking spud face as I came forward hesitantly. I turned and switched off the offending light. But Punch did not move.

'There we are,' said Makee with a weak grin, anxious to calm things down. 'That's all. I'll let it go, this time.'

Punch lowered the poker but still kept it in front of him, and continued to stare at Makee as if expecting a trap. The watchful expression stayed on his face. He leaned forward and gave a quick look up and down the street to satisfy himself there were no reinforcements. The effort of his run down the passage had exhausted him, but he did not move and did not say anything for the moment. With the poker still pointing forward, he remained menacing.

'It's all right, Mr Leggatt,' I said. I could see Makee-Learnie wanted to go and was shifting his feet uncomfortably outside. He had said his piece, now he wanted out.

'You watch it!' Punch said to Makee-Learnie. His voice was thick. Comic the incident might be, but it had evoked old feelings, was a repetition of things past.

'There's no need to be like that, Mr Leggatt,' said Makee-Learnie, sulkily. Now he put his thumb under the flap of his tunic pocket like the real policemen did.

For answer, Punch slammed the door in his face.

We went back into the kitchen. He replaced the poker by the fire, instinctively giving the brass handle a rub with his elbow. Then he sat down at the table, pointed to the cupboard built into the wall beside the fireplace.

'By there. In the cupboard. Open it.'

I opened it. Half hidden by a pile of old socks, stood a half-full lemonade bottle of rich, dark brown liquid.

'The Elderberry,' he said.

It was elderberry wine.

'Give us it, and a glass.'

I did so. Now there came upon him a great urge to explain. He must have seen my face, round, innocent, anxious to understand. He was calming as he looked at me, wiped his nose with his sleeve, squinted, then scratched his hair. He did not offer me a drink.

'They came in before, see? Black Pats.'

'To see you?'

'The boy.'

I did not know he had a son. There were photographs of himself, his wife, several dogs, but not his son.

'Our Russell.'

'Russell?'

'M'boy,' he said hollowly with great bitterness behind the word, a choking acknowledgement of this great wound from the past.

I must have been thirteen or fourteen then, beginning to understand. But everything about him was so large, his hands, his head, his long body, the staring eyes, that peculiar crop, and the noises from his chest as he spoke. He filled the little room with his presence. As he spoke, I was conscious that I had not gone immediately for the poker when commanded. Had I let him down? How would I be in a tight corner? 'No good in a bundle,' he'd said. I was ashamed of that. There were so many situations in which I did not know how to cope. But now I did what he wanted, I listened to him and the words came out, at first slowly and bitterly, and then with such heat that I began to see things for myself, images taking shape that I would never forget. Without feeling, the communication of experience is meaningless, and I learnt this lesson sitting there that night in the chair opposite him. I did not realise then, that I was probably the only person left in the world who listened to him. The neighbours did not seem to bother. People did not like him. His manners put them off. Then there was the spitting, the rough, uncouth, no-nonsense manner, a heightened sense of that truculent valley insolence, the remnants of his strength, those hands and fists, his aura remaining physical, the victim of belt, buckle and boot and the recipient of more kicks than ha'pence all his long life.

'You had a son, Mr Leggatt?'

'Yes, I had a son, and they done for him, Hickey and Galton between them.'

Those names... how I came to know them, real Constabulary men, I had to understand, booted and spurred in their time, great oafs of fellas, built like trees the pair, a helmet apiece and the silver chains they wore then, a silver mail strap coming down below the nose, the thick red necks on them, and the swelled chests, the belted gut below, and the walk they had with it, truncheons busting out of their back pockets, hands behind their backs, square shoulders, the strut of those boots, the skirts of their greatcoats swishing, and the eyes made large and knowing by the authority of the warrant and the white gloves they loved to carry when there wasn't a case in court.

'D'you see, boy?'

Did I see? Yes, I saw. I saw them, Galton and Hickey. They were beginning to take shape. He went on, detailing while I listened. Family men, they pretended to be, home-loving and fireside lovers, always a pat on the head for the officials' kids, and a clip and a belt for the collier lads, maybe a gruff 'Who's got the matches?' if there was a gorse fire, all indicative of the general two-facedness of the breed when it came to the difference between an employer and an employee. Thirty years before, didn't General Macready himself say the police were the servants of the coal owners and had less to do with justice than the military which that Churchill brought in? No, Hickey and Galton were of the same ilk, riot-busters, strike-breakers, charge-room dolly-boys with the stamp of bully writ large.

'Did I see them?' he asked again. 'Was there no difference between them?' No difference, sixteen stone apiece, all but a pound here and there, except that Hickey'd been ginger in his day, still had the ginger twsh and pink flush and quick ginger temper of the type. He was Army-moulded was Hickey, the Royal Horse Artillery in his time, and a great man for the heels-together, the standing to attention, his face up the arse of the Chief Constable the minute his horse coughed! Oh, yes, and he'd been in the Black-and-Tans on loanment so he'd that as well as the horsemanship, and the horse-doctoring making him a bit of an expert on the cruelty to animals. Two daughters, he had, never a son, but when he had his stroke, it took two of them to move him and clean up after him, a terrible death for a big man like that.

But deserved!

And Galton? Maybe a touch thinner in the face, and darker, meaner, slyer, pencil-sucker, proper Dai-Book-and-Pencil when it came to it, everything recorded, pat as you like provided it suited his book and no one else's. Bit of a gardener, was Galton, but a sly gardener like everything else he did, marrows and greenhouse and a vine that he stole sheep's heads for, never the graft of vegetables in bulk, just the fancy stuff, and for why? For the presents and the suckholing and the scraping, and the Inspectorship he might well have got if it were not for...

'Russell?' I said. I remember interrupting him. It did not occur to me for one moment that he was not telling the absolute truth. Biased or not, it was his truth. I could see

174

Galton in his greenhouse, stroking his marrow, furtively removing a stolen sheep's head from under his greatcoat. But I wanted to get at the confrontation.

'It was high jinks, that was all,' Punch said. Was there a note of regret in his voice? High jinks...

'Was he underground?' I said. 'Russell?'

'Aye, couldn't shift him. She was against it though. Went on and on at him, but pit it had to be. Couldn't wait until he had a lamp and boots. No matter what I said against it, pit it had to be.'

I can understand that now. Punch was seventy when I knew him, but as a younger man, I could see him with a lad, his silent admiration at the boy's refusal to seek work elsewhere. 'Out of the pit,' the old men said bitterly, 'the only place to be.' But a good many did not believe it, would never leave. We are attracted by the things we hate, no less than those we love. I could see Punch shifting his chaw, 'Got a lad starting Monday.' His pride...

But they transferred Russell to a different pit in company with other boys. The pits were being electrified. Russell was to receive an apprenticeship. 'By way of being a trades-man,' Punch said. The colliers, I knew, did not think of themselves as being tradesmen in the same way as skilled men above ground. It was not a negotiable craft. But you could be an electrician anywhere. The trouble was, this meant travelling, young lads on a bus. High jinks again.

'I'm not saying that they weren't high spirited, not saying that at all. I'm not saying even that they didn't need a talking to, and if there was damage done, then damage should have been paid for.'

'He had to travel on a bus, Mr Leggatt?'

'Aye.'

At the colliery, the lads finished their instruction in the late afternoon. The bus brought them home, making its way by a circuitous route, dropping off various instructors on the way. At the end of the journey, it passed by a public house called The Compasses. In the corridor of The Compasses, there were showcases of stuffed birds, the landlord's pride. Some bright spark had got the idea of rolling a bowley down the steps of the bus and into the pub along the corridor. They had done so once, maintained a spurious innocence in the face of protests, but Russell had repeated the lark when dared a fortnight later. But this time, the bowley was caught. Hickey and Galton were waiting for them in the corridor, and when Russell had been called from the bus, his mates follow-ed him. A melee followed; first words, then a scrap.

'Waiting for them! If the bowley hadn't been throwed, they'd have started something. And tell me, why two of 'em, Hickey and Galton? For a handful of collier lads?'

On a Saturday night, the policemen were inevitably in pairs. It did not seem unusual to me. But the devil of it was that Hickey'd retired from the force itself, although he still wore uniform because of his position as Colliery Sergeant, a privilege granted to the colliery policemen who were respon-sible for security and searched men from time to time. Galton must have had a complaint from the landlord of The Compasses, anticipated 'a bundle', and asked Hickey to be there.

The illegality of Hickey's presence obsessed Punch.

'Pensioned off full-time, Hickey was, and walked straight

in the same uniform in Colliery Sergeant's berth. The same uniform! Never took it off. And no warrant, d'you understand me? No warrant, and no authority the moment he stepped outside the colliery. He'd finished with the force, have you got that? The man was without authority, uniform or no.'

They must have meant to teach the lads a lesson. The lads weren't going to be taught any lesson. They were in their late teens, had faces to save, loyalties to each other, that pit-bonded empathy that welded them together in the face of any threat from authority. What was meant to be summary justice, had turned into more than could be handled by the two men. A fight took place, first outside The Compasses, then spread into the corridor. When Galton began to get the worse end of it, Hickey drew Galton's truncheon. Russell was victim. One blow, but it fractured his skull.

'The only mark on him was the bruise down the side of his ear. I knew that was the truncheon. The lads brought him in, laid him on the table there. "Fighting?" I said "Aye, it was fighting. Sarnt Hickey fetched him a right old clout." "Well, stretch him out there, let's have a look at him." The woman was out, thank God. But I didn't like the putty look he had, blue tinged it was, and the blood in that ear. Next the doctor. Didn't say anything, except don't move him. So we waited. While Hickey was up the Stipe's, old Ignatius Morgan's, the coal-owner's friend. "Provocation," said Hickey, "and the force in danger of being overwhelmed." "Coming to the assistance of a comrade," said he. But he'd no warrant. They planned it, d'you see? To give 'em a bit of a hiding, a lesson like, but although nothing official was done – they postponed the inquest, let it drag on – it was the finish of both of 'em, and Hickey was the first to go.'

He went on to describe Hickey's death agonies years later, how Galton'd moved away. He did not tell me of his wife's reaction. Russell had died two days later, never regaining consciousness. One by one the lads came to the house in their best clothes to pay their respects. The blinds were drawn all along the street. There was talk of protest, but nothing came of it. It was smoothed over in a way that was possible then. Punch's wife died shortly afterwards, and it was then that he took to the chapel.

'Oh, I seen the folly of it since, I don't mind telling you. And I done some terrible things in my time. Terrible! But...'

I can remember feeling exhausted, having heard his tale. I formed no conclusions then. I had not experienced it myself and therefore I did not know. I understood that he had been a violent man and his feelings remained violent. No doubt, a good deal of his temperament must have passed on to his son. But the man I listened to was old, embittered and plaintive, with the full force of him being dampened by age and illness. I liked him best when he was crochety, complaining about the weather, the pains in his back. Then he was more endearing, something I doubt if he had been in all his life. I liked his expression as he inspected my tin, the way his fingers shook with excitement as he reached for the delicate little cakes and sprinkled the castor sugar over them. I liked his sweet tooth, his sounds and sighs and wheezes. More than anything, I liked his total dependence upon me, his only visitor.

He died when I was fourteen. His was the first funeral I ever attended. A relative of his wife's appeared to claim the furniture, all that brass. He had insisted on being cremated. While all the others in the tiny congregation stood with their heads bowed, I watched the coffin slide away on the rollers. He was going to the flames, I thought. I was young and innocent, and did not understand why no one shed a tear, except myself.

FRILLY LIPS AND THE SON OF THE MANSE

They met in a light opera at the tail end of the war. He was eighteen and she was nineteen, tall, willowy and dark with a stunning physical elegance that was immediately displayed by the tight-fitting clothes she wore and a way of moving which was quite unlike the girls he knew who remained in school. She had poise, money to spend which was a puzzle, a predilection for black and something extra which was very special to the times. 'It', they called it then, the superficial appearance of a glamorous detachment, a quite beautiful girl who seemed altogether unobtainable to people like him. There were girls you made friends with, others you chatted to or had grown up with, but she was the one you turned around to look at, a raver whose high forehead, long black hair, large pouting lips and sinuous carriage added up to what the boys called an absolute knockout. There was also something sad about her, a note of regret, the suspicion that a part of her mind was absent and elsewhere in a strange way, but this was a feature of herself that she revealed much later. At first sight, she was immediately distinguishable by those looks, that carriage, the haughty, curving lips, her natural leonine grace, and all his life he would remember the impression he had of her walking towards him in the hallway of the Workmen's Institute where the local amateur operatic society was meeting for rehearsals. A small beginning to a major transformation.

In the first place, being present at all was rather a joke to him. The shortage of men due to the war had caused the music master at the local county school to send a dozen senior boys down to rehearse as the group were short in the chorus. He was doing Higher School Certificate then, had been working too hard, and his mother thought it would be good for him.

'You ought to mix more, Selwyn. You take far too little time off. Musically, of course, they're not up to much, but it will be something different for you.'

Selwyn was a son of the manse, dutiful and obedient, and it was typical of him that he should arrive at the rehearsal room with twenty minutes to spare. He wore his school blazer and sat in the hallway just inside the main doorway. It was the first time he had ever been inside the building of which his mother had disapproved since it also contained a bar for the sale of intoxicating liquor which was open all the week, including Sundays. It was also used for political meetings and was associated with the miners, a group for which his mother also had no special liking,

181

being country born and bred, some distance away from the Welsh mining valleys. Selwyn himself had gone to school with the boys who were now down the pit, but the break with boys of this kind had come at eleven, and there was all the difference in the world between Selwyn and these boys now. They were boys no longer and when he passed them as he sometimes did on his way home from school, they were booted and pit black, one or two of them openly sneering at the school uniform which he was obliged to wear. Now they spat and swore, and there was about them that pit-bred empathy of the working world. Years later, Selwyn would meet wealthy socialists, who had made fortunes out of the manipulation of Welsh television licences, who would insist on the classlessness of the Welsh towns, producing neat arguments about the narrowness of the wage differential then, but they were bolstering up myths that were useful to themselves. There was all the difference in the world between people, and his own self-consciousness bore witness to it all his life.

Not with her though. She came in out of the rain wearing one of those see-through plastic macs, shaking her hair loose from under a headscarf. He could see her breasts made all the more prominent by a tightly clinging black sweater. He did not know then that girls who dressed like that did so in full consciousness of themselves.

'Gosh!' she said. 'Gosh! S'raining cats and dogs.'

She looked across at him. He must have seemed a lemon sitting there, pale and bespectacled, that manse aura all over him, a tall, thin, lank-haired, stooping boy with this preoccupied student's look increased by the heavy, horn-rimmed spectacles he wore. At home, there were daily conversations over what he should do with his life. He did not feel that call to Christ as his father had, but he went religiously to chapel, had never failed an examination, and his sixth-form essays were often returned with such comments as, 'Thoughtful. I can see you have given your mind to this.' But he gave his mind now to her as she removed the plastic mac. She wore nylons, he noted, a sign of affluence or connections in a time of war shortages. Her legs were long and slim and there was something about the way she stood which was at once provocative, one leg moving consciously in front of the other so that the leg muscles were better displayed. When she moved, even the slightest movement was noticeable. She was that striking. It was something of a relief to hear that when she spoke, her accent was much the same as his own.

She came straight towards him, and in an uncomfortable way, he felt her breasts were coming first.

'Is this for the rehearsal?'

'Yes,' he said. He did not stand up. Public schoolboys stood up in front of girls. County schoolboys did not.

'The opera, is it?'

'That's right.'

'Are you waiting then?'

'Yes, there are twelve of us from school.'

'I know. The Pirates,' she said with an amused smile. The operetta was more a musical and the male chorus were to be dressed as pirates.

She had already attended previous rehearsals but they had changed the rehearsal room and this was a new meeting place. In three weeks, they were to be on stage in the Town Hall. The boys had already learnt the songs in school and Selwyn remembered a chorus.

> Give me some men who are stout-hearted men,
> Who will fight for the rights they adore.

The sentiments were somehow in keeping with the war effort, and except for those who were already committed to going to university, most of the boys of Selwyn's age had already expressed a preference for one of the armed forces. Selwyn had not and his mother was worried lest he be called up. She felt the services to be dreadfully coarsening, and although the European war was drawing to a close, there were still the Japs. If Selwyn could not positively decide on a university course, then he had better go in for the Ministry, she advised. Either the Ministry or Agriculture, since both led to deferred occupations free of the universal obligation of military service. As it happened Selwyn did not like the thought of either profession, and since he had only one science subject, it would need all the family pull to keep him out of the Forces, but he was not sure he wanted that either. He was at that stage of his life when he had begun to look at his parents' life and marriage with some alarm, and any involvement free of chapel and school and the ordered life he had known was welcome. In the present case, it might only be light opera in the most amateurish circumstances, but it was different. It was out of the house and away from the classroom.

But he was not prepared for her.

'What's your name then?' she asked, sitting down beside him suddenly with a quick, decisive movement.

He felt the closeness of her thigh against his and gave a limp smile. Her lips were parted, a full cupid's bow made larger by the amount of make-up which she wore. She held her head on one side scrutinising him and he immediately diagnosed that she was what his mother would have called fast.

'Selwyn Lewis.'

'I'm Teg. Tegwen Hughes.'

'Ti siarad Cymraeg?' he asked. Did she speak Welsh?

'Oh hell no. We've got enough at home without that.'

He liked her at once. She had that warm, slightly self-depreciating frankness which valley girls had, a way of turning down the corner of her mouth when she smiled, as if to say, take me as you find me. His mother, his mother's sister, and the Welsh-speaking girls in chapel were more careful and reserved. Of course, as a minister's son, he supposed there was a certain aura about him. As a family, they were the epitome of respectability in the Welsh sense, and a good deal of this concern for appearances had passed on to him. He was aware of being protected. Because of the family, there was a difference in the way masters at school spoke to him, and since he was always quiet and conscientious, he had slipped through school almost unnoticed, and he had never given trouble or been difficult as had so many of the wilder spirits in a trying time. The war was always omnipresent and a number of boys he knew had been killed. In Dan y Graig Street alone, six boys had died by drowning in six different ships in the first two years of the war. Each tragedy had made him think, and he did not really see how he could ever seek a reserved occupation in such circumstances. It wasn't so much that he believed in killing as that he couldn't bear to go on being unlike everybody else. But he had confided in no one, and when he came to think of it, there was no one he knew who could really appreciate quite what it was like to see this girl make a beeline for him. He was very much a loner.

She had no self-consciousness in speaking to him.

'You haven't got a fag, have you?'

'I don't smoke.'

'Would you do us a favour then?'

'Certainly.'

'Nip into the bar and get me a packet. There's the money.'

There was another problem. He had never been in a bar before, and he did not venture now either, because no sooner had she made her request, than she noticed his County School blazer.

'Oh, hell no, you'd better not.'

'I don't mind.'

'There's an awful lot gets in here. I know, my father's a club steward.'

'Awful?'

'Awful chopsy lot. Making remarks and that. They got no feelings, some of 'em. Brutes, they are.'

He was surprised at her concern for him, and although he hated to admit it, the occasional grammatical mistake in her speech made him feel superior. She was the sort of person who, in his mother's eyes, always 'gave herself away the moment she opened her mouth'. They were quite a family for such sayings. Whenever someone went away, there was often an injunction delivered over such a simple thing as taking an extra clean shirt. 'You don't want everybody to know where you're from.' It was part of the chapel people's shame at the industrial turbulence which had gone on as the century advanced, giving really rooted local people 'a bad name'. Only one of the family had 'marched with the men', in the strike period, and was much disapproved of. All these things lay at the back of Selwyn's mind, a host of warnings, stereotypes, muttered precautions, and they would remain with him until he himself cast them off one by one as so much dross.

But what struck him as so extraordinary now was that she, Tegwen, was so open and considerate of him. She was not warning him, but protecting him instinctively within seconds of meeting. She chattered casually about the opera, but always with an eye on him, occasionally tossing her hair back. She made quite a business of that.

'I don't know what it's going to be like. There's no men about at all, hardly. We won't even know about the orchestra until the last minute.'

'You've been in plays before?'

'*Desert Song*. Well it's something to do with everybody away. Where are you from then, Selwyn?'

He told her. Then, without quite knowing why, he added that his father was a Minister.

'Oh, you're chapel. I had a auntie who was chapel once.'

'What are you?' he asked simply.

'Nothing,' she said. 'Not now; I used to be, but I'm not now. Sundays, I wash my hair.'

187

She was a harum scarum then. No religion whatsoever. He could not imagine what it was like not to have a religion. What else could you do on a Sunday? If his father was not preaching at home, they often had another Minister to stay which meant a host of little disciplines like leaving a clean spare towel untouched in the bathroom, lighting a roaring fire in the front room for his after-lunch sermon preparations, and such little instructions as not asking for a second helping of tart, and generally minding his p's and q's which were ordinarily impeccable anyway. By tradition, they took no Sunday newspapers and did not even listen to the radio except for the news bulletins. Sunday was a scrubbed, holy day of sombre silence, and it was not until he was fifteen that he was even allowed to do homework on the day of rest, and then he had to fit it in between three chapel services. If he had dared to suggest anything else, it would have brought a frown to his mother's face, and while he suspected that his father would not have minded some relaxation, it had been impressed upon him that it was wrong to upset people, his mother in particular. The idea that he was being brought up to suit her convenience had not occurred to him, and despite the fact that they received extra rations illegally from tradesmen who were members of the congregation, his mother also contrived to implant the idea that she 'took food from her plate' to enable him to continue his education. It was quite untrue, but she believed it to be true, and he had not the heart to question it, fitting in with her image, her goal, 'a good boy to his mother, never a minute's trouble'. It was a classic Welsh manse situation and it bred spiders in some people's view, but of course, he was ignorant of that.

'Well, I mean, good Gawd, look what's happening every-where?' Tegwen said indignantly.

'Pardon?'

'Religion, where is it? Where does it get you?' Now she was angry, and he saw her eyebrows twitch.

It was in his mind to use one of his father's phrases and speak of a personal salvation, but he could not bring himself to do so. But it was she who controlled herself. There was a moment of sadness then, causing an edge to her voice, but it disappeared as quickly as it came. She seemed to have sensed his alarm. She was all smiles in a second.

'Oh, I'm sorry. I didn't mean to upset you.'

'You haven't upset me.'

'Haven't I?'

'Certainly not.'

'D'you always say, "certainly"?'

'You haven't upset me.'

'Good then, isn't it?' she said with a shrewd smile, tossing her hair again. 'Well done, Selwyn.'

They were left alone for the briefest of moments because a whole crowd of people soon entered, the musical director, Mr Elias, other members of the cast, and the remainder of the schoolboys who were at once put to one side to rehearse the musical scores which were already familiar to them. While they were waiting, Selwyn's eye sought out Tegwen, and he watched her whenever he could. He noticed that she was extremely popular. The men in the cast were forever at her side. Arms were linked with hers; she was petted and cosseted. She had a small part but the male lead sang a duet with her. Selwyn noticed that she had a sweet voice which

189

went up a few octaves from her normal speaking voice and when she was isolated on the stage, her glamour was even more apparent. She was taller than most of the other girls and that air of difference remained. They all went through their paces at the rehearsal and, when it was over, light refreshments were provided and the society broke up into little groups about the hall.

Selwyn was not the only one of the schoolboys to notice Tegwen.

'Who is she then? The dark piece over there? The Lana Turner one – look!'

He did not say anything but she called him by name when tea was poured. This was at once noticed.

'Hey, Sel? You're a dark horse, you are!'

He blushed.

'Here you are, Selwyn. How many sugars?'

'Three,' he said. He did not know why he said it. He never took three. He merely wanted to make her say something.

'Three? Aren't you sweet enough?'

For that, he had no reply again.

'Biscuit?'

'Thank you.'

'Catch the act, did you?'

'The act?'

'My number?' She was an ardent film fan and had all the jargon.

'You were very good.'

'Is that all? You wait 'til you see the costume.'

'I can see enough now,' another boy said, muscling in.

'Well, you can see more than you can have.'

'Is that a bet?'

'Go on. There's a law against baby snatching.'

Selwyn stood silent while all this was going on and to show that she appreciated his silence, she seemed to stand closer to him. Later, he was to enumerate the special preferences which he thought he had been shown. She had sought him out while the tea was being poured, she had excused him the embarrassment of going into the men's bar, and what is more, when the time came to say goodnight, she lingered in his company.

'Well, I'll be seeing you then? Friday, is it?'

'Yes.'

'We generally go for a coffee after.'

'Good,' he said.

'What's that supposed to mean?'

'I mean, I'll see you.'

'All right then. G'night, Sel.'

He made his way homewards thoughtfully. One thing was certain. She did not appear to think there was anything wrong with him.

'What was it like?' his mother said when he got in. She always contrived to be on her feet and busy whenever he entered the living room, as if idleness was a sin and never to be detected. She had a large round bespectacled face with his own serious regular features and greying hair drawn into a severe bun behind her neck.

'Much what you'd expect,' he said matter-of-factly, 'amateurish.'

She nodded, replacing a spoon in a Mazawattee tea container. She knew some of the leaders of the group and

191

asked after them one by one. He said as little as he could, but when he went to bed, he had difficulty sleeping. *She* was so beautiful, he thought, it made him uncomfortable. He gave no thought to the fact that she might have singled him out for attention, and there was no doubt about the fact that she was quite unlike anyone he had ever met. 'Tegwen Hughes,' he said to himself, *'Teg'*. There was a warming casualness about the abbreviation. He said it over and over again to himself.

There is no girl like the first in a young man's life and he thought about her every day until the next meeting came, and although that passed innocently enough, he made it plain that he wanted to take her out. Would she come out with him?

'Where're we going to go then?' He was not aware that she was teasing him.

'Where you like. Pictures, or...' he did not know an alternative.

'Or what?'

'Whatever you like.'

'Walk, is it?'

'Yes,' he said. He knew at once that he had to contrive a meeting at the other side of town, away from his father's parish, but if you had asked him why, he couldn't have explained it, other than that he did not want to cause his parents worry, not even a moment's hesitation about him. He knew she was 'not his sort!', the family were very probably 'not their kind of people'. But see her he had to, and see her he did.

One, two, then three weeks went by. On the night of the

first performance in the Town Hall, there was an atmosphere of tension which affected all the cast. They were to run for a week, but the first night was the most exciting occasion. It was a small amateurish affair by any standards, but their nerves were no different from anybody else's. Until the last minute, they were not certain that they would be able to muster a full orchestra, there was delay with the costumes, a leading tenor contracted a bout of tonsilitis and there were the usual anxieties, but finally the last few seconds came before the curtain went up and now Selwyn stood close to Tegwen. In the darkness beside a large scenery flat, his hand was firmly entwined in hers. It was not just their nervousness, or the camaraderie that comes to performers who face a common foe, by now he was obsessed with her. They could not stop touching each other and sometimes his grip was so fierce, it hurt her. He seemed always to be close to her, watching her protectively when he was not holding her in some dark corner. Now she opened her mouth when he kissed her, placed her arms behind his neck, ruffling his hair, and once, actually put *her* hands in *his* trouser pockets when she was cold. She seemed to set him on fire and he had experienced nothing like it. Indeed, he was experiencing all the male discomforts more often than not, and even in their pre-performance stance, he felt a full consciousness of sexual awareness which had come suddenly and violently and which occupied his mind to the exclusion of all else.

Now she wore a soubrette's costume, and in the last seconds before the curtain went up, he felt her trembling beside him. Her involvement with the production was total and he was aware that she believed in the songs that were sung and the trite sentiments they expressed, but it did not make a scrap of difference to him. He was made aware for the first time in his life that it was not just an idea which was important, but what cloaked it. He found difficulty in disagreeing with anything she said.

'You'll be great,' he muttered breathlessly. His own part in the performance was hidden amongst others in group movements and he had no real nervousness.

She turned her face to him to be kissed finally and he only withdrew his lips from hers as the curtain was actually rising. It was extraordinary to think that only that tatty piece of faded velvet substitute separated him from his mother and father whom he knew were sitting in the front stalls.

'Be sure to take deep breaths and gargle regularly,' his mother had instructed, a Gymanfa soloist herself.

He followed her advice, but with or without it, the opening night went well. All the clichés were perambulated. 'A bad dress rehearsal, a good first night.' There was prolonged applause at the finale. They had made a brave show and generally there is no more rewarding feeling than recognising your much disguised butcher carousing romantically in the arms of Jones Weights and Measures' wife. There was no doubt that the society gave almost as much pleasure to others as they did to themselves.

But for Selwyn it was the beginning of something else. He had already walked Tegwen home before, and they had been to the cinema on one occasion, but he also knew that her parents could not be present on the opening night as they had suddenly been called away to a dying relative. It meant that the steward's flat on the other side of town would be empty. He had not met her parents as she preferred him to leave her at the corner of the street, and then ran home, a strange gesture that took him quite by surprise. But now as they hurried homewards after the performance, both were conscious of the difference of the occasion. The applause had delighted them. He was glad for her. She took a second bow and there was an extra ripple of appreciation which was quite recognisable. She was a success.

They did not stay for the celebrations which went on back stage and their absence was noted, but they did not care.

'I wanted to get away,' he said.

'It was great, wasn't it?' The universal adjective.

'You were.' He'd felt his throat dry as he watched her alone under a spotlight in a pool of light. 'And everybody knew it. I'm surprised you're coming home with me.'

'Are you?' she questioned, but she looked ahead into the darkened street.

'Yes,' he said. There had been others nosing about, but she left them in no doubt. She was his girl.

'You're funny, you are, Selwyn.'

'Funny?' He did not like that.

'Tense, you are, aren't you?'

'What does that mean?'

'Oh, it's all right, I know.'

'What d'you know?'

'Don't be so soft, mun. 'Course I know.'

He did not know what to say to that, but clasped her hand even firmer, warming to the reciprocal squeeze.

'Lotta boys is nasty,' she'd said once, 'but you're not nasty, are you?'

He never knew what to say in reply to questions like that either. He was becoming aware that she was a creature of moods.

'I dunno. I just dunno what to make of you. You don't half look at me, do you? You're a looker, you are, Selwyn boy. You watches people, things, don't you? Quiet you are, but I like you quiet, not saying much.'

Then there were her comments in general. She had a way of slanting her lips scornfully.

'The people there are in this town, the minds on 'em! Sieves, they are. Oh, you don't have to tell me, I know.'

He did not tell her. He did not know. There was such a contrast between her appearance and the things she said. One night, she'd remarked about complaints made against her in the shop where she worked selling shoes. She talked too much, they said, and the delivery boy had given her a nickname. What was it? She did not like to tell him, but when he insisted, she did.

'Frilly Lips,' she said, suppressing a giggle. 'Frilly-bloody-Lips. Meaning they were never closed. The mouthy little bugger.'

For his own part, he thought it was wrong that she should have a nickname at all and said so. In a curious way, he thought, it made her less than she was and took away from the total effect of her appearance, but he could not explain it. It was as if he did not want any part of her real self to obscure or lessen the total effect made upon him by her physical presence. Perhaps, buried within him, there was a deep and little understood predisposition to prefer myth to reality, the tribal hallmark of a long-defeated people. He was that Welsh.

But at night, walking along the silent street, her arm and hand tucked into his, he stole glances at her profile and marvelled again. There was no angle of regard that took away from her and he enjoyed the rapport of her silence as much as anything else. The feel of her close to him was enough. One other aspect of her which remained unexplained was the sadness he had earlier noted and continued to detect, a part of her nature that seemed alien. He did not speak about it, nor did he encourage her to, but it was something else, a way she had of looking past him at leaves blowing by in the gutter, or at trees in the distance as if there was some reminder there of things she could not express. She did not like the sound of wind, he knew, a strange thing that, a mystery that added to her attractions and made her all the more tantalising. But for this, she might have been thought to be scatterbrained, but she was certainly not that. If anything, she was wise in the ways of relationships, an expert at putting him at his ease. He was awkward, gauche, and shy, but she did not make him feel so, although he did not count her special gift as being a feminine trait. How could he, in the light of all those admonitions and pleas which had surrounded him at home?

When they got to the end of the street where she lived, she did not leave him and he had a sense of occasion as he watched her take a key from her handbag. They had not spoken for minutes but now she grinned at him.

'You'll have a cup of something then?'

'If you like.'

'Well! There's keen!'

'Yes, please,' he gritted his teeth.

'Temper?' she said. 'We haven't seen that yet.'

She could annoy him too, but since they were usually in the presence of others, and the omnipresence of others had always been impressed upon him, he had never really given vent to his annoyance. Now he was conscious of the empty flat upstairs, that knowledge and the accompanying thickening of his blood. They would be alone together. There was no doubt in his mind as to what he had come to do and although he had a sense of profound wrong, he knew he could not help himself. From the moment they left the company of others, it had been on his mind, but for all his mind and the hesitations of his mind, there were other, more powerful urgencies, the whole strain of being with her when every part of her body caused him to want to protest, inducing a violence in him that was right out of character.

The moment the front door was closed, he seized her roughly, burying his lips on to hers, continuing to hold her and turning her back against the door so that she was forced to free an arm to protect herself. But the other arm remained around his neck and she had a typical admonition of her own, the moment she could free her lips.

'What do you think you're doing?' she said in the darkness, 'playing against me?' Her face was wicked, her eyes amused. It was a rugby country after all, and careful is as careful does, it was she who looked after his spectacles.

But he was serious.

'Come on. Let's go upstairs.'

'There is only upstairs. It's the top flat.'

'Let's go there then.'

'Wait boy... wait!' His mother might have said that, but that was all she might have said.

What he could never understand afterwards, (and which was really most obvious) was that there was an inevitability to the occasion. Of course, she was leading him on, all the way. 'As common as dirt', his mother was to say and the repercussions were mammoth, but that was later. At the precise time, he felt rather as if he were in a maze, pushing blindly at doors which sometimes opened, sometimes did not. There was so much he did not understand. Young people these days, he was to say years later, were far more sophisticated, better informed, and no doubt their instincts led them to their own pleasure and pains, but then, on that night, he was simply driven blindly by his instinct, and by his desire to be close to her, to have all that she was for himself, his need. More than anything he wanted to cease being himself, to be part of her, that close, the final and only closeness, he was to think for a long time. He wanted release too, an end to all those grubby, forbidden practices of the bedroom, but that was to take away from the total experience, to destroy what she gave to him, that knowing acceptance of his inexperience and her ultimate kindness as he lay there sobbing when the guilt came.

She had both her hands behind his head looking up at him wonderingly on a utility divan, one leg of which was broken.

'You old silly...'

'I couldn't... I couldn't help it.'

He hardly knew her as a person. Closeted in one world, he was blind to others, totally blind. He knew three facts about her, actual facts. Her father was a club steward, she worked in a shoe shop, she had a pleasing voice and was much sought after. That, and she liked him, had singled him out. But then, later, she watched him dress with a wry smile and took him by the hand into her bedroom. He had not been able to wait even for that scrap of comfort. Now he followed her wonderingly. The bedroom was incredibly small, moulded by the sloping roof and her bed was tucked under an eave. The bedspread was a cheap patterned quilt such as were sold by riff-raff in the market and her possessions were meagre. There was not a book in the room, he noted, in marked contrast to his own. But on the dressing table, there was a framed photograph prominently displayed of a young man a little older than himself with a wide cheeky grin. She picked the frame up pensively, then her sadness came on her again.

'What is it?' Now he felt embarrassed, an intruder.

She hesitated, suddenly seeming younger, even sisterly, a different person altogether. She made a regretful move of her lips.

'My husband,' she said in a small voice.

'*What?*' he stared at her frantically. He felt remorse come upon him in a wave, settling even in his stomach, like bile.

'It's all right, he's dead.' Again, she thought of him, his feelings.

'Dead?'

' "Missing presumed," at first, but then it was for keeps.'

For keeps... that was what he eventually took home with

him, the finality of that. There were other details, a whirl-wind courtship, the difficulty of obtaining her father's per-mission, the brief trip to the Registry Office, a weekend's honeymoon at a boarding house on the coast.

'Well, it wasn't actually a boarding house, it was rooms with attendance, they call it.'

He was a rear gunner. She'd met him once or twice, another one who couldn't bear to leave her alone. One or two people knew about it, but she collected her pension elsewhere and she kept it secret for a reason which Selwyn couldn't fully understand. The family didn't approve. She was too young. It would have been better to have waited. They'd had enough trouble with the elder sister when the Yanks were billeted locally. Please God they didn't have another one like her. But Tegwen's will had prevailed.

'So there!' she said. 'There... now I've told you. So now you know, don't you? Me, see?'

If anything it frightened him. It was too much to hear and as soon as she told him, he knew she regretted it. His blinking schoolboy's face gave away the enormity of it, her experience and his ignorance in the face of it. Perhaps her parents were right in wanting to keep it quiet after all. Too much can happen to you, too much in too many places and perhaps her father knew that, had a sense of the world's ills and the smallness of people who could not face up to them. There was such a thing as a propensity for bad luck, and he did not want people to know that she was starting off her life with that behind her.

Selwyn swallowed, the tears in his eyes.

'Poor Teg,' he said. He was truly close to her then.

201

Her smile was brave, accepting, womanly. It was her secret and she wanted him to know. Then it was his first time and there could be no other, that she understood best of all.

But it was not long before he looked at his watch and it was two o'clock in the morning before he got home. His father had gone to bed but his mother waited up, her eyes reddened with concern. Fortunately he had declined a drink and his breath was virginal in that respect.

'Where've you been? For goodness' sake, it's hours past midnight?'

His mind was overburdened by thought, but he was not going to change overnight. He took off his glasses and polished them, blinking solemnly.

'Oh, they had a lot of difficulties with band parts. A good deal has to be changed.'

'The band parts?'

'I had to take a whole set of new scores to Mr Elias, and then we got talking, and one thing and another.'

He was to develop an expertise in the casual additional details he invented to embellish the most commonplace lies. He would be found out, of course. Things would be 'all over town', and his mother's concern for him, and 'everything she had done for him' was ultimately no more than a subject of dismay for him. The world inside the manse could be just as cruel as the world outside. His parents had prepared him for nothing. His whole life was cocooned by their wants and wishes, more than anything by their fear of the world and their inability to change it, even clinging stubbornly to their ancient language so as to separate themselves from the main stream of the human experience. He was on the point of seeing them as small and frightened, and that worried him too, so for their sakes he began to hide his thoughts, his new self, his secret.

He lay in bed listening to his mother double-locking the back door but he did not think about her further. He had other things on his mind. Who would think that you could taste hair, taste it, and feel it and when it came down over your shoulders, it was like another world in there, the coarse, scented smell and feel of it, the touching – the touching, the little pains and discomforts and finally, actual sweat falling upon you and teeth glistening in the darkness and the final awful marvellous unthinkable release that was to be his again now; so that in a month or two when his exams had gone by the board and there was khaki looming and tears at home, he could even have his leg pulled.

'You County schoolboys are all the same. Oh, all right then. What? You're a case, you are. Get away, I knew as soon as I seen you. Never had it, and'll never want it again.'

But she was wrong about that, of course, Tegwen Hughes, child-bride, widow, wit, goddess, saviour and sage, Frilly Lips.

DREAM GIRL

Will remembered her living in the corner house of the terrace. She wore her hair bobbed then, sometimes a neat, page-boy style which rose and fell when she ran, but still remained neat, despite her mother's shouted insistence that young ladies did not run. Neat was the word for her, always neat, always a little different even as a leggy school-girl in long black stockings and gymslip. Her mother insisted she wore a uniform despite the fact that like Will she had failed the eleven-plus and, as if to make up for it, her mother made her concentrate on her appearance, and there was always a sheen coming off her, her peachy cheeks, milky complexion, that groomed, ash-blonde hair especially. The *Shampoo Girl*, somebody called her, Queen of the Dan y Graig Hairbrushers, but she was too serious for that, Dorothea Lemon.

'Dottie Lemon...' (the street kids sang then).
'Figure like a film star.'
'Face from a bottle...'

She was groomed, manicured, poised, somehow untouchable even in adolescence. From an early age, and especially after the dreadful disappointment at eleven, she was schooled in the art of keeping herself to herself, a young lady of destiny and a manufactured cut above the Dan y Graig crowd from the tips of her elegant toes to the assisted curves of her arched eyebrows. Like Will she had grown up in wartime austerity, rationing and shortage, but it was also the age of the screen star, ten foot close-ups in the Workmen's Hall, lights glistening in enlarged eyes, held poses, and glam above all. 'It', was around, written in large letters, an indefinable quality that some girls had, others didn't.

'Daft,' Will thought, ruefully recalling her name and the pertinent facts about her. With the picture of the schoolgirl and the imposed adult glamour of her appearance, Will also recalled her mother's voice. It was shrill and carping, often a complaint and a warning in it, in marked contrast to the honeyed tones of the heroines of *Screen Secrets*. Anybody'd think the world of the terraces was poison.

'You be careful who you speak to, and come home straight, mind.'

Then there was a specific reference to himself.

'Will Willis will never get anywhere. He's too half-soaked.'

If Dottie had protested, and she probably had not, the reply was duly reported, cutting him down to size.

'He's got plumber written all over him.'

His attentions were thus discouraged, but he had not pursued them with any ardour. Perhaps the old scrag was right? He was always easy going, and since he was then apprenticed to the trade, it was no great feat to assume he would serve out his time. But what Mrs Lemon could never have imagined was the urgency of the note he received nearly thirty years later.

> I expect you remember me. I saw your name over the shop and made a note of the phone number, but then lost it which is why I am writing. Could you please call personally at the above address? I really am desperate and have no one else I can ask. I've been living away and have returned. Always in after lunch.
>
> Sincerely yours,
> Dorothea.

There was only one way he could describe her handwriting and that was scatty. Great extravagant loops, curls and flourishes proclaimed her indifference to straight lines. She dashed things off, he remembered, and as he considered her request at the back of his shop which bore his name, he sucked a tooth, freeing a blackberry seed which had embedded itself in a cavity. He now went home to lunch, as did most of the local businessmen, and for years nobody had dared call him by his nickname to his face. Not that he would have much minded. Nicknames were going anyway. Will Pipes, Jones the Bricks, and their local untransferable bobby, Dai-Book-and-Pencil, were names which were part of a past that was changing anyway. The fact was that Will now had his own business and employed men, seldom laying a hand on the tools himself. Since Dottie Lemon's day when they had all been kids together, he had prospered. He was married with two boys, and if his wife, Vi, had become even more easy going with prosperity, so had he. No phrase described them better than when people spoke of them as being comfortably off. Although he wouldn't admit it, he'd made a small bomb out of sub-contracting for the council house building which had mush-roomed since the war, and they now had an office with an accounts staff of two in addition to the shop, a general foreman and the plumbing squad. But that was the ceiling. Full stop, as Will said. Cautious always, he didn't want to get too big, nor have to borrow too much. In the building trade, he'd seen enough high flyers come off the tools, only to get milked in the solicitors' offices. But not him, and if, as one solicitor had added, he probably always kept a pair of dungarees in the wardrobe, just in case, he merely smiled. Didn't it go to show that he had no side?

Of course, there'd been high days and holidays. Once, the opportunity had arisen to merge with a large competitor who had landed public service contracts and was floating a public company. There was big money to be made and talk of direct-orships. But Will had drawn back. He was told he would have been a valuable man. It was explained how many founders' shares he would have. There was a pool of building land that made the mind boggle. Stock was explained to him. The floating capital ran into hundreds of thousands.

But he shook his head. With one hand, he wiped away

the quiff of hair that frequently fell down over his forehead and grinned apologetically. They'd taken him out for a lavish expense account meal, table flowers, olives, crushed ice and gleaming silver, but he might have been in the Sergeants' Mess, and he remained unimpressed. As far as he was concerned, he still got a kick out of wearing a suit to work! He was very grateful for the compliment, but enough was enough. Fortunately, Vi wasn't greedy or pushing. They had enough to run a Jag on the business as it was.

'You do what you want, Will,' she said.

He had done, all his life, and what is more, parted on good terms with his competitor who promised sub-contracting work on the side. There were no ill feelings, and when, some years later, bad weather, the current credit squeeze and maladministration put the new company in a very rocky situation, people who knew said, 'By God, that Will Pipes has got a head on him!' But they were wrong. It was simply as he said, there were things he fancied, and things he didn't, and being his own man was important. If anything, his main preoccupation nowadays was that he had almost worked himself out of work! A morning on the telephone and he could employ his men for weeks ahead. He was so successful in his own small way, and every job he handled was so perfectly within his compass, that it ran like clockwork and left him with time on his hands. It meant he had time to think, something he regarded himself as ill prepared for, and when the note came from Dottie Lemon, he gave the morning to it.

'What's up with the Boss?' the workmen said, looking at the closed office door.

'Thinking,' the general foreman said.

It was somehow disturbing.

Will thought first of Dottie's mother, a harridan if ever there was one; and posh with it. Upbringing on the brain, that woman had. He lit a pipe and cast his mind back, slowly realising that but for one incident involving Dottie, his whole life might have been changed. It might sound a bit far fetched, but few people realised how soft he had been all those years ago. Love, he thought. Romance, he thought. And the pictures, the bloody pictures... he meant the cinema and the degree of their thrice weekly involvement on those blackout nights. In his daydreams, there had been times when Chicago seemed more real than Dan y Graig itself.

But there were more immediate images which excited his recall, the crow beak of that woman Lemon for a start. Crow beak, scrag neck, down-curved lips, hennaed hair, the perpetual reek of powder and paint. Madam Make-Up they called her, Madam Make-Up, Nancy-posh.

Dottie's mother was a shrewish widow with a small pension who had inherited a house, but from an early age, Dottie's life had been moulded with a single intention, getting out of Dan y Graig Street. With this end in mind, the personality seemed to have been screwed out of Dottie and she had been stamped and moulded in the shape of the available templates of the times, Shirley Temple to start, then moving up the Hollywood ladder. To be fair, she must have realised that there was a chance of Dottie being a beauty, and beauty had to be cultivated. Indeed, it could not be left alone, so dancing classes followed elocution classes ('speakin' nice', Will called that), and then there were winters on the accordion which put a stop to roller skating, loafing about the Bracci's cafés, or ruining the complexion in the mountain winds and the unladylike stains of whinberries which might play havoc with the lips. Dottie had a career ever in front of her, and although it took no very clear shape for years – the war interrupted a good many things – the first steps were taken when she packed her accordion and went off with a gypsy band, to a great halloo of front page glamour in the local newspaper. There was also a cheesecake photograph and a black star inset beside the headline, an afterthought by a sentimental compositor which drew a relaxed smile from Mrs Lemon's pursed lips. From such humble beginnings, stars were truly born. If only Dottie's voice had a little more volume, but then, perhaps that would come; anyway the microphone was God's gift to the whispering tenor, no less than the budding soubrette.

Will remembered it all, the sparkling sequins on the tight-fitting dance costume, the metal bars on the tap-dancing shoes, the gypsy blouse with its pretty crochet work and pink drawstring, most of all Dottie's performing smile, her lips carefully parted and the precisely calculated glance which was so levelled so as to include everyone 'out front'. Dottie did not only have *It*, she had that show business bazaaz, the illusion of life and energy when performing, that reached out over the front rows even of the Workmen's Hall.

There were also other moods, equally phoney.

'*Please...*' she sang, her head on one side, her pale little oval face straining with that smile, eyes blinking until she got used to the lights, always projecting an unrealised and as yet, anonymous self; *'Say you're not intending to tease...'*

Sweet, she was; a good turn, fair play. Winsome, was the word, as neat as a top. She'll go far.... Oh! Listen now...

'Your eyes reveal,
That you have the soul of,
An angel white as snow...'

From 'Animal crackers in my soup', she had progressed and unwittingly acquired something of the borrowed image of the girl next door, the captive blonde who never washed a dish however, but whose hair brushed your cheek when you kissed her in the moonlight, Glen Miller smooching in the background. 'And you never thought of knickers,' Will said to himself now. They were all strangely puritanical, the wartime teenagers, uneasily poised below the general disturbance. Perhaps that explained the one afternoon he had spent with her when she was free of her mother and Dan y Graig Street, one hour which stood out in his mind, perhaps the one note of reality in his whole recollection.

'Always in after lunch,' she'd written. Would he go and see her? He had certain reservations. He looked again at the note. *'I really am desperate.'* That was another poser. He was not a careful man for nothing so he rang Vi, to ask her advice, but it so happened that Vi was out. He remembered it was her day for golf lessons which she'd begun to take. She'd be out all day. He could nip home and change without a word said if he wanted to! But steady. He checked himself. It wasn't as if Dot was a what-you-call, he said to himself, an

211

old flame, did they call it? Rather the reverse. He'd never, in fact, been out with her except for that once. It was true he'd wanted to, but her mother'd put the block on it, and he was not the pushing sort. He didn't really know her at all, she was one of those girls who were always on the other side of the street really, somehow aloof and beyond him. A face, she was, and somehow as remote as a face on a poster. Except for that one day. But there was no mistaking the directness of the note. Personal, did they call it?

'Always in after lunch,' he repeated to himself, then added a thought that scandalised; 'Knock twice and ask for Mamie!'

His general foreman entered, stared at him. 'What the hell are you doing, Boss?'

He had done nothing all the morning except stare at that note and now he put it away guiltily. The effort of answering the question caused him to make the decision at once.

'I'm taking the afternoon off.'

'Oh, aye?' the foreman, who liked a predictable employer, was frankly curious.

But Will nodded curtly and went off without explaining himself – straight home to change, and since one decision involved others, he now began to take some pains with his appearance, selecting a recently bought charcoal-grey suit, an expensive blue Dior tie, a mess of intricate blurred whorls, the gift of a soft-soaping brick salesman. With his grey, button-collar shirt and sporty tweed hat, it was his best outfit, and as he looked at his short stocky frame with its friendly big-boned, blue-jowled, all-weather face, he could not resist a grin.

'Will Pipes coming out,' he said drily to himself.

He was about to realise that he had a sense of himself now, a sense of himself as a human being, but he had not always been so lucky, nor so sure of himself, and as he went out of the house and began the drive to the address which she had given him, he remembered another self almost lost now, an unsure bewildered boy without the comfort of nicknames, plain Will.

He'd met her once by accident outside the Tech where he was uneasily pursuing the theoretical side of his apprenticeship, but he was glad because he was not wearing his working clothes. They were both seventeen. She had been to her music teacher's only to find that the teacher was ill. She was never his girl really, he'd just hung about with her in the last year at school, and briefly walked her home from the youth club before her mother'd found the youth club was occasionally frequented by American servicemen. They'd walked straight into one another as they came around the corner of a subway.

'Will!' She pronounced his name with a smile, an exclamation.

He hadn't mentioned her name, just smiled. The thick-shouldered man had been the awkward stocky boy, and he actually had books under arm, and she a mandolin case. Her mother spent the earth on music lessons and while Dottie would vamp several instruments by ear, reading music was a chore to her.

'My day at the Tech,' he said sheepishly.

It was a sharp winter's day, bare trees standing behind them, a nip in the air that gave her a high colour. She wore a scarlet coat with a high cape collar. He said a very silly thing. 'Little Red Riding Hood.'

They never seemed to say anything sensible. He could reason in his own slow way, and he was gentle with everybody, a quite docile boy from a chapel home. But when she wouldn't speak to him on her mother's instruction, he had been hurt. Not being good enough was a slur and unjustified. He knew it wasn't her fault, but he wished she'd more spirit. There was nothing wrong with him then except who he was and what he was going to be, just Will. He was a nice boy whom girls took for granted, quite safe to be with, never a suspicion of going too far, but useable – useable and discardable. He didn't generate any heat and it worried him then.

Standing there that day, he was quite tongue-tied for a moment. He noticed the mandolin case was slung over her shoulders and her two hands were clasped together inside a little red muff made by her mother from the same material as the coat. She always had on a complete outfit, and liked matching things.

He should have guessed by her smile that she was glad to see him, but he just stood there silently, a half smile on his lips, a couple of tongue-tied kids.

'My lesson's been cancelled,' she said. She wore a scarf over her head and had it tied under her chin, something she rarely did because her mother said it was common and made her look like the factory girls. Perhaps it was the wind that made her relax that rule.

Finally, he asked her. 'You doing anything?'

She shook her head.

He had enough money for one coffee only and cursed himself, fingering a threepenny-bit in his pocket. She did not seem to want to leave.

'I don't have to go back,' he said, referring to his employer.

He wished he could think of something smart and snappy to say, something American. 'What's wrong with jingle bells, baby?' Humphrey Bogart had said that very week in the Workmen's Hall. But all he could manage was, 'This wind would blow you away.'

'Mum's working,' she replied. Although she was as serious as her mother in her ambitions, she managed now and then to convey a hint that she saw some of the folly of it, he remembered. At least, it seemed so that day under the subway.

'D'you fancy a walk?' he said. They were quite near a mountain slope which marked the end of the valleys and slid down gradually to the sea and to the coastal plain before it. 'There's some nice walks about here.'

Before he knew quite what was happening, he had slung the mandolin over his shoulder and they were making their way behind the technical college where there was a kissing gate that led to the mountain path. She still did not say much, just nodded as he made some awkward remarks about his course and the trade he was pursuing. But they both entered the kissing gate together, pausing at the same time. Perhaps he should have stood back to let her through first, but he did not. He had no thought of kissing her but she was obviously in a mood to be kissed. Standing there, he knew it by the way she looked at him, a real smile on her lips for a change, her oval face pale beneath the scarf, the tilt of her chin and that perfect mouth poised and ready.

So he kissed her and she put one red-sleeved arm lingeringly on his shoulder. He kissed her again and they stood there with both her arms around his neck. She was in no hurry to move, he remembered, and still she said nothing. They were innocent. There was no come-on about it. He did not feel any of the desire that was to trouble him with other girls later. He had told her once that she was the marrying sort, an extraordinary thing for a boy of seventeen to say, but she was that serious, and there was always that air about her. Despite the frivolity of her ambition and the constant aura of the tinsel costumes, she herself was often grave and silent. Perhaps it was that her mother had worn her out with instructions and constant surveillance. It couldn't be that she was just vacant? Or could it? A dumb blonde. A bit thick. How did he know? A kiss was important he remembered. The next question was, would she go with him? But he did not like to ask it. Instead, he said something that made her laugh.

'That was nice,' he said. He wiped his lips with the back of his hand, and grinned. 'I could do with half a dozen of those.'

They walked on, following the mountain path and winding their way above the opening of the valley, climbing all the time until they could see the haze of the smaller townships on the plain before them. One of the joys of living where they did, was that they could always look down on things, a pleasure that had remained with him.

But he couldn't understand the girl, couldn't get a grip on her. She seemed to have no kind of reality. She was just there, demure in red, clutching that muff, smiling at him, perfect to look at in the magazine sense.

'I didn't expect to see you.'

'Nor me.'

'You're always on your own?'

'Busy,' she said.

'The dancing, and that?'

'Everything.'

'You like it?'

'Mostly.'

'But sometimes...'

'It's hard work,' she said. 'It really is. Really.'

Her ambition...

'I know your mother doesn't like me,' he began to say.

'It's not you personally.'

'Personally? What does that mean?'

'She's had a hard life,' she said. Her eyes were a very light blue, normally expressionless, but there was a frown on her face at the mention of her mother that changed her whole expression.

'Slave driver, if you ask me,' he tried to help.

'She wants me to get on.'

'But you haven't got any friends?' he said, stating the obvious. She didn't hang around with any crowd.

She did not reply.

'I always thought you was nice,' he added. 'I called around, but your mother...'

'It would interfere,' she said.

'But the pictures? Surely, you can go to the pictures when you want?'

'I go with my mother.'

That was another thing. They went everywhere together, and once, two Americans had tried to pick them up. Officers, of course, as Mrs Lemon had related it to somebody he knew. They would have had to be officers even to have entertained the thought. Texas Rangers for all he knew. Class again.

'Well, I dunno,' he said. 'You're a mystery, you are.'

'D'you think so?'

He fumbled for words, standing there glowering like a farmer's boy in a Sunday suit. 'I'd like to go with you steady, Dot. I would. Honest.'

But her mother wouldn't have that, he knew, and kiss or not, she wouldn't rebel. It was unnatural, but he understood it well enough. In a curious way, she'd never been a child at all. Even at school, he had never seen her in the least bit upset. She never lost that composure, the silent perfect girl in the corner who never asked questions, never answered one if she could help it. It was uncanny.

He tried a joke. 'If only you was a bit more common. Like me!'

'I couldn't,' she said. He was sure she gave a little shiver.

'*What*?'

'It wouldn't be nice,' she said.

'What wouldn't be nice?'

'You're not all that common,' she evaded the question. 'Not uncouth anyway.'

'Your mother thinks so.'

Again she didn't reply.

The mysteries of human beings! She was silent for a

while until they reached the topmost point of the hill but as they walked he gave his mind to her furiously. Whatever kids did nowadays, then it was almost impossible to find words to give full extent to your feelings.

'I could go overboard for you,' he wanted to say. He really went a bundle on her, but he couldn't say that either. She was such a smasher, the identical replica of all those girls who stood on lonely tarmacs watching pilots fly off to their doom, or moved with lips sealed through the plush furniture of foreign consulates, monocled German spies in attendance. He didn't think that at the time, he thought she was beautiful, but it was a beauty curiously unrelated to anything sexual. She would have made a perfect Snow White, always trapped in a daydream.

'Why don't you answer?' he said.

'I'm going away,' she told him.

'Ah, the band,' he'd heard about that. 'What will your mother do when you're gone?'

'That's just it,' she said. Her face was suddenly hard and pouting. 'Suffer, I expect.'

'Oh, go on...'

'She's had a hard life,' she said again.

He made a note to inquire of his sister who helped on the bread round and could give you a potted biography of everyone in the town. But that didn't help him at the moment.

When they reached the top of the hill, there was an old shed called Dai's Barn which was quite often frequented by courting couples. The doors were locked but it could be lifted off the hinge on one side. He suggested they went in there to get out of the wind, but she looked at him curiously.

219

'Out of the wind, like?' he said.

'I'd better not.'

'Your cheeks are blue. I'm freezing myself.'

'You'll have to break in.' She hesitated, implying what? The law, retribution, punishment? He did not know.

'You just lift the door off the hinge.'

He demonstrated.

'You've been here before?'

'I'm not in any band, am I?'

It was perhaps the sharpest thing he had ever said to her.

As he lifted one door off the hinge to allow her to enter, she looked at him strangely.

'I'll leave the mandolin outside,' she said.

Did she think he was going to play it?

Inside, she shocked him by taking out a cigarette. He had never seen her smoke.

'My mother doesn't know,' she said. 'But it calms my nerves.'

'You got no need to be nervy with me, Dot?'

'I know,' she said. She smiled. 'I like you, Will.'

Thinking back, he knew he had one desire on that afternoon, and that was to be pals. As simple as that. He could not get close to her and he could not explain her attraction for him, unless it was that she was so well mannered. He always liked a certain kind of conformity.

There were some empty grain sacks in the corner of the shed and she sat on one, brushing it down, so that her coat would not get dirty.

'When are you going away then?' he asked.

'As soon as it's fixed.'

'Far?'

'On tour to start.'

'All over then?'

'Forces mostly.' She flicked the ash off the cigarette and raised an eyebrow to condescend to him. 'Playing to the Forces.'

It sounded glamorous then. He had seen films of troop concerts, cigarette smoke drifting through beams of arc lights, the wolf whistles of sex-starved men ogling in the dark.

He sat down uneasily beside her. It was extraordinary that they had so little to say to each other, but then they had very little in common. She did not take much interest in the street but he mentioned the name of a boy they knew who had been shot down over Bremen.

'Sad,' she said, and that was all. It did not touch her.

There was also a girl nearby who had married an air-gunner who was posted missing. She'd waited six months, then married again, only to receive the news that her first husband was reported alive, a prisoner.

'Hell of a thing,' Will said, referring to it, but he did not fully understand the situation. He had heard his sister talk accusingly of the girl as a fly-by-night. Seven boys had been killed from the fifteen houses at the end of their street alone and mourning was at a premium.

But Dottie didn't seem to take it in. She was completely uninvolved in things that did not immediately concern her.

'Are you going to be air crew, Will?'

'Army, I suppose,' he grinned. He had a vague idea you had to have County School maths to be air crew and had fixed his mind on the engineers. 'Keep your nose clean, they might let you do your trade,' his father'd said. 'Better that than cutting the barrack lawn with nail scissors.' Real Dan y Graig, his father'd soldiered in the first war, had seen the folly of it, was inclined to let Hitler vent his spleen on London before he took a view of this war. First London, then Cardiff; he'd start to worry when the street copped it.

'Haven't you any ambitions then, Will?'

He grinned again. He had not. But for some reason, she persisted.

'You're no trouble, are you?' she sulked.

He didn't understand.

'How d'you mean?'

'You don't want anything much, Will?'

'I dunno,' he said.

She finished her cigarette, sighed, tapped it out on a brick. 'Half-soaked's right then.'

He was hurt. Other people said that and he did not fully understand what they meant, except that it wasn't complimentary.

'But never mind, you're nice,' she added, madam that she was. She stood up and went towards the window of the hut, looked out, then turned alluringly towards him. One foot posed before the other. Charm was on parade again, and more than that, as ever, she was sounding her gs very carefully.

But his mind was still on the half-soaked thing. What did it mean? That he didn't rush things? That he was careful? That he did things at his own pace? Well, he had always done that. Like his old man, he wanted to be a sticker. She was still looking at him, that teasing smile playing about her lips. She opened the top buttons of her coat, continued to pose. He still couldn't understand the inference. Half-soaked, it stuck in his mind like an unpleasant note of music. 'Room for improvement... Must make more effort... Concentrates, but not enough....' His school reports ran with monotonous regularity. But she wasn't brainy. Then another thought occurred to him and he flushed. Did she mean that he was slow?

'What you got on your mind then?' he said in his low monotonous voice. 'Coming in here?'

She did not say anything.

'You're not up to anything, are you?'

She gave a little gasp of impatience.

'Will Thick,' she said.

That did it. He was on his feet in an instant. He saw it as an attack on his status and it hurt him more than anything she could have done.

'I don't know who you think you are,' he said. 'But if you got anything in mind, you can forget it. Or are you just doin' your bit of actin', havin' me on?'

For answer, she did up the button of her coat and marched towards the door. Whatever there had been between them, was over. Two kisses by the lych gate, and nothing else.

Remembering, he chuckled. There were still parts of him that were as sentimental as they come, and as far as women were concerned, it was years before he looked at them as human beings. Upbringing, he thought ruefully. He'd known nothing about girls at all. His sisters were much older than him, motherly figures at that, and he'd been virtually brought up as an only child. What a fool he'd been! She'd

223

gone out of the hut before him, made her way alone, cross with him as he'd followed in a sullen silence. It was such a problem and they were so preoccupied with it, that they'd committed a real sin by leaving the mandolin behind, and he'd had to walk all the way up the mountain to get it, and only then had she smiled as he assumed the normal and predictable helpmate's role. She went away soon after, and although he'd caught a glimpse of her across the street, they'd never really spoken since.

'Thirty years ago,' he said to himself, easing down his cufflinks as he drove towards her now. What kids they were. But still he couldn't seem to recall her as a human being somehow. It was as if she had a gift for remaining unrealised as a flesh-and-blood person. Or perhaps it was just his memory. Of course, when he came to think of it now – and he'd learned a few good things since – the whole thing was an attempt at protest, he supposed. Everything in her life up to then had been directed at the one ambition, getting out of Dan y Graig Street and doing everything her mother said. She was not only the *Shampoo Girl*, but the *Yes Girl*, and for one afternoon, she must have had thoughts of rebellion, picking him as patsy.

He found her flat and parked the car a little away from the kerb so that it would be in full vision from the house. When he pressed the bell, he could not suppress a quiver of excitement. It was a drab old world, and there was only one Dottie Lemon. Whatever you had, never altered what you had been.

Presently, footsteps shuffled towards him inside. Must be in her slippers. As the door inched open, he smelt the odour

224

of stale curry lingering about the interior of the hallway, then, as she spoke, he recognised her voice at once.

'Yes?'

She had not switched on the interior light and he could barely see her. She was wearing some kind of flowered kimono and dark glasses. Her hair was near enough the same, but piled above her head. Was it blue? A rinse, did they call it? And there was a lot more of her, bulging behind that slatternly dressing gown.

'Will,' he said sheepishly. He nearly said, Will Pipes.

She took a second to recognise him. Behind the dark glasses, the lower half of her face had become exactly like her mother's, deep drawn lines pulling down the corners of her mouth, the sallowness of her thin neck all indicating the wear of age and giving her – her of all people! – the pinched, worn look of bitter experience which he associated with those exhausted women who'd populated the terrace before the war. The exception was her hair which remained a set-piece as if it were somebody else's property. Scrag had bred scrag, he thought. The flat, the face, the down-at-heel slippers spelt penury and dismay. That career... those dreams... he knew the obvious in a second. She had failed at everything.

'Oh, hell,' he thought. 'Poor Dot....' He was not used to dismay and felt upset to see her so. She'd really fattened too, in all the wrong places. Well, whatever he could do...

' 'Lo, Dot,' he said. There was a catch in his voice. 'How is it, kid?'

She had not spoken, and indeed, seemed determined to remain a creature of disguises because she did not remove the sunglasses.

225

'I knew you'd come,' she said flatly. She opened the door fully.

He wished he hadn't left that expensive car in so obvious a position. Show-off him.

'Of course, I came...'

'You remembered me?'

' 'Course,' he said again. ' 'Course, Dot...'

'Well, you'd better come in.'

Desperate, he thought. Things on her mind, no doubt, but her abruptness now was in marked contrast to the urgency of her note.

He took off his sporty hat and followed her into the gloomy hallway. If it were not for the sunglasses which remained a barrier, he would not have been surprised if she had collapsed into his arms the moment the front door was closed. It was such an emotional moment. Had she done so, he would have said, 'There... there...'

But she did nothing of the kind. She led him past the open door of the bedsitter to a makeshift hardboard partition beneath the stairway. She couldn't be living there...

'Come here.'

He followed, his hat in his hands. If only she would take off those dark glasses.

She stood outside the partition and pointed in.

'Look at this!'

He looked instead at her face, peering into the lenses but seeing only his own reflection there.

But she waved her outstretched forefinger downward like a schoolmistress.

'Look at it!'

He did so. Inside the partition was an ancient lavatory, the pan of which had been smashed into two halves, and water trickled over the grubby linoleum on the floor.

'Look at it!' she hissed again. At last she took off the sun-glasses, but there was an expression of such fury in her eyes that he blinked.

He fingered his Dior tie. Did nothing ever happen to him that was not obvious?

'Vandals,' he said tiredly.

'Tenants,' she said. 'Students.'

'You're running this place?'

'I share it.'

'Share it?'

'The toilet!' Preoccupied, she did not take her eyes from the wrecked pan.

He swallowed. Had she nothing more to say to him? Apparently not. But what could he do? Stuck for something to say himself, he pulled a small notebook from his pocket, and began to measure up.

She stepped back into the hallway.

'Be sure you get it right,' she snapped. 'The measure-ments – everything.'

'I'll send a man.'

'Can't you come yourself?'

'Well...'

'It's been like that for a week, and I can't keep on trailing up and down the stairs.'

She did look uncomfortable.

'I'll see to it right away,' he said briskly. 'I quite under-stand.' Part of his success as a small-time jobber had been the confidential air of concern he assumed when dealing with lavatorial matters, a facet he'd observed in undertakers, and automatically the consoling note returned to his voice as he communicated his understanding of the urgency of the problem.

'Very awkward indeed.'

'As soon as you can. I shall stay in until you come.'

'Very good,' he said, controlling a sigh. What a fool he was. He'd put his good suit on for Myrna Loy, only to have his face rubbed in the pan once more. But surely, they'd have a bit of a chat? What happened to her mother? Who had she married? What happened to the showbiz?

'How've you been then?' he said when they went back into the hall.

She did not appear to have heard him.

'Perhaps you can put in a coloured suite?' she said over her shoulder. 'There's room there for a basin. I expect you've got seconds lying about the shop?'

He stared at her back.

'Seconds?' She wanted a cheap job. 'Well, yes.'

She turned and looked at him haughtily.

'And if the water's switched off, I must have notice.'

'Of course, Dot.'

It was as if he did not exist as a human being at all. Had he ever in her eyes? But then, who was she? She'd begun to doubt him again.

'You always were very slow,' she said as he put the notebook away.

Half-soaked again, he thought.

She did not show him out, but sidled into her bedsitter.

Not before he had sneaked a glance into the room, however. He just had time to see a hand of cards laid out on a green baize table, and behind it, an elaborate sandalwood chest on raised legs. The lid of the chest was open, and in the centre, beside compartments containing packs of playing cards, there was a large crystal ball protected by raised felt. Dottie Lemon had become a palmist.

He gasped as if the sudden peep into that room had given him total knowledge. 'Dottie Lemon really on her arse,' he thought. He felt a wave of sadness overwhelm him so that his throat became dry and he could not speak. But she had never really been part of his life, and would now vanish from it unknown. As it was, he soon reverted to normal.

'Toilet and suite, Number Thirty-One A, Telelkebir Gardens, ground-floor bedsitter,' he said briskly to his general foreman. 'And no plastic pipes. Use a bit of that scrap we got in the yard. Don't book it, charge it to me.'

'Will-Robin-Hood-Pipes still careful,' he thought finally, reverting to his workaday self. Give her a lav, anyhow. Even in her retirement, it was a pity to think of Snow White being caught short.

HON SEC RFC

Elgar Davies lived alone with his ancient widowed mother on the far side of town in one of those rare detached houses built in a brick-festooned style known as Rhondda baronial. It was large, squat, grey, multi-chimneyed and ugly and much too big for the widow and her bachelor son. However, there were times when it seemed that it was not large enough for Elgar who, despite all the appearances of the dutiful son, escaped from his mother when he could.

He was helped in this by his long-standing position as Secretary of the Pontlast Rugby Football Club where he displayed a love of the game and his fellows that was deeply felt, so much so that when any disagreement occurred, say, between players and officials, he would return home and seat himself in his study and ponder on the matter with intense seriousness, shutting himself away from both his mother and the world, his small podgy bespectacled little frame, short legs and tiny feet, lost in the large hide armchair bequeathed to him by his father.

Elgar was the son and the grandson of local heroes, both much decorated veterans of the wars, whose distinction had overawed Elgar all his life. 'Your grandfather was one of the tunnellers of Messines,' his mother was wont to say, and a framed Distinguished Service Order with attendant decorations was proudly displayed in the hallway of the old house. Elgar had not known his grandfather, and had scarcely begun to know his father when he died of wounds sustained when the first batch of territorials went to France in the second war.

For years, Elgar had felt rather shamefaced at his own lack of distinction since he had escaped the battlefield, and indeed, he was soon made aware that he was not the man his father was. As a child, he had been puny, given to bronchitis and was much cosseted by his mother and a bevy of aunts who had lived with them, and later, in college, where he went – inevitably, it seemed – to become a primary school teacher, he was the quiet sort who has difficulty asserting himself. Things did not improve until later in life when he began to take an interest in the administrative side of sport where his quiet efficiency and adroit bookkeeping skills were much valued, and when he began his secretaryship of the rugby club, he had at last found a position and status in life of which the menfolk in his family would have thoroughly approved.

By now, he had developed a love of the game of rugby football, and in his late forties, he spoke knowledgeably of past games and players, sometimes forgetting his own complete lack of prowess as a player. As Secretary, he was also a selector and a man of some influence, and it was in this role that he tangled with a young man known as Bashie Williams, who had recently been recruited to the club and who, while distinguishing himself on the field, had been heard in the showers to refer to Elgar as 'a bit of a pouf'. It was a vulgar and completely uncalled-for remark, Elgar thought, and it cut him to the quick.

'Not meant, Elgar boy,' said Abe Beynon, the chairman, as they walked from the changing rooms to the clubhouse itself. Abe, once praised as a forward – 'slow but dirty' – towered over Elgar's short figure and when he spoke, he could look down and see the full circular rim of Elgar's sporty pork-pie hat and a wide-skirted riding mac swishing beneath it. 'You know what these lads are. No idea of what an effort it takes to run a club. Unappreciative, is not the word.'

'I just happened to overhear it,' Elgar said. He stared at the path as he spoke, an intense stare as he scowled through rimless lenses.

'Overheard and overlooked, I trust?'

'He's not a very good forward and a lout into the bargain.'

'Oh, don't say that. He's built like a tank.'

'Robust, I give you.'

'Robust? He's got shoulders on him like a young bull. And what a worker!'

'He gives the appearance of working,' Elgar said pointedly, 'but if you ask me, there's nothing much else, certainly not upstairs.'

'Oh, come on, Elgar, it's not a dancing class we're running.'

'I didn't think it was.'

'Well, whatever he is off the field, he's a lion on it. If ever I've seen international potential, he's got it.'

'Really?' Elgar was surprised.

'Never been surer. You watch. He's one of those who'll rocket to the top. A bit of an animal around the house, I dare say, but he's not here to ice the cake.'

Elgar did not pursue arguments about the game if contradicted by so knowledgeable a person as Abe Beynon, but he did not disguise his dislike for Bashie Williams. The boy was indeed built like a tank, standing six-foot-two and sixteen stone with the short neck and powerfully developed arms and shoulders which make for mastery of the front-row trade. His face was moon-shaped and pockmarked, thick sensual lips constantly lolling open below a short cropped haircut which added to the ferocity of his appearance. In any other circumstances, Elgar would have described Bashie's forehead as Neanderthal for there was about his appearance more than a hint of things primitive. But what annoyed Elgar was the boy's truculent and disrespectful manner when in the presence of club officials. To break wind in the showers or coming off after a game was one thing, but to do it when Elgar was reminding players of the promise to wear black armbands on their jerseys to mourn the death of an old and trusted servant of the club, was another. It showed lack of respect, both for the dead and the living, and more, was no doubt a directly aimed insult, if aimed was the right word.

Then there was his insolent reply which Elgar could only term 'naturalistic'.

'I can't help it, Mr Davies, faggots it is. The old girl keeps a stall on the market.'

There had been a general titter since Bashie was the maker of statements which some found amusing, but as his coarse wit was generally at the expense of someone else, Elgar found it inexcusable. He had blushed scarlet in front of everyone, a childhood habit which he had thought long conquered, and he could do little more than turn on his heel, thereby increasing the effectiveness of the slight and no doubt causing prolonged comment behind his back. How could he tell the others that he was no prude, and always liked a laugh with the boys? He could not, of course, and had no answer for these farmyard habits which distressed him more than he could say, so much so that he dwelt upon it for weeks.

Putting it mildly, Bashie Williams was not the sort of person you liked to meet indoors anyway. He was somehow too big for rooms. When he was in them, things tended to get knocked over. Chairs creaked, sagged, split; doors slammed, shuddered and shook as if in protest at Bashie's potential for physical damage. Everywhere he went, his size created problems and everything about him was too much, Elgar felt. Bashie was a beyond-person, and big-mouthed with it. That he was a splendid forward into the bargain was a pity. They always had wilder spirits in the club. When Morlais Morgans and Dai Price had been arrested after an altercation in a Warwickshire fish and chip shop, Elgar had gone personally to see the local police superintendent and taken a brace of stand tickets for the English international with him.

'You know what these lads are, sir,' he said in a man-to-man fashion, and later everybody had complimented him on the way he'd smoothed things over when the charge sheet was kept clean. Elgar was a fixer, people said, and there were innumerable occasions when a well-chosen word in the right ear had worked wonders. Elgar had a very nice manner. He knew enough was enough. He did not take advantage and he knew when to stop asking. Then he was very good at remembering the people who helped the club, the grocer who supplied them with free tea, all the local tradesmen who helped out, and it was noticeable that the club's annual dance had progressed from a scruffy hop to a gala night with Elgar in charge and the police safely seen to in the back kitchen of the local hotel.

No one disputed his work and no one had ever publicly said a word against him, but ever since Bashie Williams had been recruited from a soccer team (and didn't that say it all really?), bringing his sixteen stone over the mountain from a foundry in neighbouring Aberdarren, Elgar had noticed a subtle change in his relationship with the boys, as they called the players. It was a change that began imperceptibly, altering little things, seeming in Elgar's eyes to spread out like rising damp from one central spot. And the core of infection was Bashie, Elgar knew it. It was not that anyone said anything specific, but that, in an extraordinary way, like the girl with body odour in the television commercial, Elgar now felt people to be moving away from him. There was one more very noticeable effect that gave him hours of regret, but again, he was slow to realise the cause.

For some weeks, Elgar noticed that his fellow committee-

235

men tended to head him off when he made his way from the grandstand to the dressing room after a match. He had thought this interruption to be a coincidence at first. He was used to being spoken to constantly, often being asked to consider this problem or that at the most inconvenient of times. He usually acquiesced so that on several Saturdays running he was buttonholed at exactly the same time, at the very moment when the players were changing in the showers, but he had thought this to be a coincidence.

Then the same thing happened before the match when the players were changing in preparation for play. This occurred on several occasions. Now another committee-man would get hold of him and Elgar became aware that he was being held in conversation for the specific purpose of preventing his entering the players' changing rooms. He was not welcome there any more, before or after a match.

At first he could not believe it for there was no atmosphere he loved more, the players sprawling about half-dressed, stamping their feet into the metal-studded boots, some rubbing themselves with embrocation – legend said Bashie Williams drank his the first time he saw it! – and one or two of the younger lads nervous if the opposition was to be feared. Hands were laid on shoulders and there was a great deal of frisky jollity, but best of all, Elgar loved the skipper Ikey Owens' pre-match instructions, and Elgar almost felt himself to be a member of the team then, standing in the background, blazered and gloved amongst the lads as Ikey spelt out the plan of the day, or enumerated the likely sins of well-observed sinners who had known criminal records.

'If that fella McCool starts anything, you bloody cool it, not him. Give him his head and leave him to me, I'll cobble him quiet.'

And Elgar would grip his gloved little hands fiercely and the downward curve of his thin lips might well be taken to mean that McCool would be well observed from the committee box and had better watch it with him.

It was on these occasions that Elgar, perhaps more than at any time in his life, felt truly at one with the boys who were sprawled attentively on the benches before him. When they got to their feet, Ikey in the lead, he watched them go out into the tunnel, savouring the roar of the crowd as Ikey led the team on. Elgar always locked up after them, then hurried to his seat in the stand. If a player were carried off with a serious injury, Elgar would open up again, and had been witness of some special in-jokes. Once he had been Ikey Owens' companion when Ikey lay there groaning with a broken leg, muttering at the boos which floated in from the terraces as the play continued outside.

'I dunno,' said Ikey as the crowd continued their disapproval. 'This is the only club in the world that plays before a hostile crowd home and away!'

It had made a good story in Elgar's annual report at the dinner, and when a year later, the offending McCool had a little difficulty seeing out of one eye, Elgar was in the know in a way that few others were. Being in the know, being indispensable, being the man to whom people turned for the keys or the cash, mattered to Elgar; and better still, after a hard match when the warriors returned, boots scraping on the concrete floor, their bodies muddied and bloodied, Elgar had his factotum, Moss Thomas, get the shandies ready and he loved it then, the chatter and the final diagnosis.

'How was it, Morlais?'

'What a cow of a ref! Braille gave him up when he went for the test!'

Then there were the complaints.

'Look at this lump by here! Good Christ, I'm moulting.'

It was sweaty, masculine, of the earth, earthy, and when they started singing in the showers, the songs were often bawdy and delighted Elgar.

> Here we come full of rum,
> Looking for wimmin who'll peddle their bum,
> In Pontlast RFC!

Certainly no prude, Elgar was in his oils on these occasions, standing near the showers long after the steam had clouded his spectacles, inventing excuses to linger on, sometimes strutting importantly with his little red cash book and gold propelling pencil, casting a blind eye upon those who were leaning heavily upon him with their expenses, and giving as good as he got when there was any backchat about money.

'Iesu Grist, Elgar, three shifts I lost?'

'Three kicks you missed too.'

'Oh, come on, Elgar, I got two maintenance warrants owing?'

'Training night Monday, then. You'd better notify Securicor.'

It was such fun there in that hothouse atmosphere with

the steam rising and the gorgeous smells of sweating flesh, liniment and sodden gear, a kind of weekly male orgy which Elgar felt privileged to savour to the full. But ever since Bashie Williams had come, trailing his other soccer uncouthness, there had been a definite shading off in the approval in which Elgar felt himself to be regarded. After three Saturdays of pointed interruptions when on his way to the dressing room, he was more than sure of his exclusion, although Abe Beynon put it very delicately despite his fractured English.

'The boys want to be on their own, I dare say. There's been too many people getting in through the doors. Kids and that. You know what the language is like.'

'I don't mind a bit of language. Good Christ!' Elgar swore impressively.

'Gets a bit overcrowded in there.'

'But there's the expenses?'

'Ikey suggests Mondays. In the clubhouse.'

'Well, I usually lock up after?'

'Moss is doing it.'

'I wouldn't trust Moss with a packet of crisps.'

'The boys prefer it.'

'The boys?' Elgar caught his breath.

'You know how it is,' Abe Beynon's lantern-jawed undertaker's face was wet-lipped and evasive. He had a large polychromatic nose, more a badge of office than an organ, and he rubbed it embarrassedly. 'They'd rather be on their own. Anyhow, be better if you opened up the club bar. They've got very slack there lately.'

Elgar, always glad of an opportunity to exercise his

authority, saw the sense of this as there was a big-bosomed, sharp-tongued girl behind the bar who needed an eye keeping on her in more senses than one, being a bit of a drop-drawers, according to Abe. But since this conversation quite clearly referred to after-match procedures and there could possibly have been some doubt about Ikey's unstated objection, it came as a double shock to learn that another member of the committee thought it would be better if Elgar supervised the ticket collectors immediately before the match.

'Ticket collectors?'

'There's people creeping under hedges – everything.'

Elgar knew that this was patently untrue.

'What d'you want me to do?'

'Well, me and the committee, like... well, perhaps, 'stead of going into the changing rooms while the boys is changing, we think that you could be very useful at the gate, like? That's the general idea.'

So there was no doubt. Elgar was being very definitely excluded from the dressing room, he, the Secretary. At first, although he took care to show as little of his concern as possible in the presence of his cautioners, his inclination was to protest openly. He could have given a polite but very firm reminder of exactly how much he had done for the club, and just how very important he was at this precise moment since he was acting as guarantor for a much-needed extension to the clubhouse proper, and without him, the bank manager would very probably have hesitated. But he checked himself. He had not survived for so long in this ultra-male world without acquiring skills and he knew that

240

a moaner was never appreciated. Never a squealer be, they said in the collieries, and it was a code that was implanted in many others besides the colliers. Also, it would not do to protest openly since there was clearly an undercurrent of feeling that he did not fully understand.

On its face value, the objection to him, for he was sure that it must be personal, could not be that he was officious or disliked as an authority figure. He contradicted no one, certainly not the players. He never expressed an opinion before a game, and generally did not contradict those who held strong opinions afterwards. His habit was to listen attentively to all, then come down firmly in the middle.

When two of the boys had been sent off after a nasty business involving a well-known troublemaker from a more famous West Wales club, he had taken the line that the referee was overawed by the occasion and had seen, not the original offences, but the retaliations. Elgar had a genuine sympathy for those punished and had made it his business to have a cheery but inoffensive word with them in the bar. Then, after a particularly violent fracas involving more than the odd punch, he might add a comment like, 'And they're sending missionaries to China!' which was a good enough crack in the aftermath of a particularly bloody afternoon, but he took care never to offend. As far as he could see, he had done nothing wrong. He had said nothing, certainly not to Ikey Owens with whom he was on the best of terms. What then was the reason for the change? And why was Abe Beynon being so tactful?

Elgar searched his mind for reasons, and he could come to only one conclusion. His enemy must be Bashie Williams.

It was at this time that Elgar began to return home earlier than usual, leaving others to lock up the clubhouse. His mother, now in her seventies, was a sportswoman herself and on Saturdays would invite her cronies into the house to play contract bridge. This group, a gaggle of women in their sixties and seventies, were sometimes jokingly referred to as The Last of the South Wales Posh for they were the widows of colliery managers or important officials, those who in the lean years had known such luxuries as maids, foreign travel, or clothes sent on approval up to their houses from the leading Cardiff stores. They were women whose investments had prospered, part of a group whose wills were the subject of great local interest. Money had been made in the old days, even considerable sums, since the wisest had not invested in the coal industry but in the booming multi-purpose stores of England, but the women had lived longer than the men, and Mrs Blodwen Davies' bridge parties were the last occasions for the display of jewelled finery repre-sented by lumpy garnet brooches and occasional Italianate cameos, the souvenirs of Mediterranean cruises of long ago.

Besides Mrs Davies, Elgar's mother, there were three other women known to Elgar by the nicknames he remember-ed as a child. Mrs Owsher-Bowsher, Mrs Eadie-Beadie Jones and Miss Caldi Caldicott-Evans, the sole spinster who seem-ed to have been a chain smoker all her life. They dressed inevitably in sombre clothes, drank the occasional port and lemon, leaving behind a mixed aroma of cigarette smoke, eau de Cologne and damp talcum powder in any room used.

When Elgar came home early from the club, it was a matter of politeness that he should put his head around the card-room door, but since this was a Saturday night world of his mother's, and one in which he had no real interest, he usually did no more than utter a few pleasantries and soon excused himself. Elgar did not play cards and now and again sensed that his mother's cronies seemed to view him with a compassionate amusement that made him feel uncomfortable.

Mrs Owsher-Bowsher he privately referred to as That Disgusting Chocolate Person since her husband had made a small fortune in the manufacture of sweets and his widow was a splendid and visible sampler of sweetmeats all her life, while Mrs Eadie-Beadie had been born poor and retained the occasional crackling malice of one who did not quite belong amongst the corpulent hoi polloi of long ago. Miss Caldi Caldicott-Evans, known as The Caldi, a doctor's daughter who had been to Roedean, was wont to chivvy Eadie-Beadie in matters of grammar or decorum, and was the thinnest of the quartet, well-known for such eccentricities as entering the local shoe shop, saying, 'Have you shoes? I mean, have you *good* shoes?' when confronted with shelf upon shelf of proprietary brands.

When Elgar entered the room, all eyes turned to him except his mother's. Only The Caldi smiled, as she always did, her spinster's heart remaining the warmest.

Elgar had a stock joke for Eadie-Beadie who held the cards between her thick be-ringed fingers as if they were enemies who might get away.

'Everything all right? They're not taking you to the laundry, Eadie-Beadie?'

'Not with tram tickets,' said Eadie-Beadie scowling at her cards.

243

'You're home early?' said Elgar's mother with a side-ways glance.

'Do with an early night.'

'Anything happened?' said Eadie-Beadie maliciously.

'We won six-nil.'

'I thought you'd be drinking when you didn't take the car,' Eadie-Beadie said.

'Always a bad sign,' said The Caldi with a fluttering, if crinkled, ageing debutante's wink.

'I walked,' said Elgar, returning her smile.

'You'll be walking if you call on a hand like that again,' said Mrs Davies menacingly to Miss Caldicott-Evans. 'If Ely Culbertson ever came down to this valley, he'd go back mental!'

The Caldi flushed while Mrs Owsher-Bowsher, replete in the majesty of her fourteen stone, said nothing and began painstakingly to count up points on the tips of her fingers.

The women, no less than the men, had the gift of repartee and while Elgar nodded pleasantly in the doorway, his mother's determination to get on with the game was quite usual. He was not going to be cross-examined. Elgar nodded at the back of his mother's head, smiled once more at Miss Caldicott-Evans who gave another coy wink, then excused himself. For years now, he and his mother had existed in a state of uneasy truce, each pursuing a separate life, coming together at meals and passing the time of day, but little else, unless either happened to be out of sorts when they would fuss over each other with habitual clucking solicitousness.

Elgar knew that she was disappointed in him, at his failure to marry or get a headship, but both subjects were now left alone by unspoken consent, and it was accepted that Elgar should live his own life between school and rugby club, with dutiful visits to chapel once on Sunday when he drove his mother to the one remaining chapel several miles away. That it was a bleak life in which the spirit was crushed by the aridity of long-established habits did not occur to him, although now and again he cast his eye on the images of the outside world as presented by the television screen, and sometimes heaved a sigh.

He had travelled little because he could not leave his mother who always left him with the idea that it was best for him to remain where he was well understood and where the family name (Davies DSOs) still counted for something. He was also delicate and there was his weak chest and the old embarrassing loss of hair which had been miraculously arrested so that he was no longer a sufferer from alopecia, thanks to the prescriptions of the local general practitioner who had expectations under Mrs Davies' will.

Best for Elgar to stay put, both had long ago agreed, while Mrs Davies, it should be said, remained in remarkably good health, a big-boned, strong woman, quite unlike Elgar in appearance, with a firm strong line of jaw and sharp piercing eyes which looked Eadie-Beadie firmly in the face when she answered Eadie-Beadie's piercing questions, stating categorically that Elgar had made his place with her and that was the end of the matter. It was a mistake to think that Elgar was deep. He was not deep, just liked the simple life at home, being a very good boy to his mother, and if she had any disappointment, it was that he was not musical as she had hoped when she first named him.

It was against this background that Elgar had found a way of life for himself which was manageable until that one word floated across to him from the sneering lips of Bashie Williams. It might have been the breach in the dam which caused the dyke to burst.

'Pouf' he repeated to himself as soon as he had left his mother and settled himself in his study chair. It was extraordinary that one word seemed to have done so much damage. What on earth did it mean? Why should it have such consequences? Why should he be singled out as untouchable when he was so companionable? If it meant effeminate, it was absurd since he was the most sporty of men and his entire wardrobe of blazers and ties proclaimed his attachment to this sporting group or that. In a curious way, it made him feel childlike to be so set apart and he had a renewed understanding of those children who were sometimes excluded by their fellows because of the uncleanliness of their appearance. It was a pariah word, no doubt about it. But what could he do?

With his legs tucked under him in his study chair, he came to a decision. There was only one thing he could do and that was soldier on, he said to himself, using a phrase of his mother's which must in turn have been passed on to her by his father.

'Soldier on, John Willy! Best foot forward!' Better still if he could manage not to give the slightest indication of his hurt. He had a number of favourite exhortations to the team when things seemed to be going against them, and now and again he applied them to himself when he tended to get down in the mouth. He stood up now and reached for his correspondence file with a typical rallying cry which he applied strictly to himself for once.

'Come on Pontlast – show your class!'

He knew he had to come back from behind, as the boys had done on many occasions, and immediately his good nature showed itself. There was something he could do for Bashie Williams as the club were about to make their annual tour of the West Country, and Elgar always made it his business to write personally to employers, seeking permission for the players to absent themselves from their places of employment. It was a formality since most of the local people accepted the penalty of employing rugby players, but it was one of those routine little tasks which Elgar did extremely well. He saw to it that the letters of application were followed by letters of thanks, and knew that the provision of international tickets was a useful lubricant when favours were required.

He decided that he would write first on Bashie Williams' behalf to the manager of the Aberdarren foundry and he settled the headed notepaper on his lap full of good intentions only to find that he could not remember Bashie Williams' Christian name. Once again an immediate good intention was abruptly followed by an irritation, as it always was when that young man's name came up. He could not put, *re: Mr Bashie Williams* at the head of his letter. But the wretch must have a Christian name. *B* was inserted in the programme and he was inevitably known as Bashie. But that would not do. Elgar decided to telephone the clubhouse which was still open.

'Abe?'

'Who is that?' Abe Beynon usually had a skinful on a Saturday night and his voice was thick and accusatory, as if a wife might have actually dared to intrude on his Saturday night privilege. 'What is it? Hurry up, if you please. It's nearly stop-tap.'

'It's Elgar. Small point. The Easter Tour. What's Bashie Williams' first name?'

There was a moment's hesitation at the other end. Elgar could imagine Abe's babyish pout at being drawn away from his bottle at the bar.

'Leave the bugger alone,' Abe said.

'Listen, I must know his name. I've got to write to his employer.'

'His employer?' Abe sounded alarmed.

'If he's going to miss three days' work, his employer will have to be notified. I do it every year.'

'Are you sure, Elgar?'

'What d'you mean, am I sure?' Elgar's annoyance increased.

'I mean,' Abe said carefully at the other end of the telephone – and Elgar could hear him sucking his teeth as he always did when suspicious – 'are you sure it's only leave of absence?'

'I'm not thinking of having him here to tea!'

Abe did not reply directly.

'Look, I've got to head the letter.'

'Basil,' Abe said finally, but clearly after deliberation. 'B for Basil.'

'And he's in the blacksmith's shop, I take it?'

'Yes.'

'Thank you. That's all I wanted to know.'

Once again there was a hesitation in Abe's manner,

another note of reservation indicating an area of concern about something that was not directly mentioned, and Elgar did not understand it. Did Abe think he was going to socialise with the fellow? If not, what did he think? Could it be that Bashie Williams had done him further harm, and did Abe think he was going to retaliate in some way? The puzzle remained and Elgar had no answer. He sighed at this latest nuance, but soon dismissed it and gave his mind to his particular expertise. As his mother always said, Elgar wrote a very nice letter. He also had a very good hand.

> Dear Mr Warbuoys, [he wrote]
> re: Mr Basil Williams (Blacksmith's)
> As you know the Club will be making its annual tour of the West Country prior to Easter Week, and I write to ask if the above-named can be released from the foundry at 12 pm on Wednesday, the 15th. I am sure you will appreciate how important it is that the Club should be well represented against the English clubs. I would like to take this opportunity of thanking you for all your co-operation in the past. As usual, I have reserved two stand tickets for you and Mrs Warbuoys for the international encounter at Twickenham, and if there is anything else I can do, please do not hesitate to ask.
> Kind regards,
>
> > Yours sincerely,
> > *Elgar J. Davies*
> > Hon Sec
> > Pontlast RFC

Elgar wrote a number of such letters and received expected replies, but in the case of Mr Basil (né Bashie) Williams, nothing was ordinary it seemed, and when the reply came, Elgar was furious.

> Dear Elgar,
> re: Mr Basil Williams
> Thank you for your letter concerning the above-named, and also for your offer of tickets which Mrs Warbuoys and myself will be only too pleased to take up. As you know, I have done everything I can to help the Club in the past, and indeed, will continue to do so in the future, as I quite agree that it is very important for us to be well represented in our annual battle with the English clubs. In the case of Mr Basil Williams, however, I cannot grant him leave of absence as you request, since he has already applied for seven days' leave of absence over the period in question in order that he should attend the funeral of his grandmother in Ireland.
> Regards to your mother.
>
> > Yours sincerely,
> > *E.F. Warbuoys*
> > Manager.

'Look at this – lying in his teeth!' Elgar said when he showed the offending letter to Abe Beynon. 'He's no conception of what I do to keep up good relations for the Club.'

But Abe exploded with laughter until the tears showed in his rheumy eyes.

'I pisses myself every time that Bashie opens his mouth,' Abe said hoarsely. 'That'll be another one for the dinner, Elgar boy.'

'The dinner?'

'Your speech, man. Grannie in Ireland... what a character!'

Wisely, Elgar did not comment. Clearly, others saw things which he did not and, as it happened, Bashie's status as a character had recently been increased by the fact that he had been returned comatose in a drunken condition to the clubhouse by an irate girlfriend who, exasperated at being kept waiting outside, had pushed him back in through the door, saying, 'You can have him back. I don't want him!' Once again, everybody thought this hilarious except Elgar, but Elgar kept his peace. If everybody thought Bashie Williams a character, then a character he must be.

Elgar soon busied himself finalising the details of the tour and in the weeks that followed, he nodded cheerfully enough to Bashie whenever he saw him, but Bashie did not speak, merely gave a caustic nod in reply, and there were times when Elgar would look down the corridor outside the committee room, hesitating to go down it unless accompanied, in case some further remark by a loitering Bashie would add to his discomfiture. Although busy, he had a sense of something building up between Bashie and himself. It was uncanny, his apprehension, and he confided in no one, but it remained, and every time he saw Bashie lolling at the bar or playing darts with the boys, Elgar had a sixth sense of danger which sometimes caused his throat to dry and he was often the victim of intense nervousness. He took care not to stand near Bashie at the bar, and once when he passed him on the way to the Gents, was forced to dig his hands deeply in his trouser pockets to disguise their tremble. Of course, it was absurd since no one in the club would have allowed Bashie to offer him even the threat of physical violence, and there was no indication that Bashie was even considering it, yet his glances seemed to Elgar to be full of threat.

Bashie had let his hair grow longer so that his forehead was crowded by an untidy fringe and he appeared more uncouth and villainous than ever. In an odd way, Elgar felt that Bashie had found him out, and if he had no clear idea of exactly what Bashie had diagnosed, his huge aura of bustling masculinity seemed to contain an explosive charge when it passed Elgar's puny little frame. It was quite absurd, and yet it was quite real. The man's presence was like a taunt which was repeated whenever they met and yet there was not a further word spoken.

One night, Elgar dreamt about Bashie. The two of them were locked in a cage with people coming to visit them, and in his dream Elgar saw Abe Beynon standing complaining to other spectators outside the bars. The complaint was that it was not fair to put the two of them together and, as a spectacle, the fact that they were together was in some way a cheat on the public purse. No violence was offered even in the dream, and while Elgar would not have confided with a living soul about this extraordinary occurrence, his obsession caused him to resume the sleeping tablets which he had long abandoned. Indeed, he packed them when the time came to leave on the tour of the West Country and he was aware that he must have given something of himself away because his mother affected a rare concern for his welfare.

'Are you sure you're all right, Elgar?'

'Of course I'm all right, mother.'

'You look pale, and you're very restless in the nights.'

'Nonsense.'

'Yes, you are. You're up at the crack of dawn, and there can't be any good in you drinking all that water.'

When under stress, Elgar drank water continuously. It was one of the giveaway signs of his tension.

'You're not doing too much are you, Elgar?'

'Probably.'

'Well, give yourself a bit of a holiday.'

'I will.'

'Eadie-Beadie can't come to Llandrindod Wells for the Bridge Convention.'

'Oh?'

'She reckons she'll be rooked. Mean, if you ask me.'

His mother's mind soon passed on to her own concerns and, when the time came, Elgar was relieved to see her off in the hired car which she shared with Owsher-Bowsher and The Caldi. Owsher-Bowsher, of necessity, sat in the front with the driver while his mother and The Caldi sat firmly apart, proudly demonstrating the room between themselves in the rear, the latter's lined and dotty face wreathed in cigarette smoke as they gave him a final scrutiny before the car pulled off to be driven at a prescribed speed along a prescribed route.

They went to one or other of the watering spas every Easter while Elgar joined the boys, taking his seat at the

253

rear of the Club coach, with Abe Beynon, flagons clanking in the outside pockets of his poacher's overcoat, his gay check trousers and co-respondent's shoes in strange contrast with the hoarse solemnity of his cracked voice as they sang their way up and out of the valley.

'Tonic solfa on the brain,' Abe would complain every year, but he underscored 'Sanctaidd' and the more maudlin of the Welsh revivalist hymns with the rest. They began with the hymns, careful to hit the right note under the caressing voices of the tenors, making their getaway like cliché-haunted actors in a television commercial, the repertoire changing to a cheerful obscenity at the first sight of the Severn Bridge and foreign England. Here, Abe and Elgar hooted wantonly with the rest, and with no more than an hour or two's separation in time from his mother's firm admonition to check that the sheets of his bed would be properly aired that night, Elgar, bright-eyed and pink-cheeked, would bawl in his high piping tenor with the others:

'I done her standing and I done her lying,
If she'd have had wings, I'd have done her flying!'

It was true abandon, one of the joys of Easter, and for Elgar, happy to be on the move once more, it should all have been normal. But why was it that even now, safely tucked up beside the faithful Abe, he imagined hostile glances were being cast in his direction? Bashie, seated far down the coach at the front, was constantly visible since by some bizarre coincidence his face appeared in the interior driving mirror, and as if that were not enough, Bashie actually turned from time to time and peered down the length of the coach. His eyes seemed to seek out Elgar and rested scornfully upon him so that Elgar looked away, at the same time crossing and uncrossing his neatly trousered legs and smoothing their creases with a nervous gesture. Throughout the trip, Abe Beynon gave him puzzled sideways glances, and even when they trooped into the hotel which was persuaded each year to accept them, Abe continued to watch Elgar with a genuine concern that added to Elgar's embarrassment.

It, said Elgar to himself, whatever *it* was, was beginning to show.

Immediately, they had other problems. There had been flooding in the area, the hotel could not accommodate them all and the party had to be split up. The hotelier had made alternative arrangements. Would Elgar care to inspect the rooms in the adjoining boarding house, and would he also decide which members of the party would use them? At first, Elgar suggested that the committee be separated from the players.

'Oh, hell, no,' said Abe reproachfully. 'There's got to be someone responsible in each place.'

Elgar had a sudden terror of being in close proximity to Bashie Williams.

'Perhaps you and I could go with a few of the youngsters?'

Abe was anxious to remove his shoes since his feet swelled on long journeys.

'You go, Elgar.'

'But...'

'Just nip down, have a dekko.'

255

The whole party now stood in the foyer of the hotel and the baggage was being unloaded on the road outside. A decision was needed at once.

'Quick, Elgar. 'Fore they gets the gear off the bus.'

But Elgar could not decide. Through the doorway, Abe saw the last bag come out of the boot of the coach.

'Here,' said Abe. 'Mog, Dai, Mush, and you, Bashie, get hold of your gear and nip down the road with Elgar. What's it called, this place?'

'Harbour Rest,' said the manager.

'That'll be changed,' Abe said knowledgeably. 'Go on, Elgar, I'll sign us in by here.'

So Elgar found himself leading the party through the streets of the little Cornish town, Bashie bringing up the rear, the toothbrush which he described as his luggage sticking out offensively from his top pocket. The Harbour Rest was a tall Victorian boarding house set in a terrace and the landlady believed in making space go round since normal bedrooms were partitioned into two, with single beds jammed up against each partition. If Abe had intended that Elgar should inspect each room, he had not reckoned with Elgar's apprehension for no sooner had the party entered the building than the players began to deposit their luggage, and it was all Elgar could do to ensure that he had a room of his own on the ground floor. The players were anxious to rejoin the main party, so there was no inspection and Elgar began to unpack his suitcase with a continued sense of his own inadequacy. Once again, the presence of Bashie Williams had disturbed his sense of equilibrium. He simply must pull himself together.

'Where the hell you bin?' said Abe when he returned eventually to the others.

'Perhaps he's got a bit of stuff there already?' Bashie said loudly.

Elgar was silent. Normally, his practice when confronted with suggestive remarks of this kind was to give a sly wink and mysteriously imply that the jester was closer to the truth than he realised, but with Bashie, he had no such confidence. What might the fellow say next? Bashie, as it happened, was distracted by the arrival of a pint, and Abe drew Elgar to one side.

'I didn't mean you to stay down there yourself.'

'I could do with an early night.'

'Yes, you're looking a bit peaky.'

That night, Elgar dosed himself with tablets and awoke in a drugged stupor which had the effect of lessening his unease. Surely his fear must be a grotesque product of his imagination? What was needed was a return of his old confidence. If only he could find some remark which would cut Bashie down to size. He remembered his silence on the previous night in the face of Bashie's snide remark and tried to rehearse replies which he might have made.

'Perhaps he's got a bit of stuff there already?'

'Not under the same roof as you!'

That was better than silence. How he envied those like Abe to whom remarks of this kind came as second nature.

'You are,' Abe once said in a famous reply to an offender, 'about as much bloody use as a chocolate fireplace!'

If only he could sharpen his tongue and learn to defend himself. He would do well to learn from Abe, but then Abe had a street-corner facility for repartee. Perhaps the best he could do was to continue to make himself indispensable to the club and seek whatever shelter he could beside Abe who knew very well how much he did for them all.

'There are some,' Abe said on one occasion, 'who could talk the robin off a packet of starch, but our Elgar is a worker; I say no more.'

Such praise as this, proclaimed when the committee was in full session, Elgar with his head modestly bowed beside his chairman, was for the Hon Sec the ultimate in acclaim, and the memory of it after a night of assisted sleep marked a return of confidence which was immediately bolstered by an odd occurrence at the breakfast table. Bashie, as might be expected, was late getting to breakfast. When he did arrive, bleary-eyed and unshaven, he sat at the end of the table in his shirtsleeves, blinking at the remainder of the party who were already beginning to eat the bacon and eggs which formed the main course.

The landlady approached Bashie with some diffidence and held a menu card in front of him. Elgar feared that he might come out with some uncouth remark, but as he studied Bashie's scowling face, he saw his lips move unfamiliarly as if trying to form the shape of a letter. Out of politeness, the landlady, thinking perhaps her hand-writing was causing the difficulty, read the menu aloud.

'Would you like cornflakes, cereal, fruit juice or grapefruit?'

Bashie glowered once more at the menu, then at her, then cast a resentful glance up the table where several rashers remained on other plates.

'Wassamatter?' said Bashie aggrievedly. 'Can't I have bacon and eggs like the other boys?'

Elgar gave a little gasp. Bashie's thick lips bending themselves about the letters on the menu card was an oddly familiar gesture and Elgar suddenly realised that Bashie could not read. He was probably totally illiterate for Elgar now remembered his attempts to evade making his signature on the accounts book on several occasions, and when he did, he made a hasty scrawl, one foot in the door as if anxious to escape. So that was it... Elgar's own isolation from his fellows had given him a certain understanding of the problems faced by others, and now it occurred to him that Bashie's belligerence was explained by this inferiority. Would you expect him to be anything else but hostile to a schoolmaster? Perhaps the whole thing was an educational matter.

When the opportunity arose, Elgar dropped the news casually to Abe.

'Can't read?'

'No, he couldn't even manage the menu.'

'You didn't say anything, did you?'

'Of course not.'

'All I hope is, it don't put him off his game.'

Abe had other worries and their first game did not go well. Bloodied by visits from other Welsh clubs, the local side had made preparations and the first half was fiercely fought, a ball-denying contest with many abrasive confrontations up front, frequent whistling up by the referee whose nervousness far exceeded that of the players. It was not a game for the connoisseur, maul succeeding maul, scrimmage following scrimmage, and kicking up field predominated so that the ball-to-hand agility of such stalwarts as Ikey Owens, who in the past had displayed a thief-in-the-night quality when outwitting opposing outside halves – he had previously been named Ali Baba – was not obvious. It was grey football on a grey day, and Abe Beynon complained and complained and complained.

'I wish I never got out of bed.'

'Come on Pontlast – show your class!' entreated Elgar courageously from the side of an opposing committee-man half his size.

'Boneless,' said Abe, all loyalty vanishing. 'If they was dogs, I wouldn't give 'em house room.'

'Up and under Pontlast!' shrilled Elgar. 'Vary it a bit.'

'Vary it?' said Abe. '*Vary it*? Vary what? With what?'

'There's still time.'

But Abe grunted. He was inclined to take the game with religious seriousness and when it passed below minimal expectations, would brood in a sullen sog of memory, images of better days flowing through his mind while his face took on the saturnine appearance of a man confronting total and expected disaster of Asiatic proportions. In the vintage years, when there had been violent arguments over the respective merits of two world-famous Welsh centres known to him as Bleddyn and Dr Jack, he had quarrelled with his brother-in-law and not spoken one word to him for two whole years, thereby putting his undertaker's business in jeopardy since his brother-in-law had county council connections and was instrumental in passing over the bodies of paupers and mental defectives at two-pounds-ten the single journey. It had cost Abe dear, this passion for

Bleddyn, and when a game went wrong as it did now, Elgar often felt that Abe was grieving, seeing not the present but the past, although Abe still maintained his capacity for cutting everyone down to size.

Elgar tried a new shout.

'Feet and take!' he yelled squeakily. 'Feet and take!'

Abe's eyes swivelled from under his cap.

'They're planting rice,' he said. 'Didn't you know?'

Elgar concentrated on the game. Now the play seemed to be cemented under the Pontlast posts which rose like two sombre headstones above the steaming packs of forwards. Ikey Owens, hands on hips, stood with his back to his own line, but the bodies in front of him might have been digging their own mass grave and as the forwards slithered about, ball lost and never seeming likely to emerge, Elgar saw Bashie's face break from the rear of the maul, his mouth hanging open as he gazed blankly before him. On this occasion, he packed on the blind side, the side nearest the touchline, but his appearance for once was devoid of threat. All promise of a game had vanished. Even the rough stuff was carried on in slow motion as if by men suffering from influenza and Bashie's gaze resembled that of a foraging cow. Elgar saw him detach himself from the maul and wander forward, passing the centre line in his search for the ball, still moving forward while the ball was dextrously held by the opponents and kept invisible, and now both Elgar and Abe saw the trick coming, one of the oldest in the book.

'Oh, look at him! Look at him! What's he waiting for? Milking time?'

They watched helpless as Bashie wandered offside and

kept their silence as the referee blew and the inevitable penalty was awarded and kicked. Now ragged cheers from the few remaining supporters rent the air. Pontlast had lost, penalty goal to nothing.

Abe shifted his false teeth a notch, readjusted them, then sucked his breath as if rationing saliva for the remark that would immediately come.

'I always said he didn't have much upstairs,' Elgar said as they walked over to the dressing rooms.

Abe made no reply.

'Of course, he's big enough, but, well... is he worth the trouble?'

Abe continued to make no reply.

'I mean, of course, it was a pisscutter of a day,' said Elgar using a graphic phrase of Abe's. 'But I mean, the oldest trick in the book?'

Abe walked on bitterly, hands ground into his overcoat pockets. Flecks of mud splashed upon the flanks of his sporty check trousers, but again he held his tongue.

'A bad start to the tour,' Elgar said gravely. 'And needless. I mean, a draw would have suited us fine.'

Abe seemed inconsolable, did not return an opposing committee-man's cheery 'Well done!' and Elgar followed him into the visitors' dressing room where the exhausted players lay in various attitudes of despair about the benches. Bashie, as it happened, was standing examining various marks about his body and displaying certain scratches, the consequences of binding, as if these wounds were in any way an expiation of his cardinal ignorance. Offside under the posts... was there any worse crime?

Bashie saw Abe enter, Elgar beside him, shark and pilot fish together.

'Oh, don't you bloody start,' Bashie said defensively to Elgar but the fact that he had picked on Elgar first was itself an indication of weakness.

'I've nothing to say at all,' said Elgar. But it was untrue. He felt decidedly perky. Now Bashie Williams positively looked as if he couldn't read. 'In fact, you're not even on the menu,' Elgar said sharply.

Bashie made no reply and Abe, overcoat open and thumbs to his braces, leant forward to look into Bashie's face, his eyes narrowing and lips curling, creating another Pontlast legend as he delivered the *coup de grâce*.

'Basil,' said he, using the name which young Bashie must have dreaded in street-corner confrontations as a child. 'Basil, my son, blind side don't mean shut your bloody eyes, you know!'

Bashie flushed, then turned away sheepishly. They would all change their views, of course, since the rugby world would come to know Bashie Williams, from the high veldt to the packed stadiums of the Pyrenees, as there were honours, both amateur and professional, awaiting him, and Abe's initial judgement was right, but now the lizard-like stare of Abe did not leave its prey, and Elgar, taking courage, capped Abe's remark with a pearler of his own making.

'Yes,' said he, also going for the throat. 'On reflection, it would have been better if you had attended your grand-mother's funeral in Ireland.'

If ever there was a Pax Britannica, it did not extend to

Pontlast RFC at home or away, and the event marked a temporary decline in the career of Bashie Williams, for that night a chapter of accidents occurred that were not believed afterwards. Fifteen pints down, Bashie blundered by mistake into the landlady's bedroom, an occurrence that was made worse by his entire sixteen stone being in the nude. The landlady summoned the police. The police would not come. Then she roused Elgar and Elgar summoned Abe. At three o'clock in the morning a committee of investigation was set up.

'What was you doing in the altogether?'

'I thought it was the lav.'

'But she says you got hold of her?'

'Yes.'

'Well, then?'

'I thought she was the light.'

'Thought she was the light!' said Abe disgruntled. 'You're not in the foundry now, you know? How much had you had?'

'Fifteen.'

'Pints?'

'Yes.'

'And shorts?'

'No shorts.'

'Thank God for small mercies, anyhow.'

'Leave it to me,' said Elgar.

'Entirely in the altogether,' said Abe disgustedly. 'I mean he's got a stalk on him like a cauliflower even in the cold showers. What was the poor woman to think?'

'I'll have a word with her,' said Elgar blushing.

'After that penalty, this is the last straw,' said Abe.

'Please,' said Elgar.

'No, no, no,' Abe said. 'One thing leads to another, and as for that penalty...'

'As it happens, I've got a box of Mintoes in my case,' said Elgar helpfully, 'and we passed a flower shop on the way here. I've got my Barclaycard and...'

Now Bashie Williams looked more humble than Elgar had thought possible for he eyed the floor between the investigators like an abashed lout outside the headmaster's study.

'Well, what have you got to say to Mr Davies by here? Where have he got to now and on whose behalf, if I may ask?' fulminated Abe in his vintage county council English. 'Well, *Basil?* Say something, or have your tongue got mixed up with your what-d'you-call?'

'Sorry, Mr Davies.'

'I should bloody think so too. What a start to a tour! Go on, Elgar! Go to it. Tell her he was born in the workhouse, didn't use a knife and fork till he was ten. Tell her he's an animal and we'll chain him to the coach for the rest of the tour. Tell her what you like. I'll leave it to you. I mean, Good God, it's not as if he'd met her before, is it? Never mind, go to it, Elgar. Bleddyn or no Bleddyn, all I hope is that Cardiff try to book in here next week.'

Elgar went to work and it was one of those occasions and one of those feats for which the Hon Sec was justly praised.

'What he done at the material time,' said Abe when the full committee were assembled, 'was to take charge at once. No messin', no adgin'. Without him, we'd have had a rape case on our hands more'n like, very unsavoury and not at all for the good of the game.'

A vote of thanks was in order and a vote of thanks was given.

'Well, did you enjoy the tour?' said Mrs Blodwen Davies when her son returned.

'Drew one, lost one, won three,' said Elgar. And that was all.

'D'you know, I think he's put on weight?' said The Caldi from behind her inevitable Benson and Hedges. 'Look at his little cheeks!'

'Nonsense!' said Eadie-Beadie.

'Yes, he has, he's positively glowing,' said The Caldi, coughing continuously.

'I have found out certain things about that woman,' said Mrs Davies darkly when the visitors had gone. 'Public school indeed! She is the sort of woman who needs a recipe for toast.'

Elgar paid no attention. Remarks, remarks, remarks, he thought. They were surrounded by remarks which cut about their ears like knives, but remembering his own improved performance, he smiled. Not bad, that one about the funeral of Bashie's grandmother in Ireland. He had turned that to his own advantage, and it would keep. Then he might also dig up something about a box of Mintoes being as essential on tour as Mush's embrocation. Having learned to bite, there was suddenly no end to the number of points he might make in his speech at the annual dinner.

The reinstatement of the Hon Sec was complete.

DAI CANVAS

It began, perhaps as more deadly conflicts have begun, with
a doubting of potency, a seed of fear planted in the mind
which remained there, growing into a decision.

Jecko eyed his brother-in-law and said with a rehearsed
and calculated innocence: 'With your build, Benja, have you
thought how good you'd be with the dukes? I mean, if you
really tried?'

Benja was a short, squat, cocky, young man with the
braggadocio of the hard-drinking, fist-fighting collier. It was
he who had made public his knowledge of Jecko's private
hurt, breaking a confidence to do so, and laying Jecko open
to humiliation of the worst kind. For Jecko's wife had told
his wife and she had passed it on until it became a public
matter and a juicy excuse for the sniggers of the braggarts.

'Jecko can't do it,' Benja'd reported when the miners'

267

club contained its full complement of appreciative listeners. 'She jest lies there pantin', and Jecko can't do nuthin.'

'Short of greens?' a listener jocosely suggested.

'Aye, the sap's gone right out of the little flamer if you asks me.'

But this was a year ago and Jecko had disguised his hurt and given his mind instead to revenge. He'd *get* Benja. He'd find a way to humiliate him which would cause the tongues to wag even more assiduously than at his own demise. Had he not been made to weep in public, to suffer the lewd appraisal of his inadequate stature, and worse, the brutal jests of his fellows?

'Trouble doin' your old tart, Jecko? Feed her up and tap the wall for me!'

There was no compassion, and Jecko, a thin-faced colliery fitter, bound by habit and temperament to the pit, now believed what he had always half-suspected, that misery and humiliation were part of the inheritance of life. Robbed of status and a sense of belonging, he brooded as each grey day went by until finally, he made his sense of hurt a positive thing and decided he would avenge himself. Bastardy, impotence, lack of physical strength in a physical world... there was so much to be avenged.

But the more he thought about it, the more he found that it was no easy matter for Benja had a capacity for triumph in all things familiar. He was a coal-cutter in the colliery, a forty pound a week man, *in* with the Union, *in* with the Management, and there was no possibility of inflicting harm or ridicule upon him in work. He was, in his way, an artist with the coal-cutter, and if adequately directed, there was no one on the coalface who could compete with him. Outside of work too, Benja was a free-spender, generous with beer and fags and as good as gold when a touch was wanted for a double on the dogs, or when one of the boys had a bump. He could have all the women he wanted, had he wanted them, and in so many respects, he seemed to Jecko to be the complete man. It was a problem.

But he did not despair. He worried at it until eventually he came to the conclusion that the only solution was to be found in some exploitation of Benja's prime qualities, his physical strength and his dullness. A fella like Benja could only get really above himself with the dukes. Put the gloves on him, he might be conned into thinking the world was all his own bottle. This done, he would have to be shaped up for defeat, directed above ground as well as below. It would need care and allies, and above all, it would take time. The seed to Benja's vanity would have to be sewn with delicacy and dropped into that unfertile mind and left to germinate with the least obvious aides to cultivation.

'What I mean,' Jecko repeated slyly when the appropriate moment had come; 'is that very few people have got the build and shoulders like you have. You got them for a start, I mean.' He sat with several cronies in the darkened television room of the club awaiting an amateur boxing tournament.

'Got to be fit,' Benja said. He had seven pints safely gulleted and had forgotten Jecko's animosity. 'Must be fit.'

'Anybody can get fit, but they can't hit or move with any craft unless the body's made for it.'

'Ah, naw,' Benja said suspiciously.

'Well, I think so, I do,' Jecko said.

269

Benja grunted and pointed to his gut, a swelling mound of beer muscle that bulged above his belt. 'I bin on the pop too much. And you got to have wind for the fight game. I haven't got the wind.'

Len Beynon, Benja's helper who owed his job to Benja and was by way of being a favoured retainer, nodded sagely. 'Wind is very important.'

'Wind you can get,' said Jecko.

'Nah,' said Benja cautiously.

They were talking in the commercial break between the televised bouts, sitting smoking in the darkness. With them were the two Jones brothers, Ivor and Llew, from the same street as Jecko. Obligingly, they took up the refrain.

'What Jecko says is right, mind. You can train a mole, but he won't go far if he haven't got it in him natural.'

'Exactly. The real stuff have got to be there at the beginning.'

Benja eyed their flushed, beer-drinkers' faces for any sign of mischief, but none was present. Like Jecko, they were half hidden in the darkness and now they nodded their heads in unison, two short, valley jokers with the shonihoi's inbred instinct for calamity and the victimised faces to go with it. But now they looked merely wise.

'Nah... ' Benja gave a surly smile and said no more.

But as Jecko well knew, he had the kind of *slow* mind that was capable of feverish acceleration when a cord of vanity was struck. There'd been a good crop of fighters from the valley. No less than three champions of the world had been born within a radius of six miles of where they sat. In a pub down the road, there were signed photographs of all three,

270

Tom Thomas, Freddie Welsh, Jimmy Wilde. And hadn't they all fought their way over the tips and out of the pit in the first instance? It was a local tradition with which they had all grown up. Weren't they, after all, rather special people?

Although Benja said nothing, he flexed his shoulder muscles self-consciously. Of course, when he came to think of it, he did have the build for the fight game, and of course, you could train any bloody thing. He'd trained dogs himself for years. It was a matter of stick and graft, and what Jecko'd said was right, he could hit and move. He had the strong legs, narrow hips and exceptionally developed shoulder muscles of a boxer. That was no fancy. Benja was, as it happened, one of those men who lose no opportunity of displaying themselves in the nude. He was always last out of the colliery showers, towel about his midriff, always indulging in various kinds of semi-lewd horseplay. He was a physical man, hard knock, as they said locally, and of such stuff, champions are made.

'Champions be Christ!' he thought. He could just see himself under the arc lights in the Gardens like old Tommy Farr up the road. It would take a Taff to hang one on the Louisville Lip. He could also see himself putting it across the blackies. And think of the birds! Madison What-you-call? What was that big stadium over there? But he'd better put the block on it and say nothing.

'Good Gawd, look at that!' he said eventually when the fights had restarted and he watched a pair of ill-matched welterweights fumble and miss in front of him.

'Kid stuff,' Ivor Jones said flatly. 'Pure boys' club, it is. There's no footwork, nuthin special about them at all. D'you mean to say you couldn't do better than that, Benja?'

271

'Oh, I dunno,' Benja gave a self-depreciatory scowl, but then unaccountably volunteered the information; 'I hit a hole in a oak door once.'

'Ah, but you would,' said Ivor Jones knowingly. He leant across and held Benja's elbow testingly between palm and thumb. 'I would've 'spected it. If you got a arm like that, you got what they calls a shorter distance from the fulcrum. I mean, it's a natural.'

'A six-inch punch,' his brother Llew said, nodding agreement. 'Louis had one, Sharkey had one, and Tunney. But it's nuthin to do with size, it's what our kid said, the distance from the thing.'

'Oh?' Benja looked at them mystified.

'It's the force you can swing at the shortest possible distance,' Ivor said, poker-faced. 'You heard of forces? Well, some people can hit very hard without a big swing. From the elbow, see?' He demonstrated a vicious chop.

'Oh, aye,' Benja said. 'I done that with the door. I hit right through it.'

'Well, there you are then,' Ivor said, and settled back.

Jecko was careful to say nothing further, and, to Benja's disappointment, the subject was dropped. When the fights finished, they adjourned to the bar where Benja plied them all with drinks and insisted on accompanying them part of the way home when the club shut.

'You comin' with us?' Ivor Jones said. 'Bit out of your way, isn't it?'

'I feels like a walk,' Benja said sheepishly. 'You comin', Bine?'

'Aye, may as well,' Beynon said. His thick eyebrows

twitched as he glowered at the three men from the other street. It was as if he felt some unaccountable danger and could not fathom it. They had never accompanied anybody home.

Jecko silently brought up the rear of the little party, his close-set eyes glittering malevolently as they made their way up the street towards the path alongside the tip. He could already sense the difference in Benja. There was something girlish about him as he awaited further compliments.

'D'you really think...' Benja began to say.

'Uh?' Jecko said sharply, affecting ignorance. 'What you say?'

'I mean, d'you think I could...' but Benja could not complete the sentence. Already the prizes kept interfering, names flashing through his mind like the signboards of railway stations on some hallucinatory journey, *Dan y Graig, Rhondda, Chicago, Madison Square, cock and glory all the way!*

Jecko looked sourly away past the tips at the leaden sky over the other side of the valley.

'Come on, boys,' he said gutturally. 'It's goin' to piss down any minute.'

'See you around then,' Benja said when the time came for them to separate. The two coal-cutters were just in earshot to catch Ivor Jones' muttered observation to Jecko as they made their way to a section of terraced houses known as The Gulch.

'He could, y'know. Be a bloody world-beater at the weight.'

Jecko grunted and made his way in front of them, his

273

head bent, peaked rat-face pinched with the night wind, scowling inscrutably into his upturned coat collar. No one saw the expression on his face, and the Jones boys, swollen with beer, puffed with the success of their co-operation, and even more pleased with the unusual restraint they had shown, stopped to urinate, eyeing the disappearing figure of Jecko through the steam.

Now there was a queer little fella, off to the unwelcoming thighs and scornful mouth of the shrew wife, poor dab. Twisted a bit too, but there you are, it took all sorts, all sorts of snakes to make a snake world. Poor sod couldn't shaft, they said. Well, well.... There were some foul strokes about when you came to think of it. Oh, jawl, yes! And now he was bullin' Benja. Well, they'd done their best for him anyhow.

Indeed, they had. In the week that followed, Jecko became aware that Benja wanted to speak to him, even took the trouble to seek him out, not directly perhaps, but by a strange series of coincidences, Benja visited the places which Jecko frequented, another club and pub in the neighbouring village. But Jecko took care not to be there, and smiled when the visits were reported to him. He avoided Benja for the express purpose of not mentioning the conversation they'd had together. In his way, Jecko was playing Benja like a fish, allowing him slack once the hook was secured, then tiring him out on his home territory.

Meanwhile, Jecko continued his own life much as before. He worked, drank, and ignored his wife with the same habitual disinterestedness that he maintained in all routine activities. He was the expected underdog, hard done by, bitter, chips accumulating on his narrow shoulders as if drawn there by some malevolent magnetism of fate.

'Poor dab,' the Jones brothers had described him and he looked one. The merest glance at that haunted face, those cold, defeated eyes and downcast lips sneering in their belittling way and you would find it difficult to believe that Jecko had ever been young. Perhaps it was the environment in which he was inevitably seen, pub, pit, or terraced street, for he seemed to take their colour, the greyness of the industrial valleys, and below them, the anarchic wilderness of machine and tunnel with its own bizarre geography and permanent dark. Pit-bonded, he seemed never to have had any connection with natural things.

But in the weeks that followed the birth of Benja's ambition, Jecko developed a new light-footedness. It could not be said that he was light of heart. His face, his scowls and grunts, were all unchanged, but he walked a little more carefully, and there was a confidence in his steps. He now walked cat-footed with a sureness that was quite unlike him. It was as if he too had had his run of fancy, as if every step he took was a calculated feint towards the loins of his adversary. He walked cat-footed with a purpose.

After a week of avoiding Benja, he ran into Beynon in the club on a day when Beynon was on the sick. Beynon had broken three fingers by carelessly jumping off a moving tram and now hung about the club all day, waiting for them to mend.

'Er... Jecko?' Beynon lumbered up to him with a pretence of casualness; 'You know what you said the other night?'

'*I* said? What d'you mean, *I* said?'

' 'Bout the boxin' caper.'

'Oh, that,' Jecko shrugged his shoulders indifferently; 'Stuck in your mind, haven't it?'

'It have stuck in Benja's,' Beynon said grimly. 'It have stuck there, burrowin' like somethin' live. He don't talk about nuthin else.'

'Benja?'

'Aye, he's not the same. There's somethin' goin' on in him,' Beynon said uneasily.

Jecko gave a non-committal grunt as if to say, 'I can't help that, can I?'

'Well, he's got serious,' Beynon caught his sleeve. 'It's goin' on in his mind all the time and he can't get it out. He must have a bash at it,' Beynon said hoarsely.

'Well, he wants to train then, don't he? Cut out the pop and fags and get the roadwork in. It's a hard business.'

'Yeah, that's what I told him,' Beynon said. 'But he don't know how to get started.'

'Simple,' Jecko said with an amused smile. 'The am'teurs, join the am'teurs.'

'The am'teurs?' Beynon said dubiously. He considered it with a worried frown. 'I don't think that's quite what he had in mind, like.'

' 'Course, it's kid stuff at his age, but it's a start. He could try the NCB in a month if he's really serious,' Jecko said, referring to the Coal Board's annual sports which were held every August. 'It'll be ring practice for him.'

Beynon considered it. 'Aye, all right. I'll tell him.' He looked at Jecko accusingly. 'He's looked in here a few nights, hopin' to run into you.'

276

'Well, I bin around,' Jecko said, and turned again to the darts match without further conversation. That was that over.

Jecko met Benja in the club a few nights later. Again, Jecko was in a crowd, standing his round when Benja entered. Out of the corner of his eye, he watched Benja sidle up to the crowd and hesitate diffidently on the edge. He smiled to himself and looked away from him. It was curious how the roles of the two men had mysteriously changed already. Previously, Jecko had been the loiterer, the hanger-on in the crowd, forever at someone's elbow and never in receipt of any favour, while Benja was the very opposite. If Benja hated anything, it was silence and he never stood for it, injecting it with the poisons of his viperous tongue when there was ever any danger of discomfort. But now, such was the total involvement of his mind with his ambition, he was already beginning to appear as a different man. He was obviously preoccupied, and his coarse, red neck was bent as if with the physical pressure of such an unaccustomed thing as thought. He frowned continuously. His eyes were nervous and darting, permanently on the lookout for ridicule, and when he spoke, instead of the arrogant rasp of old, there was now an obsequious lightness of voice and a hesitancy to his words that was as sweet as a favourite melody in Jecko's ears.

'Jeck'?' Benja called. 'Er... Jecko?'

Jecko affected not to hear him and laughed over-loud at the merest of quips from his neighbour.

'Jecko!' Benja said in a louder voice. He craned his short neck forward. 'Got a minute, have you? Jest a sec!'

Jecko laughed again, running his eye over his neighbour and bursting forth with a convivial comment.

'You're a hell of a boy, aye!' he said, taking care that his field of vision ended just short of the spot which would include his brother-in-law. His comment caused several of the colliers to look at him with surprise. Jecko laughing! It was a rare sound, and indeed, there was suddenly a new Jecko in their midst. Instead of the defeated rat-spirit, a more benevolent and whiskered rodent cast its aura over them. Life was full of surprises.

'Jecko...' Benja said again. 'Jeck', mun?' The voice was growing desperate.

'Oh, hello,' Jecko turned at last. 'Good Gawd, where've you bin?'

'Come here a minute, will you?' Benja said hoarsely. The confidential nature of his tone was such as to indicate a death in the family.

'Oh, all right,' Jecko said. He excused himself from the colliers and went across to the bar, but Benja was diffident of talking within earshot of the others.

'Come over by here in the corner a minute.'

'Uh?' said Jecko, affecting alarm. 'What's up then?'

'Nuthin's up,' Benja hissed.

'Oh, well, have a drink?'

'No, I'm off it.'

'Off it?'

'Aye,' Benja gave a sheepish smile. 'Trainin'.'

'Oh?' Jecko feigned a stare of surprise. 'Oh, that...'

'Yeah, I thought of nuthin else since you mentioned it.'

'I only said...'

'But you're right, that's the point,' Benja said quickly. 'I'd thought about it myself, of course, but never mind who thought about it, I want to get on with it, the trainin'. I've cut out the pop and the fags and I... well, I don't know what to do next, like. Not specific, that is, but I... ' he leant forward to hiss the supreme confidence into Jecko's ears. 'I put my name down for the NCB prelims.'

'Have you?' said Jecko carelessly. 'Well, that's a start.'

'Welterweight,' Benja said, his eyes gleaming. 'I got to lose a stone, I reckon, maybe two, but I got my name down, and, well, I was goin' to ask you, like, bein' as how you suggested it...'

'You done the real thinkin',' said Jecko coldly.

'Yes, yes, but what I was goin' to ask you was, if you'd help me with the trainin'?'

'Beynon,' Jecko said automatically. 'He's your boy.'

'That swine is useless, he's had a bump,' Benja said venomously. 'Jest when I needs him, he goes and smashes up his hands.'

'Oh,' said Jecko. 'Well, in that case...'

'It's the roadwork and the weight is the problem.'

'Weight?' said Jecko carefully. 'Hm... yeah.' He was weighing every word.

'Yeah, I got to get it off,' Benja eyed his beer muscle.

Jecko thought, clenched his teeth, sucked in the smoke-laden air with a shrill whistle, then puffed out his cheeks again. 'Diet,' he said eventually. 'You'll have to diet, like they do. *Cut out*, that's what you'll have to do.'

'But what?' Benja said. He leant forward avidly. 'Cut out what?'

'Meat,' Jecko said without a flicker of an eyelid. 'Meat, cut it right out. Fill up on fruit and glucose – no fats at all.'

Benja gave a little pant. 'Right! And after? It's three weeks before the bouts?'

'Roadwork,' said Jecko earnestly. 'Night and morning. Roadwork and diet – you've got to flog yourself. You can punch all right, you've got the shoulders. But you've also got to take the weight off your legs. That's imperative, see?'

'Off my legs?' said Benja blankly.

'Pump up the speed, see? You don't hit with your legs.'

'Oh, aye, of course,' said Benja. 'But there's one thing... I don't know how to ask, really, but I was wonderin' if you'd give us a hand, like, on the road?'

'Oh, I couldn't,' said Jecko sadly with an aggrieved pout as of old. 'I couldn't afford the time.'

'I'd pay you.'

'It's not only that, I couldn't take it, not if you do it proper. I haven't got the frame.' He affected an expression of regret. 'Sorry.'

'Oh,' said Benja. The frame.... There was no way out of that. He had, after all, always regarded Jecko as a bit of a weasel.

'I could er...' Jecko began.

'What?'

'Well, I could come out with a stopwatch, time you, see if you're improvin'? I mean, it's on the road it's won. I mean, look at Farr, look at the Bomber? Look at all them Yanks lately. Where do they win it?' said Jecko rhetorically. 'On the road. The nigs is mustard on the road.'

'That's what I want then,' said Benja. 'If I gets a watch, will you act for me?'

'Yeah, all right,' said Jecko, but there was a rider: 'Provided you're goin' to take it seriously?'

Benja gave a hollow, trapped laugh. 'Oh, you don't want to worry about that. When I do get my teeth into somethin', I do never let go.'

In the days that followed, they met in the early morning at a rock known as the Pig's Back set high above the valley and overlooking a bleak stretch of moorland which extended for miles to the northern mountains where the coal ran out. Jecko was given a stopwatch and insisted on payment for his services. They had the first and only argument over the fee. Jecko insisted that he should be paid the equivalent of the minimum day wage rates of an NCB surface worker. He made play of the fact that he was not claiming the same as an underground worker and Benja, who only wanted to give a token few quid, was forced to accept this curious logic. There was no real rate for the job and while Jecko could not put up a case for lost time, he argued that the exposure to the early morning winds and the hazards of the unfamiliar open air surroundings stood him in poor stead for his menial tasks underground. He was not all that strong, he said; as Benja ought to know.

But Benja was too concerned with himself to argue for long. He was not going to spoil the fruits of victory arguing about coppers at the outset. Besides, the days of abstinence since the clinching conversation in the club had given him a physical confidence that added to his obsession. Although only in his twenties, his life had been almost entirely an indoor one if you included the pit. From the age of fourteen, despite his involvement in physical things, he was very much the town man. He had not the temperament for team games and apart from the periods of his youth when he used the moors for the rapid and unsophisticated seduction of girls, his life had been a short circuit between club, pub, billiard saloon, cinema and pit. Like Jecko, he was a valley animal, and once the initial act of belief in his ability was achieved, Benja found himself moving more and more into unfamiliar places where the natural confidence of movement and thought which he normally took for granted, now left him, and he became increasingly dependent on Jecko.

It was an ancillary happening that Jecko could not have foreseen and whereas he was at first cautious in his encouragement, preferring to take the familiar role of non-committal observer, he soon found that he could say almost anything and Benja would heed him. He had advised a meatless diet without considering how dangerously near the absurd he was moving, but once Benja had accepted that – what training for a boxing bout! – he would accept anything.

They soon began in earnest and for the first mornings, Benja ran half a mile, sprinted for a hundred yards between two cigarette packets slotted in twigs which Jecko placed at the measured distance, and then ran a further half mile over the clumpy moorland. It was a gruelling run for a collier who, like a sailor, develops certain muscles at the expense of others, and when Benja protested at starting off with such a stiff training course from scratch, Jecko looked at him peculiarly.

'Why not? You're made for it,' he said dourly. 'I mean, look at you?'

Benja wore shorts and singlet, and heavy boots. His

pockmarked face beneath its unkempt, greasy mop was tinged with blue as he stood awkwardly in the boots, shivering with the combined effects of exposure and effort.

'But it's too much, mun?' he panted. He had given up the first run at the end of the hundred yards. 'I mean, from scratch? I can taste the bile already.'

'Swallow it then.'

'But look at my legs?'

Jecko inspected them. They were trembling with fatigue, one or two blue coal scars scattered under the knees giving them an oddly invalid look. 'There's nuthin wrong with 'em from what I can see at a casual inspection,' he said. 'It's not all that cold, is it?' He was himself mufflered in a new donkey jacket and balaclava. 'Perhaps your legs is not up to it?'

'No... it's just too much to start, that's what I'm sayin',' Benja said aggrievedly.

'Hm...' Jecko spat a thin stream of saliva expertly between a gap in his front teeth. 'Look,' he said flatly, 'either you're bloody serious, or you're bloody not?'

'But...'

'Well, are you?'

'Yeah, but...'

'The *whole* course then,' said Jecko savagely and waved a hand to dismiss the appeal. 'You'll be knackered for a few days, but once you've got it under your belt, you'll do double that and laugh.'

Benja stared at Jecko. He had never considered Jecko an extremist in anything, but now his face had taken on a flinty look that obscured his previous seediness. His bony cheekbones shone, the downcast mouth was hardened into a line of determination and the colour brought back into his pallid cheeks by the wind all combined to give him a new fixed expression. Not yet maniacal, there was a visible inscrutability and a complete absence of all evidence of past failure. It was no longer the face of a man who had been third best at every activity which life offered. He even moved differently, discovering a blunt eloquence of gesticulation as when he jerked a thumb insolently at the uninviting moorland and watched the sweating Benja turn and begin to plod with hunched shoulders over the uneven ground. One movement of the thumb and he, Jecko, was another man. But he did not smile. His eyes never left that lurching, booted figure.

'On!' he seemed to be saying. 'On! On!' And part of this maniac urging communicated itself to Benja and coupled with his own ambition so that the two of them were for days like parts of a whole, the one driving and the other driven. And as Benja's booted feet slammed into the springy turf or hammered and sparked on the rough stone track, they were, these two typical men, suddenly untypical, bigger than themselves, aware only of each other and no one else.

'*Tom-Thomas, Tom-Thomas, Tom-Thomas!*' Benja grunted to himself as he ran. '*Champ!*'

While Jecko muttered as he watched his charge striding out over the grass; '*Mush! Mush, you bastard!*'

Down below in the silent streets, their wives lay abed and slept on. At first ridiculing, their scorn changed to indifference and they did not even bother to wake when the men turned out. The men's world was not their world, and

284

except in the most personal of matters, they had no say. Although when they happened to meet – there had been little traffic between them since the confession of Jecko's impotence – they felt even more uneasy with each other. It was as if they sensed trouble brewing, as if, with the low cunning of excluded Arab women, they felt that the slightest indiscretion on their part always rebounded upon them. So they lay abed and said nothing, while above them, morning and night, the contender Benja, meatless and liquorless, pounded his strength away under the unflinching gaze of his adversary.

The weeks passed. The week of the contest arrived. Benja had shed a stone and although he was finding the going easier, if anything, he was more aware of his weakness than his new found agility. He had done no ringwork and had not even donned a pair of gloves.

'But I must have gloves,' he said one day. 'I'm goin' to buy a pair.'

'Buy a pair? The Welfare've got gloves,' Jecko said disapprovingly. His tone suggested that Benja was guilty of wild extravagance.

'But I must, mun. Got to.'

'Salt water,' said Jecko firmly. 'Work it into the knuckles, soak your hands every day. Then rub it into your eyebrows, toughen 'em up. Gloves indeed...'

But Benja ignored him on this occasion and soon presented himself to Jecko with a string of purchases; black, heavy contest gloves with nylon laces, black silk shorts with a white electric stripe emblazoned down the sides, and unaccountably, the bill. It was just short of twenty pounds.

Jecko gave an involuntary smile. 'I can see you're not sparin' nuthin.'

'Take a look at them gloves,' said Benja proudly. He thrust them into Jecko's hands.

'Not bad,' Jecko did not want to look at them too closely. He felt a spasm of feeling overtake him. He fondled the gloves feeling like an arsonist glassy-eyed before the flames. What could he not do next? He handed them back with a grunt.

'Gloves don't do nuthin for your legs, mind. The legs is the boys to watch.'

'But my legs is fine,' Benja protested.

Jecko folded his arms implacably. 'What did we say in the beginnin'?'

'Never mind that. I haven't been in a ring yet and the prelims is Thursday,' Benja said hoarsely. There was a shrill note not far from hysteria in his voice. He had only just realised it. 'Never in a ring!'

Jecko gave the faintest shrug of his shoulders. 'We've said it's won on the road, that's where the stamina's made,' he repeated. 'And just 'cos you got a pair of flash gloves, you musn't let up on the roadwork, not for a second!'

'But...'

'Poncin' about in them fancy nicks,' said Jecko cruelly. 'Is that the way champions is made?'

'No, I don't suppose...'

'There you are then. You can't let up on the roadwork. You daren't. Once you let up, you're finished,' said Jecko harshly.

Benja looked at him and said nothing. He had been

about to remonstrate with Jecko, to raise the matter of his increasing tiredness, but just as he had often steeled himself to work a double shift in the past, so did he screw up his determination now. Secretly, he felt a curious satisfaction in punishing himself, seeing virtue in exhaustion, and pain as a cleansing thing. Once he had worked with a young lad who was too close to his mother. One day, after some traumatic adolescent experience, the lad attempted to castrate himself with a razor blade. The mother accompanied him to hospital and while she deplored the extent to which the boy had gone, she still saw virtue in his action. He had gone too far, as she said to the appalled caseworker, *but it was on the right lines*! And hearing the tale, Benja saw her point. He recalled it now with a smile.

'Yes, by God,' he said to Jecko, 'if we're not out-and-outers, we're nothing!'

Jecko agreed. They were of all Celtic stock and there was something about them all that glorified in totality. It was not just a case of going the whole hog, but that the extremities of their nature were unexplored poles, and escape from this bereft place was only possible by the total experience. It needed courage, it needed the blindness of obsession, and above all, stamina, and Benja began with all of these things. The fact was, in the exercise of his imagination, Benja had grown above himself, becoming the archetypal successor to those in this same place who had fermented massive religious revivals as far removed from the person of Christ as can be imagined. If his gods were other gods, he still felt the oceanic swell of the blood that led him onward remorselessly to total redemption. He had, after all, felt a call.

287

He sighed and laid down the gloves on their brown wrapping paper. 'Right,' he said grimly; 'You're a driver, Jecko, aye!'

Jecko replied by doubling the distance of the sprint, and Benja pushing himself to the hilt, completed it in a time that surprised them both. This redoubled activity, they repeated morning and night and it was not until the last morning on the day when the preliminaries were to take place that Jecko allowed Benja to put on the gloves. This they did in the final kitting-up preparations in the back parlour of Benja's house.

Benja stood in the parlour resplendent in shorts, vest, gloves and elastic-sided boxing boots, posing beside the electric fire, one foot on its imitation log front. Jecko sat opposite him, still wearing the donkey jacket and cap, scrutinising his prospect.

'Well?' said Benja anxiously.

'Hold on a minute, I'm thinkin'.'

Despite the outfit, Benja could not have looked more unlike himself. The rapid loss of weight, the intense activity, the sudden change of diet and probably the most debilitating thing of all, the abrupt stoppage of at least seven pints of fluid per day, had given him that dehydrated look of the advanced consumptive in pre-chemotherapy days. There was an inflamed area at the back of his neck where a crop of boils threatened to develop and the skin sagged on his jowl, causing hollows beneath his eyes where before the full face had thrust itself aggressively forward.

'Well, how do I look?'

'Great!' said Jecko. 'Like a champion. You got that raw

look you never had before. Hungry, it is. And nasty with it. Very nasty.'

Benja grunted with satisfaction and examined himself in the full-length mirror he'd brought specially downstairs for the purpose. On Jecko's advice, he'd had no sexual relations either with his wife or other women for the three weeks prior to the bout.

'You can't,' Jecko said. 'Definitely out.'

'But...'

'Listen, why d'you think the champs have the trainin' camps miles from anywhere?'

'But Jeck', once a week?'

'Out of the question. Douse yourself with cold water, sleep on a hard bed. Good Gawd, the smell of a woman is bad for you. Put it right out of your mind!'

Benja sighed. 'All right, greens is out.'

They smiled at each other, madmen!

Everything had passed beyond the point of reason – everything. The fact that the local NCB sports was by professional standards a molecular affair for which few people trained seriously was beside the point. They did not think of that, nor of the grubby, ink-blotched programme, cyclostyled on an office machine, nor the makeshift boxing ring in a cleared skittle alley – these were inessential details. So was the opponent. Incredibly, Benja did not give him a thought. Although they did not discuss it, they knew that the names were taken out of a hat and the contenders turned up to fight off the heats in preliminary contests. There were normally few entrants, but no doubt there would be an opponent. It was another thing to be taken for granted and left to Jecko.

And Jecko would not fail, not Jecko. Benja now thought of him as the supreme leader in the same way as his predecessors might have thought of John the Baptist, or the firebrand trade unionists of old. He had turned into a little trump, there when he was wanted, steady as a rock. The first big purse Benja got, he'd split it right down the middle, fair dos.

The time came for them to leave the house and proceed to the skittle alley. Benja's wife had been banished until after the contest and the children were being looked after by a relative. Jecko stood at the front door awaiting his protégé who was upstairs in the narrow bathroom, making his final toilet. Now Benja ran his eyes over the room with the feeling of a man viewing familiar things for the last time. He would fight his way out of squalor like the others before him. His eye fell on a torn sock which one of the children had discarded, and suddenly tears came into his eyes and he choked back a sob. It belonged to his eldest son, a boy he hardly saw. They did not hit it off. But now, Benja felt a welling-up of emotion which caught him unawares.

'From now on, you shall have pure gold, my boy,' he said aloud.

'We'll be late,' Jecko called from downstairs.

But still Benja hesitated, clutching at the sock and staring out of the window, past the ash cans in the uncultivated garden to the slag heap beyond. Oh, they'd see a difference in him, when this was over! In a second, he felt all his acts of selfishness flash before him with cinematic clarity. What a life, he'd lived. Self, Booze, Cock and Belly, it could be summarised in those four words.

'You haven't got chicken up here on the lav'?' said Jecko, appearing in the doorway.

'I'm jest thinkin',' said Benja slowly. 'Thinkin' what a pig I bin... a pig to myself, a pig to my fam'ly, a beast!'

Jecko considered him coldly. 'Have you done what I told you with regard to the bowels?'

'Yes, they're as dry as dry.'

'You sure you've had nuthin to eat for twenty-four hours?'

'Only lemon juice every four.'

'Undiluted?'

'The enamel's nearly come off the spoon.'

'Rightho then,' Jecko rubbed his hands together briskly. 'A good fast walk now, and you'll be right on top of your mettle!'

The contenders were required to change in a billiard room adjacent to the skittle alley where the ring was erected. They were mostly young colliers who were out to impress girls, or who had entered for a lark, and there was nothing ominous about the procedure. But Benja held himself apart with the aloofness of a professional. Once changed, he retreated into a corner and did a series of leg exercises, flexing and unflexing the muscles in a pre-match routine that he had observed on the television. Stripped and resplendent in his new kit, he was hardly recognisable as the old Benja, and when the moment came for the weigh-in, he passed an old workmate who looked at him blankly and walked on without a word. Surprised, Benja looked at Jecko.

'Jealousy,' Jecko said. 'It have started already. You'll have to watch that.'

An official came up to them and checked Benja's name on the list. 'You've drawn Danny Biggs, Cwmparc,' he said. 'First contest, is it?'

'Yes,' said Benja scowling.

'Well, don't be nervous.'

'I'm not,' said Benja. 'Only for him.'

'Well done!' said the official warmly. 'That's the spirit.'

They went from the billiard room into the skittle alley where the ring was set up. There were now a dozen or so spectators and when Benja entered with Jecko beside him carrying the gloves, there was a burst of comment.

'Good Gawd, who's that?'

'There's pants!'

'Got a 'lectric flash.'

'I fancy them socks.'

'Bet he hired the gloves.'

'Bit of class tonight by the look of it.'

As they weighed in, a routine business with each boxer stepping on and off the scales and whispering his name to another official, Jecko cast his eyes around the audience. He thought there was no one there whom they knew, but just as he was about to give up looking, he saw the two Jones brothers seated behind foaming pints and eating chips out of a newspaper. They could not see him because he was hidden from view behind the scales, but he soon saw them eye the changed figure of Benja whose satin trunks dazzled the room. He gave a satisfied smile as he studied them. There was no trace of recognition on their faces. Benja had become unrecognisable.

Jecko then saw the back of the other boxer, Danny Biggs,

disappear behind the back of the referee and he grasped Benja's arm, leading him to the corner where he bandaged his hands and put on the gloves before clambering up into the ring. As he tied on each glove, laying it into his midriff to lace up, Jecko spoke his final piece.

'They're here, all of them,' he whispered to Benja, 'to see you lose.'

'I got it,' Benja said thickly. His eyes were now continuously narrowed and there was a rime of spittle around his lips. He had his head down in an aggrieved cowlike stance.

'So you'll have to box clever, glove to glove.'

'I'll box clever.'

'Let him get the first one in and pull yourself on to it. Just get his measure with the first.'

'I'll get his bloody measure all right.'

'And remember to let him get the first punch in, lull him on, see?'

'He's lulled,' said Benja. He gave a demented smile and slapped his gloves together. 'Don't worry...'

Jecko shook his head quietly. 'I'm not.'

The timekeeper wielded an enormous school bell, purloined for the occasion.

'Mr Benja Francis and Mr D. Biggs... if you please, my lucky lads!'

Jecko pushed in the gumshield and helped Benja up into the ring where the referee made a cursory examination of the gloves. Danny Biggs was a thick-set, red-necked electrician with strong shoulders and a barely concealed paunch. He nodded sheepishly to his father, a wasted silicotic who sat way up on the edge of the skittle alley.

'Put a cork in,' his father shouted, 'or that gut'll be comin' out of yer ears!'

There was some good-natured laughter and the referee began his speech to both boxers.

'Now you all knows the rules, keep your elbows up, punch hard, break when I tell you, let's have a good, clean scrap. All right, go to your corners and come out fighting!'

Biggs nodded at Benja and turned to his corner where he again winked at his father. There were some further shouts of, 'Come on, Biggsie,' 'Put 'em up or hang 'em up!' or just 'Biggsie boy!'

Benja hesitated, saw Jecko's impassive face for a second – it was obscured as an NCB photographer manoeuvred to get into position – and then he glowered around the hall, taking up his stance and moving on to the balls of his tired feet as Biggs made a cumbersome advance. They watched each other carefully and the crowd became silent.

Biggs had noted the new shorts, boots and gloves of his opponent with considerable alarm and grew more terrified as each second of the bout progressed. He was fighting for a bet and regretting it for he expected at any minute to be met with such a flurry of blows as he had never encountered in his life. He had already decided to make a go of it for one round and to fall awkwardly in the second, and with this purpose in mind, he wore an elastic knee bandage. But the sight of Benja hesitating and muttering to himself was confusing. He flung out a half-hearted right and followed it with a heavier blow hooked to the body which Benja blocked. For almost a full minute, there was not a blow squarely struck.

But Benja, slant-eyed with a glowering rage, suddenly gave one almighty shudder and rushed for his man in a spasm of temper, throwing a wild uppercut that grazed Biggs' forehead and caused him to send a haymaker in frightened retaliation. He grunted as he did so, wincing as the contact with Benja's jaw sent a shooting pain up his arm. To his surprise, it landed plumb on target, but even more incredible, still blinking through moistened eyes, Biggs saw Benja stiffen as he fell like a clothespeg on to his back on the floor.

There was an amazed gasp from the crowd and before the derisive shouts began, Biggs, flushed with embarrassment, said thickly through his gumshield, 'I didn't mean to... honest...'

But the referee began to count and the photographer's flash bulb caught Benja's glazed eyes and inert body sprawled in that ludicrous position, his new gloves unmarked. He was out for the count, first punch.

Then the crowd began to laugh. Ever vociferous, now they excelled themselves.

'Iron man,' one shouted. 'Iron man – glass jaw!'

'What you got there, Biggsie boy – a coconut?'

'It's a carve up. The poor bugger don't look as if he ever bin off the sick.'

'Bring back the soup kitchens!'

'It is Benja,' said Ivor Jones to his brother. He stood up and peered into the ring. 'It is, it bloody is. And behind there... Jecko, the bastard!'

But Jecko had turned to go. He did not see the need to wait. They could have been scooping up Benja's limbs, he would not have stayed, nor felt one second's regret. He felt free, released, a new vigour coursed through his veins and he strode with a unique confidence, his manner and walk, the newly acquired flush of colour on his cheeks, all indicative of a body wholly alive with the pleasure of conquest. Benja defeated, Benja a shell, splayed out like some absurd novice, cooked by his own vanity, and a photographer there for good measure. He would take pleasure in purchasing that photograph, Jecko knew.

Ah, victory... he could taste it and it was good. He picked his way unnoticed through the crowd as the wits were beginning to rise to the occasion. Strangers carried Benja, still inert, to the dressing room.

'Boots, gloves, nicks, 'lectric flash – and never struck a punch! Down-i-oh'd before the bell had stopped.... What a flamin' sell!'

'Who is he?'

'I dunno his name – Dai Canvas if you ask me!'

Jecko smiled. He caught that. The wits were his only ground for patriotism. *Dai Canvas*... it would stick.

He made his way home jauntily, surprising his wife in the bathroom and laying himself upon her with a violence that was not altogether displeasing to either. And after, satiated, the sweat standing out in globules on his forehead and his loins limp with the pleasurable aftermath of his rare abandonment, he withdrew, did up his fly, replaced his cap, and went back out into the street without a word. It was still early. By the look of him, they wouldn't get Benja round for hours. His wife would be in now and the children were with relatives. Jecko smiled, spat, and made his way there thoughtfully, regaining his appetite as he went.

He could see himself regaling them in the club: 'Dai Canvas, and a bit on the mat chucked in for good measure!'

They say it never rains but it pours. And when a wrong has been publicly vented, it can sometimes be put right in private.

THE SCANDALOUS THOUGHTS
OF ELMYRA MOUTH

Elmyra Mouth did not like BBC Wales. Either on the box or off it. Although she dutifully watched the programmes which involved her husband as assistant cameraman, she was always conscious of a great disparity between them and her. She did not like the announcers for a start. The women looked like something out of a Sunday School vestry and the men sounded phoney, half-London, half-Welsh, neither one thing nor the other, with the most unacceptable of getting-ahead acquisitions, posh accents.

Then again, on the few occasions when she went down from the valleys to Cardiff and waited for Davie in the staff canteen, Elmyra had increased her dislike for what went on behind the scenes. Take the bosses. They treated the more lowly technicians' wives like dirt, either looking through you, or rambling on amongst themselves in deep, book Welsh.

Always jabber-jabber, it was, never mind whether you understood or not. They had no manners, Elmyra concluded, but that was not the worst. From what she had heard from Davie who was inclined to exaggerate to please her, the place was a hotbed of sex. You never knew who was sleeping with who, and for all the air of sanctity which somehow got on the air, behind the scenes, Elmyra was sure, the place was like a rabbit warren.

Wasn't it full of strangers? Glamorgan people lost out all the way along the line. You seldom came across anybody from the valleys, or Cardiff even, just the *in* Welshy-Welsh, catarrhal BA'd North Walians down for what they could get, Ministers' sons from everywhere, and girls from farms by the look of them, legs like bottles, all sitting around endlessly in the canteen, heads bent together and the hum of gossip rising like steam above a football crowd. Some of them *lived* in that canteen. It was an unhealthy atmosphere, Elmyra felt, and definitely not her style.

But there was another side to it. Her Davie had a good job by valley standards. On top of what he was getting in take-home pay, he always managed a few bob on top, what with car allowance, expenses and subsistence – it was as good as the Police from that point of view. But she had put her foot right down when there was any talk of moving down to Cardiff. Her grandmother had left her a furnished house, the corner one in the terrace, and where they lived, they had a view over the town that was worth waking up for.

From the bedroom window, she could see right down Dan y Graig Street, over the rows of terraced houses below them, right down to the memorial park where the trees formed an avenue beside the confluence of the Rivers Rhondda and Taff. Further away, familiar grey mountains and brown tumps stood sentinel over other valleys, and everywhere she looked, Elmyra felt at home. Here she had a position and status, and although they used to call her Elmyra Mouth because of her not being backward in coming forwards in that direction, she was well content to be at home. She was a valley girl, was she not? She knew every brick of Dan y Graig Street, every shadow of the courting gullies behind the terrace, every blade of grass and cwtch on the bare mountain and tip behind, and although now you didn't hear the tramp of miners' boots in the mornings and the little front-parlour shop around the corner no longer sold lumps of chalk for the colliers to mark their drams as they did in her mother's day, it was still home and here she felt comfy. So when Davie'd proposed moving to Cardiff as it would cut down his travelling time, she had a cryptic and typical answer.

'Travel you bugger,' she said flatly. 'You'll not move me a inch!'

For his part, Davie did not much mind. He was from further up the valleys, easy going, placid, glad enough to be in any kind of job when it came to it, and the extras that came his way from the travelling allowance allowed them an income that made life more comfortable. He had met Elmyra in a dance when home on leave from Malaya. One of Templar's boys, he'd caught a packet the sharp end, a burst from a terrorist's gun that left him with a slightly stiff knee, and when Elmyra looked at him, handsome and sunburned with the fusilier's dark patch hanging from his battledress, he didn't have a chance. She liked a man who was a man, and the wound, the campaign medals, the air of experience about him, and his close-cropped hair and engaging shoni's wink were enough. She also felt she could manage him, as her mother had managed her father, also an old sweat. Give the valley boys a good look at the world and it did them no end of good, and like many before him, Davie had returned home from the wars with that certain air which Elmyra found irresistible. The best Welshmen belonged to the world. They didn't stay at home picking their noses in beautiful Welsh.

Of course, Elmyra was a catch herself. Now at thirty-two, she could still go down the shop without a bra under her jumper and nobody'd know for sure. When she got her war paint on, with her slim hips, long, sexy legs and wide, insolent mouth, she had her mother's Saturday night at the Vic look, cocktail lounge, not the Two Foot Six, a touch of the Lauren Bacall's, in short. And despite her nickname, she never went too far with Davie. Marriage and two children had calmed her in that respect. Now she thought more and said less. She was perfectly happy, thank you very much, no need to give her a thought. But she did sometimes worry when Davie was out late. It was not that she feared competition – she'd go through the BBC canteen like a knife through butter if she'd occasion to – but there was an end to her patience in waiting. She didn't mind when he was away on location, but lately, waiting up for him had got on her nerves. It was the age-old wives' complaint. It was when he was not in when he said he was going to be in, that was the rub. So when Davie informed her he was going to be late one Friday night, she had a caustic reply.

They were sitting at breakfast, lolling about on one of his

rest days. Karen and Sabrina, their two young daughters were in school.

'Oh,' Davie said, 'I forgot to tell you. Friday, I'll be late.'

'I thought it was your rest week?'

He took care to keep his eyes casually on the centre pages of the *Mirror*. 'It is, but you know Fred Eckersley? He's off to London, a promotion, and we're going to give him a bit of a send-off.'

'Fred – who?'

'Eckersley. You know. He's going to *Panorama*.'

'You don't have to kid me with none of that stuff,' Elmyra said sharply. '*Panorama*? You can keep it. You know you usually take me out Fridays?'

'Well, he's going on Saturday. It's just a send-off with the boys from the Unit.'

'That Film Unit!' Elmyra said in much the same way as her mother would have said, 'That pit!' or 'That club!'

'Well, I could hardly refuse, could I?' Davie said mildly. 'Fred's one of the best. It's just a get-together, that's all.'

Elmyra scowled. She knew the charm of that phrase. It could mean anything from a few pints and a game of darts to the back door stove in and him banished downstairs in a Worthington fug, a bucket and sheet of newspaper ready beside the settee. Lifeboat stations, as they said. About once a year, she knew, Davie let himself go as her father had done and still did. They were both capable of drinking without reason, stomach to stomach in the four ale, and then returning home with flushed red faces, hoarse from singing and as full as eggs. BBC Wales would be sorry to know that the songs they sang were 'Mexicali Rose' or 'I

302

have been a Rover', but that was beside the point. Where they got the capacity from, she did not know. She was a Snowball and Babycham girl herself. But she was careful to control her objections. If her mother had taught her anything, it was not to be a nag.

'Oh, well, I suppose you'd better go then,' she said resignedly. 'Just men together, is it?'

'Just the boys in the Unit.'

'Mind to be home at twelve then. Twelve *sharp*.'

'Oh, good Gawd.' Davie returned to the *Mirror*. 'I'll be home long before that.'

'You have to be up early Saturday, mind? I want to go shopping and Sabrina's got to have new pumps for her dancing lessons.'

'Rightho,' Davie said. And that was all.

But when the time came for him to leave and drive the twelve miles down to Cardiff, she noted he had his drinking suit on. It was an ancient Burton's Donegal tweed which he fondly believed did not show stains, but despite this optimism, she felt she knew the signs when it was produced. He wore it on the *beyond* nights and it looked like it, had stayed crumpled where he fell, spillages on lapels to boot.

'Twelve sharp then,' she repeated. 'And remember the breathalyser.'

'Oh, if I have a meal, it'll kill it. A good hot curry'll do the trick.'

He went to give her a goodbye kiss. She'd done herself up. All the more desirable to come home to!

'So long then, kid,' he let his lips linger on hers.

She studied him gravely.

'You watch your bloody self. I know the signs.'

He repeated a family joke. 'It's not the drink, Auntie, it's the company.'

'I can see that by the veins on your nose.'

'Go on...' he gave her a playful squeeze.

'Stay if you want,' she kept her hands behind his neck.

'No, I can't. It's Fred's last night.'

She bared her teeth and released him. Men, she thought; animals. If he didn't come up the stairs cat-footed, she'd turn the tap off that night. Shut shop it would be, him and his drink and his Fred! As her mother'd advised, there was such a thing as frostbite after closing. But like her mother, she didn't want to be thought a bad old sort. So she merely grunted; 'Get on with you. And come home with more than your bracers!'

When he had gone, she heard the familiar clunk of the car's gears outside and lit a cigarette before getting the children to bed. There was nothing for her on the telly as usual. With all the money they spent on it, you'd think there might be a show she'd actually enjoy now and again. Sometimes there was a serial or a play with which she could identify, but it was never from Wales and usually had to do with the Midlands or the North. Locally, she did not count, she supposed. Not that she gave a monkey's. Davie said you had to go to Bristol to get the Welsh edition of the *Radio Times* because nobody took it locally. But why should they? It had precious little to do with them, any more than it did the other commercial lot, who weren't even worth mentioning except for a passing sigh for the Dorchester film stars worrying about South Wales on their yachts. Who was kidding who? They were no bottle from the start. Mouths shut, remember the divi, and don't offend Bristol again. Where were the valleys in that?

She finished her cigarette and went up to inspect the bathroom which Davie had recently tiled. It contained a coloured bath, pink, with matching accessories, and luxury of luxuries, a separate shower attachment. Elmyra could remember what it was like not to have a proper bathroom and she thought her coloured suite a whizz and no mistake. Now she looked proudly at the hand towels, the matching floor mat and lavatory cover, and thanked God for Embassy coupons. It was the most hallowed room in the house.

Presently, she called the children in, and having bathed them and settled them down in their nightdresses, decided to bathe herself. If Davie but knew it, she spent hours in the bathroom, wallowing in the suds, endlessly combing her hair, and surveying herself in the long mirror she'd insisted upon. She often took her measurements. Two kids and hardly an inch on or off at either end. Boy, she was too good to waste, she thought. It was a good job she was faithful. There were always plenty of chances. She couldn't go down the market Saturdays without what seemed like a visiting team trying to look down her dress, but she'd developed a look that killed, she fondly imagined. And anyway, she wasn't interested. They said a slice off a cut loaf was never missed, but not her loaf, thank you very much. She was took, a one-man woman.

She did not dress after her bath, slipped a robe on and went downstairs where she attempted to read her horoscope from a woman's journal, but somehow she couldn't concentrate. She didn't know quite what it was, but her mind was on the itch. Was their marriage getting boring? Did they take each other too much for granted? She'd caught Davie looking at pin-ups a lot lately, his eye flashing to the ripe page of the *Mirror* before he so much as crackled a cornflake. What if his eye was beginning to wander elsewhere?

At first, she put the thought out of her mind and turned to the broken-hearts column which she also read avidly. People's troubles were incredible. The best required a stamped addressed envelope for a confidential reply, but she was adept at reading between the lines. Some men were so crooked, they'd fox their own shadows. And slimy with it, pure slime. But not her Davie. She couldn't understand how she even gave it a thought. He was as good as gold always. As open as the day is long.

And yet it nagged, this thought. For some reason, her natural confidence began to ebb away. It was the BBC that did it. Of course, it was ridiculous and the Cardiff lot were nothing like the London lot in any respect, but it was the showbiz world even if most of it was all in Welsh. Oh, why couldn't he get a job in the chain works or on the trading estate? Why couldn't he get a job at home? They said travel broadened the mind, even twelve miles a day, but there was all the difference in the world in those twelve miles leading down to Cardiff. She saw them stretching out in her mind's eye, Treforest, the Estate, Taff's Well, Whitchurch, and then the environs of the capital city opening up like the red-light district in some lurid American film. Downtown What-You-Call, she thought. She'd give him Downtown!

Bloody Cardiff... it was so cold compared to the valleys. Oh, why couldn't he get a job at home?

Then suddenly, her mind began to panic. It was as if a spring had begun to unwind, a coil slipping slowly from its point of tension, then exploding, thoughts expanding like rings of steel and spilling into every corner of her mind.

What if he was on the knock? All those stories about Malay girls. What did they call them? Taxi Dancers. And what about the divorces in showbiz? The Boss of the whole BBC had had one and now he was working for the commercials! There was no such thing as bloody loyalty any more. You only had to sit in that canteen to listen to them tearing each other's programmes apart to know that. Everybody got stick, and the South Wales boys who were coining it on *Z Cars* in London got the most. That was one thing, another was that she'd refused to go to the Christmas party on principle. The poor bloody technicians always got the raw end of it with the bilingual production staff and the bigwigs ruling the roost. She didn't fancy being squeezed, pawed or patronised in that crush. It was like Machynlleth zoo. If they had a zoo in Machynlleth. And if they did, Glamorgan and Monmouthshire people had to pay for it. Like the bloody language. And as for what went on down in Make-Up after some of those Ychafi programmes, disgusting wasn't the word. Sometimes, they had actors there, and actresses, and the Make-Up girls said anything went. It was no good putting in to see Controller (Wales) either because he said London was worse and Glasgow the best, according to what somebody had told somebody who told Davie. At any rate, it was no place for

307

a self-respecting valley girl. Even if they didn't have queers which Davie said were everywhere else. Like some places he knew where you had to stand with your back to the wall as soon as you got into the lift, by all accounts.

But what about Davie? If Fred What's-His-Name was on transfer to *Panorama,* he'd be ready to let himself go, wouldn't he? They'd probably have the riggers out drinking with them, and the scene shifters, and there was a commissionaire who could tell a story or two, she knew about them. Once they got the beer into them, there'd be no telling what they'd do. If they weren't at it with the Welshy lot, they might be down the docks and that was almost as bad, if not quite. The trouble was, once you got near Cardiff, the values changed. You could get drunk up the valleys like a man, but after stop-tap, home you had to come, boyo, one foot behind the other, or no place for you but the gutter. And there was something very comforting about the gutter. There was seldom room for two in it.

But Cardiff, the docks... she thought about them obsessionally now. What she hated most was her sense of the city's anonymity, those cold wide streets, actual architecture, people pushing, sometimes stuck-ups with yet another accent and the girls in the better shops trying to sound like a lot of lezzes and looking down their noses at you if you ever had to leave your address.

'Dan y Graig Street and up yours too!'

What was good about the valleys from her present point of view was that there many a fly that was never unbuttoned because it would be all over town the next day. You couldn't bend down to straighten your tights without half the street pricing your underclothes. Walls had ears and bricks had eyes, and it was a good job too, made you feel part of the family, and keeping the old Adam down in all but the wilder spirits and they were usually Poles or County School boys. There was no creeping off and having it on the sly if you were married unless you were the Invisible Man or something. What worried her now was the thought of them all together, egging each other on. They said there were some rugby clubs who actually had a competition when they went on the Cornish tour. Who'd be the first of the married men to click! Thank Gawd for that Malayan terrorist anyhow! He'd put the shot in just the right place.

By eleven-thirty, Elmyra was convinced that her marriage was threatened. If it could happen to Diana Dors, it could happen to her, couldn't it? They must be on the razzle. Must be.

As a matter of principle, she never kept drink in the house, except at Christmas. It was not that nobody called, but rather, that she knew very well who might call, and the men there were around here, you couldn't give them one drink. Oh, no. With them, it was one drink, finish the bottle. They were as Welsh as Welsh in that, out-and-outers, the bloody lot of them. It so happened that there was a half bottle of rum which her father had given Davie for his chest in the winter. She brought it out and poured herself a liberal tot and drank it with a swallow. She'd give him a going-over when he came in. If there was a hint of another woman, she'd give him a beating, the like of which the street had never known.

There'd been some famous cases, one erring husband

sewn in the bed sheets and laced with a broom handle in his cups, another wrapped up in wet wallpaper and pasted all over like a snowman before he got his. They didn't believe in sulking, the Dan y Graig women. Defiantly, she poured another tot, swallowed it, and then another. She'd give him sox!

But by one o'clock when there was still no sign of him, her rage turned like the weather cock to self-pity. She was drunk now, wallowing in remorse. All these accusations. It was her fault, she'd refused to move to Cardiff in the first place. What was the good of blaming him if he didn't have a home handy? All the temptations were put in his way. He was a boy-and-a-half as far as his attractions went. A wife's place was to follow her husband. She'd jibbed at the first thing he'd ever really asked her. And now what was she doing? Never a quitter be, her father always said, true to the pit always; neither a quitter nor a squealer. Now she was both.

By two o'clock, she'd finished the bottle. She got to her feet and staggered to bed. Now she was maudlin, disaster's victim. Dead, she thought, he was dead, neatly incised on the motorway, or crushed under some truck. He'd told her once he'd seen a man cut in half by a lengthy burst from a sten gun, actually in half. Now she transferred the image into her own mind, but it was too horrible. He was norm-ally the most careful of drivers, but then, they were the sort who always copped it. She could not remember going upstairs, or what she did when she got there, but she already saw herself as a widow, pale and grief-stricken in black with the entire street turned out for the funeral and perhaps a sight of one or two of the BBC celebrities who might be there. It was all over in her mind. Perhaps they'd fiddle it to say that he was working so she'd get a pension, no doubt Controller (Wales) would find a few words of English to cheer her up, but she was a widow all right. She *felt* like a widow. Thank Gawd her grandmother's left her the house. She sobbed herself to sleep finally, lying naked on the coverlet, her long, black hair hanging down by the side of the bed.

It was in this position that Davie found her at three o'clock in the morning. He smelt the rum on her breath with some annoyance. There was no call for that, nothing wrong with her chest, but he said nothing, stripped and eased himself in beside her, taking care to throw the coverlet over her in case she would catch a chill.

In the morning, it was he who attacked first.

'You were lying there looking like a bloody book jacket. What if the children had come in?'

She felt dreadful, a mouth like a birdcage. Her temples throbbed as she looked at him blearily. She'd decided on something before she fell asleep, but now she could not remember what it was.

'You said twelve...'

'I was late because I had to drive everybody else home.'

'Twelve, you said.'

'Well I wasn't much after, but before you go on at me, have you seen the bathroom?'

'The bathroom?' she caught at her throat. She had a vague memory of disturbance, a sense of sin.

'Were you swinging on the light cord, or what?'

311

'Swinging?'

'The plaster's flaked on the ceiling by the switch, and the matching accessories are stuffed down the pan.'

'The pan?'

'The lav,' he said accusingly. 'What did you have, an orgy all on your own?'

In her frenzy, she must have tried to wreck her own creation ! Ychafi! And even as he accused, the fact that he did not couple her with anyone else shamed her all the more. Thoughts was awful things when you came to think of them: nasty.

'Oh, lor'... sorry kid,' she said guiltily.

'I should think so too.'

She thought for a moment, then looked at him. 'It's the bloody BBC. I get worried. I don't know why you don't try and get a job at home.'

He looked at her startled.

'Hey?'

Then she said what everybody knew and Honours Graduates denied: 'You know you won't get on there. It's all clicks, and with your shoni's Welsh, what chance?'

He said nothing. They had discussed the matter before and what she said was right. It was just that he was easy going.

But now she pursued it.

'A little photographer's or something?' she said suggestively, as only she could. She slanted her eyes in a look she privately called, The Japanese Goodnight. 'If you had a shop, you could come home dinner times. When the kids are in school. You know...'

He sighed. He knew the signs. From now on, she'd get her beak on it like a jackdaw at a nut. Might as well say yes to a shopkeeper before she dressed.

'We'll see,' he said comfortably. 'Leave it at that for the moment.'

'Great,' she said happily, and later a sweet, intimate poem in monosyllables: *'Oh... Oh... Oh, Duw-Duw! Oh, help! Oh, Malaya! Oh, smashing!'*

Further up the street where the houses had bay windows and the occasional colour television they said Elmyra Mouth was as common as dirt, but the most endearing thing about her was that she thought him, her husband, the most desirable man in all the world. He was hers, and apart from him and the children, she had but a single thought. 'If you was from the valleys, stay in the valleys.' Nothing else made sense.

THE FORMER
MISS MERTHYR TYDFIL

Nothing is more regrettable than the speeches we compose, and never make.

'Art be buggered!' Ivy Scuse Lewis would have liked to have said. 'Art, painting, and his bloody gouaches, or whatever he called them. It could take a long walk off a short pier – and the St John's Wood mob who went with it.'

Half of them were queer anyway, she was convinced. Never mind the condescending looks they gave her once they had heard her speak.

'Oh, for a man who simply put his hand up your dress!' she might have said. Well, you knew where you were with plain lust. There was something wholesome about it, like brown bread.

But she said none of these things, smiled her professional, full-lipped, front-of-rostrum smile, and guiltily reflected instead. And more shame on her she thought, considering where she was from and everything.

The truth was that she felt herself threatened by Melville's painting, and also by the new people who had begun to call at their little flat in NW3 since his exhibition. The people were not of her world and defied her understanding. Half of them spoke to her as if she were the maid, she felt. *In service*, to use her mother's dreaded phrase. *Them and their Pouilly Fuissé!* They were English, of course, people he'd met on these courses of his, and at the gallery, but it wasn't a question of nationality, Ivy knew, it was the art-lark, prattle and paint, all excluding her and everything she stood for, meaning life, being yourself, having an identity of your own.

It was not that they didn't pay her compliments. One of them said she was beautiful. Said it straight out.

'Her dark Celtic good looks,' he emphasised knowledgeably through a mouthful of pâté, standing there against the stereo, six foot of skin and bone in aubergine corduroy, his touched-up, greying sideburns needing a nightly rinse by the look of them.

How could she say she'd turned down the chance of being Miss Merthyr Tydfil years ago? She wasn't from there, but she had her visitor's qualification through her aunt who worked in Hoover's. Then as now, she knew she was fancied and she'd kept her 38-38 at the operational ends, but it was such a wet thing to say, as if she wasn't a person in her own right at all. It seemed they had to pay tribute to her appearance, but that was where it ended. 'Open your legs and close your mouth!' she'd said to herself, her sense of humour always shocking in Melville's eyes. Not that he'd said a word, not so much as a wink coming from his taut little face. If the lights had fused, she wouldn't have been surprised to see them all holding hands in the dark. It was a problem, them, her, and Melville's newly acquired weekend gear, the Breton beret, fisherman's shirt, worn *espadrilles*, and the overall aroma of bare feet and *gauloises* which marked the retirement of the primary school teacher every Friday at four pm sharp.

But then again, this last she could have laughed at. It was a change from him sitting scowling over his marking. What was more disturbing, was the way he now had of looking through her with the pained expression of a man whose wife had become his burden. At thirty-six, she no longer understood what made him tick.

'Self-self – bloody-self!' her mother would have said, in no doubt whatsoever, but then her mother was a tartar who'd remained back home in Aberdarren, ginning up on the corner stool of the bar they called the Two Foot Six, making occasional trips to London to see them, and one thing husband and wife continued to have in common, was a sense of relief when Ma returned home. They were always glad to see the back of her. About her ravaged face, outrageous wink and festooned hats was the ever-present whiff of a past that was best left buried. A war widow, she'd gone wild when the Black Yanks hit town; or so the story went. Gossip, riotous nights, slammed doors, vanishing lodgers, the weekly visit of the police court missionary and a long-departed brother who'd done time, all formed the backdrop of Ivy's crowded memories. She was fond of saying that the street had brought her up. She'd had hearths other than her own to comfort her, and was shrewd enough to discount a good deal of what her mother said. If she'd had any ambition, it was to create in her own life what had been so clearly lacking in her mother's: order, stability, and some fixity of purpose. It was why she'd married Melville, conscious always of the difference in their backgrounds and ever hopeful that things would be different.

But the melody lingered on, she thought bitterly. She lay now in her black apache outfit, white headband and skin-tight sleep suit on the G-plan divan which Melville had insisted on buying, an extravagance which they could ill afford at the time, but then, when they'd got married, Melville had been more houseproud than arty, and again, she had dutifully fallen in with his wishes. The fact was, she'd tried to be a good sort, and had exhausted herself in the attempt to find some kind of rapport with a man whose face was even more of a mask now than when she'd married him. By arrangement, they'd had no children, then when they'd changed their minds, they hadn't clicked, and the lengthy process of adoption had yielded nothing except Ivy's embarrassment at the social worker's inquiries, and now Melville's painting seemed to dwarf her and everything else.

If she swore at the art-lark, it was as at a rival. His canvases represented his escape from her. Nightly, he was making a world of his own in which she had no part, and the last straw was that he had now adopted a permanent pretence that she was incapable of understanding anything he said.

Their recent row was a clincher and only went to show.

It wasn't only the art-lark, it was something else. Although they had lived in London for the ten years of their married life, Melville maintained the Welsh connection in traditional ways. He was a member of the Exiles' groups, attended St David's Day dinners, and frequently spent his Saturdays at the London Welsh rugby ground in whose clubhouse he was inclined to spend a beery Saturday night in the company of like-minded fellows. They frequently had a skinful and Melville would come home hoarse from singing, an aspect of his life that was quite different from his activities with the new people in the art-lark. As it happened, she did not mind a traditional Saturday night out in the least, even went with him on occasions. A man and his beer she could understand. She was no prude, but then again, it was not as simple as that since the very Welshness of the occasion tended to get up her nostrils. Melville spoke Welsh and she did not, and another sign of the times was the way even the London Welsh were quietly separating themselves up into groups so that she tended to be left out and often declined to accompany him as she had done recently. It was an absence she now regretted for it seemed that two worlds had collided when Melville met a prospective buyer who enthused about his painting. Melville had received, as he said, a certain invitation, but she'd bridled at the very phrase.

'A certain invitation?' she said. What a way for a husband to speak to a wife! His speech was so careful, it might have been carefully thought-out evidence given before a magistrate.

'If you must know, it's Clayton-Hayes.'

'Who?'

'Spencer Clayton-Hayes. He's a millionaire. From Treorchy originally.'

That took her breath away.

'Oh?' she said. If there was one reassuring thing about money, it was that, unlike politics or religion, it contained the possibility of change.

'And he wants me to call up at his flat tomorrow night.'

'Tomorrow night's Christmas Eve.'

'That's why he's so anxious for me to call. He's looking for something to surprise his wife and was delighted he ran into me. He wants me to bring as many things as I have framed.'

'He's heard of you then?'

'He's seen some paintings at the Walter-Thomases.'

'What about Ma? She's coming tomorrow night?'

'I can't possibly meet her now. You'd better get a taxi.'

'On Christmas Eve?'

'You can order it here and go with it to the station.'

'What if the train's late?'

'Then it's late,' Melville's pale green eyes stared at her intensely, his round little face slightly flushed by his irritation. 'I should have thought you'd have been glad for me. If he buys my work, it will be quite a breakthrough. He's a collector, a man of taste and discrimination.'

She bit her lip. That went home.

'Look,' he repeated; 'Don't you see? It's such a chance.'

She wouldn't have minded if she could somehow have accompanied him. What was wrong with a wife being an asset to a husband? A millionaire too. She had a vague feeling that money and sex went together. Why couldn't she be a help? She was short on one, but the other was lying fallow.

'Couldn't you fix another night?'

'It's out of the question. I can't dictate to him. Anyway, you'll have to meet your mother.'

They normally spent Christmas in Wales, sharing themselves out between her mother and his people, but this year her mother had expressed a wish to come to London and Melville wanted to use all his spare time for painting. The irony was that he'd completely changed his style since his exhibition. Now he painted Welsh industrial scenes exclusively and his little canvases were all expressions of some aspect of valley life. Pit wheels, ravaged coal tips, cameos of gaunt chapels and back-to-back houses now made neat little patterns whose colours somehow formed an idealised picture of a way of life that was gone. There was something immensely nostalgic about his work, however. It had a prettiness and charm and clearly evoked memories in which people still delighted. It was as if part of experience had been reduced and falsely crystallised into manageable proportions, and although she could not quite express it, Ivy was aware of a parallel with those glass baubles she'd seen as a child. When you shook them, they produced artificial snowstorms, snowflakes swirling down upon some miniature log cabin and showing a little world enclosed with all the properties of a cosy dream.

'I'm going to ask fifty pounds for the larger framed,' Melville said. 'All the Treorchy pieces.'

Ivy was respectfully silent. Money was money.

But that night, she found it difficult to get to sleep. Her anger at her rejection had given way to melancholy. It was not often that she succumbed to self-examination, but when she did, it was usually at these lonely hours of the night, and she had a dismal conviction that, all her life, she had been surrounded by lies. Sex was a lie, marriage was a lie, art was a lie. Living itself was nothing like it was cracked up to be. There came a time in your life when all you could do was look back and then images floated into your mind without rhyme or reason, all combining to make everything that ever happened to you seem disconnected and meaningless. At these hours of the night, there seemed to be an overshadowing greyness to her powers of recall which affected everything like a blight. Take her marriage...

Melville's parents, who were ironmongers in a small way, very chapel and self-contained, had raised the earth when they knew who she was. She remembered all the phrases, 'as common as dirt', 'no background to speak of', 'no education', and the most damning of all, 'worked in a factory'. She also 'went to no place of worship' and the very name of the street in which she lived filled them with horror.

Poor old bloody Ruby Street, she thought now. It was in the worst area of Aberdarren, over the tramlines near the canal. Originally, it had received its bad name from the immigrant Irish but the arrival of the Black Yanks had really clinched it. There was a famous incident when the local constable, Ikey Price, had been ordered by his Inspector to investigate number 33 which was suspected of being used as a brothel. Ikey was told to cover the back entrance in anticipation of a raid on the front. Unfortunately, he had climbed over the wall too soon, and upon taking up his station at the lavatory out the back, was at some pains to remain undetected. Fearing discovery, he had crouched down in the lavatory with his cape over head. ('A very smart disguise in the blackout when you came to think of it!') But two Alabama Joes sauntered out and peed all over him, the Inspector's master plot forcing him to be silent all the while. Mind, it was done unwittingly, but in the subsequent raid there were arrests made and Ruby Street was placed out of bounds to US Forces. The irony, as far as Ivy could remember from her mother's account, was that half the blackies were Methodist anyway, and flooded the Sunday Schools with chewing gum and goodies from the PX store. But the damage was done as far as Ruby Street was concerned, and Ikey Price, far from being a hero of the hour, told his story and became the laughing stock of the district.

The Aberdarren wits came out like flowers after the rain:

'Turned out a bit damp again today, Ikey?'

What a thing to remember, Ivy thought. Her mind was like that. She had an uncanny facility for remembering incidents of that kind which made Melville's short body twist uneasily in his chair when she revealed 'the fur coat and no knickers' side of her nature.

'God bless America!' Ivy always ended up saying when relating the story. It was one up on the police, but Melville did not really share the joke and, at the time of her wedding, his mother had actually hinted that she fill in a false address on the registrar's book! She'd been obliged to get married in Melville's chapel, and the few pews which contained her side of the family were probably disinfected afterwards. The Scuse Lewises had taken care of everything. He was, after all, their only boy and if ever there was a case of the groom going to the slaughter, this was it, she thought.

But that was from the outside. She belittled herself when she thought of it like that, taking what you might call the street view of things. The chapel was no different from the street in that sense. Neither affected your insides or your deepest needs. It was as if the outside world coated your real self and blanketed your aspirations, coarsening them in the process. The fact was she'd had a real sense of Melville's needs and more than anything, his need to escape from their cloying respectability and awful concern for appearances.

He'd told her once that he was eleven before he was allowed to tie his own shoelaces and the stories of his mother waiting up to smell drink on his breath would have kept Ruby Street agog if she'd ever related them. The Welsh Mams in Ivy's book should have been turned over to the SS and given to the Gestapo for training. They ate their own young by all she'd heard.

She herself was not that kind of Welsh, but of the earth, earthy. In the old days, they'd talked about it and, although they'd lived in London for years, the old ties were still there, and recently Melville had started to drift back to Welsh haunts. She had made new friends, learned hairdressing and mixed with everyone, but recently Melville's discovery of the Welsh streets in his imagination had set his feet moving along ancient trails. There was not a terrace or a pit shaft that escaped him now, it seemed, and his best-known study, a group of lads playing dick-stones outside a blacksmith's shop with a haulier and blackened colliers in attendance, had been bought by a famous London Welshman who'd described it as 'indicative of the true spirit of our people'. She'd been there when he said it, as had Melville's mother, but what relation it had to anything Melville had ever known about, Ivy could not imagine. If his mother had seen Melville even talking to a collier in the old days she'd have phoned the police! But there it was, these memories which were now paying off a treat. Everybody was very complimentary, including his mother, whose attitude towards Ivy had softened over the years. Now she spoke of Ivy as one who'd overcome tremendous odds. You'd think she was from Biafra, not Ruby Street, but there, they were all alike in their incapacity to see things as they were.

In Ivy's view. As it was, she could understand the snobbery bit, not wanting your precious to ychafi himself, and she also understood their reserve about Ruby Street; but now, in addition, there seemed to be this other harass-ment, the Welshy bit whose lot had miraculously found the guts to get bolshie according to the paper, some of them very nasty with it too. Educated people, mark you. But try as she would, she could only see it as a new madness. Nothing changed, it seemed. First the Revival, then the Band of Hope, now everything in bloody Welsh! Well, fortunately, she was far away now, except that Melville, after years of feathering his nest with the LCC, seemed to have turned the full circle and returned to what he had earlier rejected so conclusively.

'From over by there to by here,' Ivy thought, 'and getting bloody nowhere!' It was the definitive Ruby Street sentence, and having summed the matter up so succinctly, she promptly fell asleep.

But in the morning, there was a telegram which brought her quivering up to the bedroom where Melville had determined on a lie-in.

'It's from Ma. She can't come.'

Melville did not answer. Things had been strained lately and he was inclined to brood over what was said.

'She's broken a bone in her arm: club outing.'

'Oh dear... is there someone looking after her?'

'The people next door, I 'spect. She says she'll phone. She sounds all right. Wishes us all the best.'

'Perhaps we can go down after Christmas?'

She knew he was avoiding what precisely concerned her. The news meant that she was free to accompany him on his visit to the millionaire.

'Look, cock. You know very well what I'm on about. If you're going to see this fella...'

'No,' he said. He understood at once. He stretched out his hand and lit a *gauloise* nervously, his round little face tense with the pain of having to tell her. 'It's not what you think,' he began, his concern obvious. 'It's just that, well, with luck, I'll catch him in the right mood.'

'Catch him?' she caught her breath.

'I want him to study my work in, well, silence.'

'What d'you think I'm going to do?'

'It's nothing to do with you,' he said gently by way of explanation.

'Oh, I bloody know that.'

'It's just him and the paintings.'

'Are you going to sit outside on the lav, or something?'

He frowned. He painted the streets but their directness had escaped him.

'It's selling, that's all.'

'Selling?'

'Yes. A certain mood has to be created.' He smiled, as if that were the end of the matter, picked up his reading glasses and put them on. Now the prospective headmaster seemed to look at her, pink-cheeked and reproving. 4C again, she thought; her mark.

She still stood awkwardly in the doorway.

'You won't say, will you?' she bit her lip.

'Look, he's an old man, and he's got memories.'

'Memories?'

'It would be better if there were just the two of us.'

'You sod!'

Now he was aware of the intensity of her feelings, she could see, but she did not wait for him to speak.

'I shan't say anything. Honest. What d'you think I'm going to do – talk my head off? Well, do you? D'you think I'm going to tell him about Ikey Price or something?'

'He'd probably like that.'

'Well, then?'

'I'd rather you didn't.'

'I'd rather you didn't!' she minced, but while there was still a chance, she kept her cool. 'All right. Look... Supposing I was to drop in after? Say I was on my way from shopping?'

'At six-thirty at night?'

'I'll leave it until late, then we can go and have a meal?'

'We can have a meal anyway,' he smiled.

But she wasn't having that.

'You know what I mean, don't you?' It was very simple. She wanted to see the millionaire! And he knew.

'But he's a perfectly ordinary chap.'

'From Treorchy?'

'Originally.'

'Then what's wrong with me calling in on a perfectly ordinary chap from Treorchy originally?' she said breathlessly. 'After you've done your bit of business?'

He took off his reading glasses once more. His eyes were hard and uncompromising and she felt she knew his answer before he spoke.

'You won't say what you mean, will you? I'll let you down, that's it, isn't it?'

'Nonsense.'

'It's not nonsense. Every time we mixes with your sort of people, I can see you wincing. You insult people, you do. Just by looking at them. Me, I mean. Yes, you do.'

'Ivy...'

'Look at you, you can't even get out of bed to have a decent row, can you? All right, I'll tell you something else. I don't know why you married me, I don't. At all!'

With that, she flung herself out of the room. God, how she'd tried. Tried and tried. When he'd made no effort at all. From being a petty irritation, a squabble which she could handle in her own way, it now seemed to be much more, as if a match had been struck only to light up greater areas of unhappiness than ever she'd imagined.

In the other room, she heard him get out of bed and begin to dress. She knew that he would attempt an apology, but it made no difference. She'd answered her own question. She was sure that part of the reason why he'd married her was to get away from the dreadful clamminess of his upbringing, but the moment he'd done so and the initial pleasures of conquest had worn off, he'd begun to regret it, as if he, too, were searching for something and had not found it.

When he came into the room, his face was solemn and his tone of voice indicated that things had gone too far.

'I'm sorry, but it's not personal. It's nothing to do with you at all. It's just that I see this as a chance and I don't want anything to go wrong. That's all.'

She did not reply, kept her thoughts to herself once more and served him breakfast in tight-lipped silence through force of habit. She felt weak and exhausted suddenly. He made her think too much. She did not want to think. She just wanted to be liked. Couldn't he understand that?

Apparently not, but when the time came to leave, he still affected concern.

'I don't like to leave you like this.'

'Why don't you just go?'

'Ivy...' he put his hand on her arm.

'Leave me alone.'

'Look...'

'It's very common to say "look" all the time. I wonder where you picked that up from?'

'Please...'

'Oh, why don't you just go?' she said again.

'Not like this.'

'Listen,' she was already tiring of it and just wanted to be on her own. 'I've got the turkey to stuff.'

And that did it. He was out of the room, off on the art-lark, his suitcase of canvases under his arm like a rep with a foot in the door.

Men, she thought. But she couldn't generalise. It was the Scuse Lewises and their offspring. But the extent of her feeling in the bedroom startled her. Was she right about her marriage? There were some doors that were frightening to open, but having opened them, you had to decide whether you wanted to follow your inclination and proceed further. So she hesitated. The curious thing was that, despite the intensity of her thoughts, she still felt there was something missing, a key to her understanding of her husband which still eluded her. Why was he like he was? Why did he behave in this way?

She poured herself a large bacardi and coke and put a Frank Sinatra on the stereo.

'Only the Lonely' the record sleeve said.

'You wouldn't bloody nob it!' Ivy said to herself. But it was not like her to sulk for long and she was recovering continuously. To tell the truth, she did not have the energy for a prolonged row. There had been tears in her eyes, and only one thing was certain. Once you got past thirty, you couldn't cry without your eyes giving you away. She felt she looked like the victim of the dentist's apprentice, and for no reason that she could think of, decided to get herself up, doing the best she could with her eye shadow and slipping into a sheath dress, her backless and breathless. She was thus dressed to kill when he returned.

'Well?' she asked. That mask of a face gave nothing away. But his voice was choking.

'Nothing,' he put down the suitcase and came blundering into the room, and she saw his lips quiver as he blinked at her.

'How d'you mean?'

'Nothing,' he said again. 'I didn't sell a picture.'

'Was he in?' She didn't understand.

'Yes, I had difficulty getting to him, but he was in. He... he told me to lay out all my canvases on the floor.'

'*The floor?*' she said incredulously.

'Then,' Melville nodded and his face became enraged; 'then he put out all the lights and examined each picture with a pencil torch. It took him twenty minutes. He said he didn't like my brushwork. I didn't get a drink – anything. Not even a cup of tea.'

'But I thought it was practically certain?'

So did Melville. But it was not.

Normally, she would have comforted him with a remark or two, but she was not in the mood. She watched him sit opposite her and loosen his collar, his face still numbed as he stared in front of him.

'It's the end of something,' he said melodramatically.

Lor', what was she going to say? 'What did he look like?' she asked in a low voice.

'Small, bald and mean. But I don't want it mentioned,' he turned his eyes to her.

She shook her head, biting her lip to hide her smile.

'I mean, I don't want anyone to know. Especially your mother.'

She nodded again. She understood that. They sat in an uneasy silence. She had a little picture of the millionaire scrabbling over the floor with the pencil torch and thought it rather a scream, but she did not dwell on it. Evidently, she was required to say as little as possible, but the mention of her mother caused her mind to stray back to Ruby Street once more, and again, she had a vision of the other crouching figure, the suffering uniformed Ikey Price, his peeved face glowering beneath his dampened cape, and then she had a flash of intuition which went to the heart of the matter. The trouble with Melville was that he'd never been peed on before. All his life, he'd been protected in one way or another, all his expectations were ministered to, and despite his attempt at escape, there remained a niceness of conventions, the confident expectation of a style of life and a sameness of manners and language which surrounded him like a comforting mist. She had thought it especially Welsh, this conditioning, but it was merely a dressing and in any case, did not affect her. Never been peed on, she thought again. That was it, the trouble with the lot of them, the art mob as well. Her intuition had divined a condition of life that existed irrespective of countries and national boundaries.

'A good job your mother's not coming,' Melville said.

She noticed that he was looking at her anxiously. She was not often silent and she had not stuffed the turkey.

'What have you got yourself done up for?'

She smiled, and for a moment, smelt his fear. Whatever she was, she was all he had.

'Nothing,' she said and went presently into the kitchen

331

and put on an apron in preparation for her chore. But for the goodness of her heart, it would have been a right Ruby Street Christmas, she thought: poached egg, flagon and a fag! But that was another dog-end she'd better keep behind her ear for after. As it was, without even seeing the man of mystery, she felt in an awed way that they had both received a salutary lesson in what it took to be a millionaire.

There was a movement behind her in the kitchen doorway and although conscious of Melville's eyes upon her, she did not turn round. Now her strong deft fingers began slowly and confidently to tear the innards out of the turkey.

Foreword by Des Barry

Des Barry, born in Merthyr and now living in Cardiff, having travelled much of the world in between times, is the author of three novels: *Cressida's Bed*, *A Bloody Good Friday* and *The Chivalry of Crime*. His short prose has appeared in *The New Yorker*, *Granta*, and various anthologies. He teaches Creative Writing at the University of Glamorgan.

Cover image by Terry O'Neill

Terry O'Neill achieved his first success documenting the fashion, style, and celebrities of the 1960s. He attracted attention for photographing his subjects in unconventional or candid settings. In addition to photographing the elite of the decade's showbusiness icons, such as Judy Garland, Frank Sinatra, Richard Burton, The Beatles and The Rolling Stones, he also photographed members of the British Royal Family, and several prominent politicians, showing a more natural and human side to these subjects than had usually been portrayed before. Examples of his work hang in the permanent collection of the National Portrait Gallery in London. He continues to work professionally and is revered as one of the great British photographers.

LIBRARY OF WALES

SERIES EDITOR: DAI SMITH

'This landmark series is testimony to the resurgence of the English-language literature of Wales. After years of neglect, the future for Welsh writing in English – both classics and new writing – looks very promising indeed.'

M. Wynn Thomas

WWW.LIBRARYOFWALES.ORG

LIBRARY OF WALES titles are available to buy online at: